Someone Like You

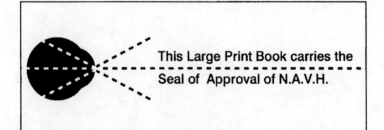

This Large Print Book carries the
Seal of Approval of N.A.V.H.

Someone Like You

Barbara Bretton

WHEELER
PUBLISHING

Published in 2006 by arrangement with The Berkley Publishing Group, a division of Penguin Group (USA) Inc.

Wheeler Large Print Softcover.

The text of this Large Print edition is unabridged. Other aspects of the book may vary from the original edition.

Set in 16 pt. Plantin by Ramona Watson.

Printed in the United States on permanent paper.

Library of Congress Cataloging-in-Publication Data

Bretton, Barbara.
    Someone like you / by Barbara Bretton.
      p. cm.
    ISBN 1-59722-145-7 (lg. print : sc : alk. paper)
    1. Mothers and daughters — Fiction. 2. Aging parents
— Fiction. 3. Domestic fiction. 4. Large type books.
I. Title.
PS3552.R435S658 2005
  813'.54—dc22   2005026963

Someone Like You

As the Founder/CEO of NAVH, the only national health agency solely devoted to those who, although not totally blind, have an eye disease which could lead to serious visual impairment, I am pleased to recognize Thorndike Press* as one of the leading publishers in the large print field.

Founded in 1954 in San Francisco to prepare large print textbooks for partially seeing children, NAVH became the pioneer and standard setting agency in the preparation of large type.

Today, those publishers who meet our standards carry the prestigious "Seal of Approval" indicating high quality large print. We are delighted that Thorndike Press is one of the publishers whose titles meet these standards. We are also pleased to recognize the significant contribution Thorndike Press is making in this important and growing field.

Lorraine H. Marchi, L.H.D.
Founder/CEO
NAVH

* Thorndike Press encompasses the following imprints: Thorndike, Wheeler, Walker and Large Print Press.

Then

He was a blue-eyed guitar player with big hands and a wicked grin, and she was the last eighteen-year-old virgin in Idle Point, Maine.

Their eyes met across the smoke-filled auditorium during the annual Valentine's Day Dance, and forty-eight hours later Mark Doyle and Mimi Brennan found themselves standing before a justice of the peace in Bel Air, Maryland, vowing to love each other forever.

As it turned out, forever only lasted seventeen years, seven months, and twenty-seven days, but for awhile it was almost enough.

Once upon a time, in a very different world, Mark and Mimi Doyle were famous. They hadn't set out to be famous; they set out to make a difference, but they ended up famous just the same.

Every family has a legend that defines it

to the rest of the world, but not every family sees that legend on the cover of *Rolling Stone* the way the Doyles did, and with quotes from Dylan and Baez to back it up. Their love story was as famous as they were, part of who they were and what they were trying to do with their music and their words. Mark's talent made the music possible, but try to explain why fame hadn't come his way until he married the shy teenager from Idle Point with the heartbreaking catch in her voice.

Maybe it was because she loved him enough for both of them, enough for the entire world. Maybe it was because when she looked at him in those heady, early days, he believed anything was possible, and when you believed anything was possible, that was when miracles happened.

For a little while they had it all, but then it began to slip away from them like rainwater between their fingers. The world changed. Or maybe they did. Who could say? But they both knew that the trouble started when Mimi found out she was pregnant with Catherine. Their great big Technicolor love only had room for two, and when they tried to expand it to include their newborn daughter, it began to crack under the strain.

They weren't stupid people. They understood cause and effect. But somehow Catherine's arrival came as an enormous surprise. They hadn't planned for her. Although they never admitted it, not even to each other, they hadn't wanted her. There was no place for a child within the framework of their marriage, no understanding of what it meant to refocus their attention outward beyond the limits of their own relationship.

By the time Joely was born ten years later, the cracks were wide and deep and beyond repair.

On a crisp and sunny October morning during the Carter administration, Mark Doyle shrugged on his faded leather jacket and said he was going out to buy a new string for his favorite acoustic guitar, an old Gibson that smelled vaguely of cherry pipe tobacco and Jack Daniel's. They were living in Pennsylvania at the time in a little cabin that Arlo and Ramblin' Jack had snagged for them. The days of sold-out concerts and *Rolling Stone* covers had come and gone. These days they were lucky to score a gig at an oldies revue for people who asked, "Didn't you used to be famous?" But their old friends were good friends, and somehow the Doyles always managed to have a roof over their heads and food on the table.

That morning Mimi was subbing for a waitress friend at the diner two towns over. Joely, who was barely a toddler, slept soundly in her crib while ten-year-old Catherine stood guard by the front door. Mark used to laugh and say his girl was trying to keep the bad guys out, but they both knew the truth. What she was really trying to do was keep the good ones safely inside.

He stopped on the front porch to adjust his collar, his big graceful hands skimming across the supple leather the same way they skimmed across the strings of his guitar. Cat was a quiet kid, watchful and observant, a changeling in a family of extroverts and exhibitionists, but even she saw nothing different in his manner, no hint of what was about to happen.

"It's cold," he said, and he ruffled her bangs with the back of his hand. A ripple of happiness, pure as the first snow, moved through her narrow chest. "Go inside and put on a sweater, Kit-Cat."

She nodded silently, but she didn't move an inch. It wasn't often that she had his full attention, and she savored the moment the way another kid would savor a hot fudge sundae. She held her breath and waited for him to ask her to walk with him to the music store the way he sometimes did. He opened his mouth to speak, and her heart almost burst through her chest.

"Take care of your mother and sister," he said.

She nodded again. Of course she would. He didn't have to ask her to do what was right.

He ruffled her bangs one more time, then strode off down the block.

That was the last time she saw him.

Joely was too young to know what had happened or to feel the loss. If Mimi felt the loss, she wasn't saying. In fact she wouldn't even admit that he was gone. She insisted Mark would be home any second with the guitar string and a pack of Marlboros. For the first few months, every morning Mimi woke up her girls with the words, "This is going to be the day! Daddy will be back by suppertime. Just you wait and see."

And every night the three of them ate supper without him.

Still Mimi persisted in her optimism. The bad times hadn't happened yet, the dark depressions, the lost years. Back then Mimi was just an optimist, one of those people who were born believing in eternal sunshine, blue skies, and happy endings.

Seven months and three weeks after Mark walked out the door, Mimi packed their belongings into the old VW bus and took her daughters back home to Idle Point. She had tried to keep things going, but the gigs had finally dried up and so had the kindness of strangers. When Mark left, he took the magic with him.

The only thing left was family.

Chapter One

Loch Craig — Now

Joely Doyle woke up a little before five on the morning of the summer solstice to sunlight streaming through the sheer curtains at her window and an explosion of birdsong. This was her sixth summer in Scotland, but she had yet to accept the fact that nightfall was little more than a gathering dusk that lingered a few hours then gave way once again to daylight. A Scottish summer, beautiful as it was, left her feeling unsettled and nostalgic for the inky blackness of childhood summers in Maine when she and her sister Catherine would lie on the beach near the lighthouse and sleep beneath a blanket of stars.

Her earliest memories were of her sister's voice, the gentle touch of her hand. Their mother had been a shadowy presence when she was growing up; it was as if Mimi knew that Cat would do a far better job of mothering Joely than she could ever manage. Mimi was an ineffectual creature who had tried reality on for size and found it wanting. She lived in a construct of imagination and hope, a place so antithetical to Joely's professional world of pure immutable fact as to be incomprehensible.

Joely wasn't much for nostalgia. Looking back had always struck her as a bloody waste of time and energy, but on that particular morning, she awoke on the edge of a dream about home that lingered like morning fog on the heather. She saw the two of them as they had been years ago. Fifteen-year-old Cat struggling to get both herself and five-year-old Joely dressed and ready for school while their mother slept off another night of regrets.

Joely had been in diapers when their father walked out on them. Her memories of him were secondhand, gleaned from old record albums and articles in *Rolling Stone*, from her sister's stories, and her mother's endless yearning for a man who could be many years dead for all they knew. Sometimes she thought her mother's internal clock had stopped ticking the day Mark Doyle left. There were times when Mimi actually seemed surprised to see them at the breakfast table, as if the stretch marks and the endless labors had never happened, and her daughters had been sprung on her like a pair of subpoenas.

Joely rarely remembered her dreams, and when she did they were usually one-dimensional replays of a mathematical problem she had struggled with at work. But this dream had been very different, so rich with image and detail that for a second she thought she was back in Idle Point, looking for a way out. Relief took a few seconds to catch up.

Yawning, she stretched and bumped up against the tiny form sleeping next to her.

Annabelle was curled up on William's side of the bed. When he was away on business, the child had taken to slipping out of her own room in the middle of the night and climbing into bed with Joely. Annabelle was a sound sleeper, happily oblivious to the assault of sunlight and birdsong that would keep Joely awake until September. Her right thumb was curled close to her mouth, the one surviving remnant of her baby ways.

How far away those days seemed. When they first met, Annabelle had been a bundle of "Look at me!" and "No!" yelled from the top of toddler lungs. That toddler was now only a memory, and a little girl with very specific likes and dislikes and requirements had taken her place. A beautiful, tiny individual who delighted Joely's soul simply by breathing.

Next to her, Annabelle buried her face deeper into her father's pillow. She was seven now, a beautiful child with hazel eyes and soft curling brown hair. Where William was analytical and precise, his daughter was fey and mercurial. Annabelle believed faeries sheltered in the heather. She was convinced a pixie had taken up residence in the cupboard behind her bed. She saw angels dancing where Joely saw nothing more than fog settling over the craggy hills behind the house.

While there was nothing inherently wrong with a no-strings relationship between consenting adults, the truth was that the rules changed when children were part of the picture, and they changed again when the child started growing up.

Over the last few months Annabelle had grown curious. She wanted to know why Joely still kept a flat in Glasgow. She wanted to know why she didn't have a cat or a dog or a baby brother.

She wanted to know why she couldn't call Joely "Mummy."

They treated her questions with respect, and they tried to answer her honestly. But there were limits. You couldn't tell a seven-year-old that nothing was permanent. You couldn't sit her down and say that sooner or later everything changed, because she wouldn't believe you.

And you wouldn't want her to. Part of childhood was the ability to nestle securely in the now, knowing it would never change. Annabelle wouldn't understand that the people she loved most in the world were changing right in front of her eyes, in ways that would alter her life forever. She was only a little girl, after all, and she wanted them to be a family like her friend Louis's family. The kind that shared a name and a history and a future that was as real and solid as the hills beyond the house.

For weeks Annabelle had been entertaining them with stories about long-ago solstice festivals, charming blends of fact and folklore that had made William and Joely smile at each other over her head. They let her talk them into allowing her to stay up late tonight to celebrate the longest day of the year. They planned to pack a

17

picnic basket and take pillows and blankets up the hill and maybe some of the ancient magic neither one believed in would find its way into their hearts.

William was in Japan, finishing up the last of a series of seminars on the effect of personal economical growth on a country's GNP. He had been gone for two long weeks, but during last night's phone call he had promised he would make it home in time to join Joely and Annabelle on the hill tonight. And William always kept his promises.

He was a wonderful father who kept in close touch with both of them when he was away. E-mails and digital photos for Annabelle and a phone call every single night, no exceptions.

Joely wished she could pinpoint the moment when she realized how much she dreaded those nightly phone calls. The easy companionable silences they had once enjoyed were now uneasy stretches of meaningless small talk. At times it seemed the only thing they had in common was their love for Annabelle. Joely had the terrible feeling that they might have reached the natural end of things.

The thought came close to breaking her heart.

Annabelle mumbled something, then flopped onto her back, her stuffed Tigger clutched to her chest.

Joely was wide awake. She wasn't in the mood to read, and she was too lazy to head downstairs to watch one of the morning chat shows. Her laptop rested on the nightstand and, careful not to disturb Annabelle, she reached over and pulled it into bed with her and connected to the Internet.

The new-mail symbol flashed from the bottom of the accessory tray, and she clicked over to her e-mail program. Cat had promised to send her a scan of the cardi Sarah Jessica Parker planned to wear on *Letterman* next week, and there was the off chance that there might be some news about funding for the next stage of testing at Clendenning, which would translate into a return to work for her.

She hadn't told William yet, but her old research team in Glasgow would be re-forming next month and she had been asked to take over the lead. A few months ago the thought of going back to work would have filled her with joy. Loch Craig was an easy thirty-mile commute from the city, which meant she could have the best of both worlds: a job she loved and a home she adored.

Except she was no longer sure there was a place for her at home.

Her bosses at Clendenning had been surprised when she expressed interest in the new team they were putting together for the Surrey facility. "We don't want to lose you here," Gareth Stewart had said to her, "but if you're serious about moving down to Surrey, I won't stand in your way."

At least she didn't have to make that decision today. She was almost relieved there was no news about Surrey in her in-box. Instead there was the requisite bucket of spam and a two-liner from Cat saying she was on her way down to New York to deliver a batch of sweaters to the costume designer at *Pink Slip* and would send the scan when she got back.

She sent the monthly alumni newsletter from MIT spinning into the trash. She wasn't in the mood to read a laundry list of her classmates' weddings, new babies, and professional successes. She was about to flip over to her browser and surf eBay for Barbie doll clothes for Annabelle's birthday when her computer chimed, and a new message popped up in her in-box.

TO: jdoyle@clendenning-bio.uk
FROM: w.bishop@globalfinance.uk
DATE: 21 june
SUBJECT: itinerary

Sorry: change of plans. Harris fell ill (emerg appendectomy) so I'm taking over Kyoto. Sending from rail station. Bullet boards two min. Will call when settled w/details, hotel, etc. Kiss A for me. Hope she's not v. disappointed. Talk later. Miss you.
L,
W

"Damn it," she whispered, shutting down the laptop and closing the lid. Annabelle would be heartbroken when she found out her father wouldn't be with them tonight. They had had so much fun planning the goodies they would pack in the picnic basket, speculating about what they would see on the hill tonight as the sun slowly dimmed in the sky. She knew he would have moved heaven and earth to get back home to them — to Annabelle — and that this burst of anger toward him was both unreasonable and undeserved, but it was there just the same.

There were times when it was hard to

figure out the boundaries. They looked like a family. They behaved like a family. But were they really a family? Annabelle and William belonged together, but where did she fit into the mix? She was like one of those houseguests who came for the weekend and forgot to go home. There were no blood ties between them. No legal bonds. Possession might be nine-tenths of the law when it came to the family silver, but did it count for anything when it came to your heart?

How did you do it, Cat? How come you never stumbled into a family of your own? Her sister was thirty-eight years old and blissfully independent. She lived alone. She owned her own business. She kept an eye on their mother without being drawn into Mimi's craziness. No messy love affairs. No messy children. No broken heart along the way. *Tell me the secret, Cat, because I'm drowning over here.*

She knew she couldn't call Cat. For one thing, she wasn't home. Her sister was running around Manhattan doing glamorous things with glamorous people. Besides, the last time she'd dumped her problems in her sister's lap she was thirteen years old and wondering why boys only liked the girls with big boobs and

Chapter Two

New York City

"Look at them," Catherine Doyle whispered to the man sitting next to her. "I'm old enough to be their mother."

Michael Yanovsky's gaze traveled the waiting room. "Older sister maybe, not their mother."

"You're a lousy liar." She leaned closer. "See the way they're looking at me? They probably think I'm here for hormone replacement therapy."

He laughed out loud, and a sunburst of lines crinkled the outer corners of his eyes. Lines like that would send most women running for Botox, but they brought his face to life. Men had all the luck.

"Now might be a good time for a little insincere flattery," she said, not entirely kidding. "I'm still trying to recover from being called an 'elderly primigravida' by that high school cheerleader at the reception desk."

"I already tried flattery." He reached for her hand and laced his fingers with hers. "You told me I was a lousy liar. Remember?"

She stifled a groan. "Karen warned me about pregnancy brain, but I didn't think it would show up for a few more months."

He didn't laugh this time, just gave her one of those looks that made her think he knew her thoughts better than she did. Her voice sounded high and pinched, like a parrot's idea of human speech. And that laugh — who was she trying to kid? That laugh wouldn't fool anybody. She sounded scared out of her elderly primigravida mind.

"Your hand's cold," he said.

"It's the air-conditioning."

He sandwiched her hands between his and rubbed briskly. The gesture managed to be matter-of-fact and intimate simultaneously. She wasn't the kind of woman who knew how to accept comforting gestures. She fought the urge to pull her hand away and make some smart-mouthed comment designed to deflect any unseemly displays of emotion. She was emotional enough these days for both of them.

"You're good at this," she said, aware that six pairs of eyes were lasered to them.

"If the writing doesn't work out, you can always get work in a day spa."

"I'll keep that in mind."

He was the only man in Dr. Colfax's waiting room, and if it bothered him, he didn't let it show. She had expected to see men sprouting everywhere like toadstools. Didn't couples share everything these days? Where were all the happy expectant fathers with their empathy bellies and camcorders?

And, come to think of it, where were all the other elderly primigravidas she was always reading about in the women's magazines? She had at least ten years on the oldest mother-to-be in the room, and that was giving herself the benefit of the doubt. Here she thought she was joining a great parade of older mothers who were out to change the world, and instead she was a one-woman band.

"You really don't have to stay around," she said. "Why don't you grab some breakfast at the deli around the corner, and I'll meet you there when I'm finished."

He squeezed her hand. "How about we grab some breakfast together when you're finished?"

"And I have the best idea of all," she said, wishing the other women weren't watching them like they were the last episode of *Sex and the City.* "How about you see the doctor, and I make a break for it."

He laughed again, and she was struck for maybe the hundredth time by what a great laugh he had. Warm. Mellow. The kind of laugh a woman wanted to hear from the father of her child.

"We're in this together, Cat," he said so only she could hear him. "I'm not going anywhere."

And he believed every word. She didn't doubt it. He was the kind of man who invited you to hand over your problems so he could give them back to you all nice and solved. But Cat knew life had a nasty habit of changing the rules on you when you weren't looking, and she believed in being prepared. Sure, Michael seemed like one of the good guys, but then so had her father, and that hadn't stopped him from walking out on his wife and kids.

Still, there had to be something different about him, or she wouldn't have made the crazy life-changing decision to have a child with him. They weren't married or even thinking about it, but what they had found together was still more than either one had ever expected to find.

They had met almost two years ago

when she came down to Manhattan to deliver some hand-knits to the costume designer of the latest HBO hit, *Pink Slip*. Michael was leaving a meeting as she was going in. They smiled at each other, murmured a few words, and when she came back out an hour later, he was waiting for her by the bank of elevators just as she'd known he would be.

Neither one believed in magic, but when two average-looking people managed to find each other in a crowd of eight million supermodels, it was worth taking note.

He kept a loft in SoHo and rarely left the island of Manhattan, while she lived in Idle Point, a little town on Maine's central coast. She came down to the city every three or four weeks to deliver finished knitwear, take meetings, oversee fittings, be wined and dined by the producers, and sleep with her lover.

Next to her pregnancy, their relationship was her best-kept secret, the one thing that belonged to her and her alone. She loved climbing behind the wheel of her Jeep and heading south on the Maine Turnpike, Billy Joel and Madonna blaring from her radio as Idle Point disappeared in her rearview mirror. Responsibilities, expectations, her mother — she left them all behind. For a few days every month she didn't have to answer to anyone.

He knew about her design work. He knew it had something to do with yarn and knitting needles and the occasional sewing machine. She had told him a bit about the group of talented spinners and needlewomen who gathered daily at her house to create the costumes that were building her reputation in the industry. But he knew very little about Mimi and Joely and nothing at all about her father.

She hadn't invited him up to visit her in Maine, and he hadn't asked. He didn't press her for more, and she never volunteered. So far the arrangement was working well for them, but it was anybody's guess what the next seven months would bring.

She tilted her head in the direction of a small refectory table to their left. "I think I saw a rogue copy of *Sports Illustrated* under that stack of *Lactation Today*."

Public displays of affection had always made her uncomfortable, especially when they were aimed in her direction. Michael didn't think twice about holding hands, a quick kiss, walking down the street with his arm draped across her shoulders, while she had to fight the urge to hide her face under her jacket like she was making the perp walk.

She leaned forward and rummaged through her tote bag for the project she was working on, a pair of sparkly black-and-silver leg warmers. She felt antsy and unsettled, and knitting calmed her mind and soothed her soul. Some women turned to yoga; others disappeared into the pages of a romance novel. She found her bliss with sticks and string. It also didn't hurt a bit that knitting paid the bills and had put her name on the cover of *In Style* last month.

"Excuse me." A ripely pregnant young red-haired woman leaned forward and said, "I love that sweater you're wearing. It reminds me of the sweaters Allison wears on *Pink Slip*. Where did you find it?"

She caught Michael's grin in her peripheral vision. "It's a hand-knit."

The young mother-to-be rolled her eyes. "I know it's a hand-knit. That's why it's so cool. Where did you find it?"

"Actually, I made it."

Three other pregnant women looked up from their copies of *Modern Baby*. Their expressions ranged from disbelieving to awestruck.

"I tried to knit once," the woman

nearest the door volunteered. "It was such a disaster I ended up in Barney's, maxing out my Visa."

"Don't get me started." The tiny blond next to her seemed transfixed by the motion of Cat's hands. "My mother taught my youngest last year. I still can't figure out how to cast on."

"Cat could help you." Ten pairs of eyes turned in Michael's direction. "She designs the sweaters for *Pink Slip*."

By the time the nurse called Cat's name, she had given minilessons in the long tail cast-on and attempted to unravel the secret of double points.

"Want me to come in with you?" Michael asked as she dropped her work into her tote bag and stood up.

"And have you find out how much I weigh? Not on your life." He could join her in the doctor's office after the exam was over.

The nurse, a no-nonsense type who looked more Queens than Upper East Side, eyed her with open curiosity as they walked down the corridor to room three. "The last time I saw such a commotion we had a soap star in the waiting room."

Cat laughed, but her heart wasn't in it. Reality was finally beginning to settle in with a vengeance. Getting pregnant had seemed like the smartest decision she had ever made. Being pregnant, however, was starting to scare her.

"Do you always travel with knitting needles?" The nurse motioned for Cat to step onto the big ugly scale in the corner.

"Occupational hazard."

"Hate to be behind you on line at the airport check-in."

She kicked off her shoes and debated the wisdom of taking off her watch, her earrings, and her sweater. She settled for exhaling, then climbed aboard.

"You might as well breathe," the nurse said as she slid the weights left then right. "Air's not going to make any difference."

"You're lucky I didn't take off my sweater."

"You wouldn't be the first." The nurse scribbled a number on Cat's chart. "Don't worry. You don't look it."

Cat tried to think of something suitably witty to say — this was Manhattan after all, and wit was the coin of the realm — but her mind went blank. Hard as it was to believe, in a few months she would think of that number with fond nostalgia.

"You can hang your clothes in the closet behind the screen," the nurse said. "You'll find disposable slippers and a robe on the chair."

"And a mint on my pillow?"

The nurse flashed a sympathetic smile. "The first visit is the hardest," she said. "Once you get past this, it's clear sailing until delivery."

"Can I have that notarized?"

Another sympathetic smile. "The doctor will be with you in a few minutes," she said, then vanished.

Everything about the room was designed for the physical comfort and emotional well-being of the patient. Soft peach walls. An ivory privacy screen. Pleasant watercolors of nameless beaches placed at eye level. The requisite diplomas and certificates and awards meant to reassure a woman who was lying flat on her back with her feet in stirrups while she waited for a total stranger to snap on the latex gloves and go to work.

This wasn't her first visit to the gynecologist. She was thirty-eight years old. You would think she would be used to it by now. She had a history of annual pelvic exams, birth control checkups, occasional visits for problems that always turned out to be blessedly minor. Her health was good. She was there because she wanted to be there, because after much thought and consideration, she had decided to have a baby with a man who very much wanted to be a father.

Her hands shook as she folded her sweater and slid it onto the shelf in the closet. How odd. She couldn't remember ever seeing her hands shake like that. What was it her friend Karen was always telling her to do? Breathe deeply. That was it. Talk about basic information. Empty your mind of everything, and draw in the deepest, longest breath you possibly could without thinking about anything at all.

She tried, but it didn't work. Her hands still trembled as she slipped on the pale peach cotton gown. This wasn't an annual Pap smear, something she would forget as soon as she left the office. Her old life stopped right here. After today, nothing would ever be the same again.

She thought about that as she hopped up onto the examining table. Wasn't that the point? If she had wanted her life to stay the same, she and Michael wouldn't have made a baby. You didn't decide to have a child because you wanted your life to stay the same forever. You decided to have a child because you wanted your life to be better, to have more meaning, because you were so filled with longing for a family of your own, a child to lavish with all the love that had been building all these years, that you decided to close your eyes and take a leap into the future, even if you weren't exactly sure what that future would hold.

Three hours later Cat and Michael faced each other across a tiny table at Aquavit. She had ordered her all-time favorite Swedish meatballs with lingonberries, but so far all she had done was push the berries from one side of her plate to the other and ignore the meatballs altogether.

"You haven't touched anything but water," he said.

"I don't see you making inroads on that salmon you ordered."

"I'm not eating for two."

She picked up her fork, broke off a piece of meatball, then popped it into her mouth.

"There," she said. "Are you happy now?"

"Sorry." He looked suitably chastened. "Next time tell me to back off."

"I will."

She took a sip of water and leaned back against the padded banquette.

"Still queasy?" he asked.

She had had an episode in the doctor's office, a combination of nerves, no breakfast, and the fact that she was in her first trimester.

"Queasy?" She considered the question. "No, but if you ask me if I'm scared, elated, or overwhelmed, you might get an entirely different answer."

He reached for her hand across the table, but she grabbed for her fork. "Screw the meatballs," he said, and she laughed. "I'll order you some ice cream."

"I know I'll regret leaving these meatballs behind tomorrow when I'm halfway between here and Maine."

"So take them with you."

"I don't think they do doggie bags at Aquavit."

To her surprise they not only did, but they managed it with high style and grace. Her entrée was neatly packaged and replaced with a towering dish of snowy vanilla ice cream, a dazzle of lingonberries, and an icy silver spoon.

Michael ate some of his salmon, then pushed his plate aside. "You're right. Nutrition's overrated. Eat dessert first."

"Grab a spoon," she said, "and help me out."

The waiter appeared next to them with

an urn of coffee. Michael nodded, and so did Cat. Then she remembered and opted for more water.

"There's so much to remember," she said with a shake of her head. "No caffeine. No wine." She tugged at a lock of hair. "Good-bye highlights, hello dark roots."

"That talk about amniocentesis and genetic counseling took me by surprise."

"Same here," she said. "I don't think we have anything to worry about, do you?"

He shook his head. "We come from good stock. He's just being cautious."

She knocked lightly on the wooden table. "From your mouth to God's ear."

"Superstitious?"

"Cautious," she said. "Like the doctor."

He took a giant spoonful of her ice cream, then followed it with a slug of black coffee. "Colfax seems like a good doctor."

"Great reputation," she agreed. They had done their homework before making the appointment. Harvard Medical. Interned at Johns Hopkins. Chief of ob-gyn at Columbia-Presbyterian.

"So why aren't you going to have him deliver the baby?"

Michael Yanovsky was a terrific guy, but clearly geography wasn't his strong suit. "For starters, how about the fact that he practices in New York and I live in Maine?"

"You're down here every month," he said. "Sometimes more."

"Right, and the baby will check my schedule before entering the birth canal."

A remark like that might have dimmed another man's enthusiasm but not Michael. "No problem. You can move down here."

Before that moment nothing had ever come between her and a bowl of ice cream. She dropped her spoon into the bowl, creating a vanilla wave. "You've got to be kidding." She loved the fierce creative energy that was the lifeblood of the city. A five-minute walk in any direction provided more food for her imagination than her brain could absorb, but there was no denying that she was a country girl through and through.

If he was kidding, he had forgotten to tell his face. He looked frighteningly serious. "I've been thinking about it. You could land a plane in my loft. Finding a space for you to set up your spinning wheels shouldn't be a problem."

The urge to run — a Doyle family trait — was almost irresistible. She fought it down as best she could. "I don't know what to say, Michael." *Don't ruin every-thing, Yanovsky. Didn't we agree we liked things the way they were?* "You know my business is in Maine."

There were times she wished he was a bricklayer or a truck driver, anything but a writer. Michael had this way of cutting through the layers of bullshit and going straight for the heart. The same gifts that illuminated his work made him tough as hell to lie to.

"Your business is like mine," he was saying, and she clicked back into the conversation. "It's portable."

"Not exactly." She took a fortifying spoonful of ice cream. "I own a dozen sheep. Wonder what they'll think of city living?"

It wasn't often a girl from Idle Point shocked a native New Yorker speechless.

He took a few long seconds to regroup. "Did you say sheep?"

"Twelve Romneys," she said, reaching for her tote bag. "I have pictures if you'd like to see them."

"You carry pictures of your sheep?"

She laughed out loud. "Don't look so scared, Michael. One of the producers at *Pink Slip* grew up on a sheep farm in central New Jersey. He wanted to see my stock."

40

Poor man. The thought of sleeping with a shepherdess clearly threw him for a loop. She had seen him adjust to random gunshots on Sixth Avenue faster.

"What the hell are you doing with twelve sheep?" His expression was priceless.

"I haven't been spinning straw into gold," she countered. "I need fleece, and it has to come from somewhere." She didn't tell him they lived on a farm three miles from her home. His shock was too delicious.

He gulped some more coffee. He probably wanted to mainline it. "I figured people bought it."

She was starting to enjoy this. "You mean like at a fleece store."

He knew when he was being played and grinned. "Yeah, a fleece store."

"I don't suppose I mentioned my four alpacas and two crias."

"Okay, now you're scaring me, Doyle. What the hell is a cria?"

"A baby alpaca, the cutest thing you've ever seen in your life. We bred two of the females and got lucky first time out."

"Bring 'em on," he said. "If the writing doesn't work out, I'll sign on as your shepherd."

They fell silent as the waiter made another pass with the coffee urn.

"Colfax gave me the name of a good doctor in my region. That's where my house is. That's where my business is. People depend on me. I can't let them down."

He was censoring himself. She could tell by the way he drummed the tabletop with the ring finger of his left hand.

"If you have something to say, say it," she urged him. "We're not going to come up with a perfect solution to our geography problem, but we can work something out."

"Listen, Cat, maybe —"

The sound of reveille poured from her tote bag. "I'm sorry. I forgot to turn off my cell." She reached down to silence it, then caught sight of the caller ID display. "Karen's my business partner," she explained. "I'd better take it."

She stood up and hurried to a hot spot in the corridor between the kitchen and the restroom.

"Where are you?" Karen asked without preamble.

"Standing in front of the ladies' loo at Aquavit."

"You're still in New York?"

"Yes. What's wrong?" Few things were more frightening than silence when you needed words. "Karen, say something. You're scaring me."

"There's been a fire, Cat. Your mother's in the hospital. You'd better come home right now."

Michael heard a commotion coming from the rear of the restaurant. He glanced around, but nobody else seemed particularly concerned, so he settled back into demolishing Cat's bowl of ice cream and didn't notice the waiter until the guy practically climbed onto the table to get his attention.

"Sir, your lunch companion isn't feeling well."

He jumped up and clipped the poor guy with an elbow. "Where is she?"

"In the ladies' room. She said —"

He didn't wait for the paraphrased version but barged into the women's bathroom, where he found Cat stretched out on a chaise longue in the anteroom.

"I'm fine," she said before he could form the question. "Don't look so worried."

"Do we need to call Colfax?"

"No!" That brought a splash of color to her cheeks. "We just left his office. I'm two months pregnant. It comes with the territory."

"So what happened with the phone call?" he asked.

"A — um, a problem back home."

"Yarn emergency?"

"Something like that." She swung her feet to the floor and tugged at the hem of her sweater. "I'm sorry. I have to leave."

Understandable. They were in a public bathroom. He wanted to leave, too.

"We'll go back to my place," he said. "You can take a nap."

"No, no. You don't understand. I have to get home." She swayed like a sapling in a hurricane, then sat back down again on the edge of the chaise.

"You're not driving."

"I'm fine."

"You almost fell over."

"Give me a minute. I'll splash some water on my face. I'll be fine."

"It's a three-hundred-mile drive." *She drives it every month, moron. She knows the mileage.*

"I'll pace myself. I have to get back this afternoon."

"Let Karen wait. You can drive home to-morrow."

"No," she said. "I have to leave now."

"What's the rush? I have a phone. I have a fax. I even have a computer. You can handle whatever you need to handle from my place." He tried not to notice that she

44

hadn't told him what the emergency was.

"Look, I know you mean well, Michael, and I really appreciate your concern, but it's unnecessary. I'm a big girl. I'll be fine."

She didn't say "case closed," but she might as well have. He knew every centimeter of her body. He knew parts of her body she had never even seen. She was carrying his baby, and he still had the feeling they were strangers in all the ways that mattered.

"So are you going to tell me what the emergency is?"

She actually looked surprised, like it hadn't even occurred to her that he might have a need to know. "It's a family thing."

He placed a hand on her flat belly. "So is this, Cat. Tell me what's wrong."

"My mother," she said, then stopped. "My mother had a — there was a fire —" She raised her hands in a classic gesture of helplessness. "They rushed her to the emergency room, and it's not looking good."

"Okay," he said. "We'll go to my place and get your things, and then I'll drive you up to Maine."

"Listen," she said, "I appreciate the gesture but —"

"It's not a gesture. It's what you do when

someone you care for needs help."

"I don't need help."

"Remember that the next time you find yourself hugging the floor in a four-star restaurant."

She handed him her keys.

Chapter Three

Loch Craig — Late Afternoon

Annabelle pouted for a good thirty minutes after Joely told her William wouldn't be home in time for the solstice picnic, but then her sweet nature returned and with it her excitement. She talked nonstop about what would happen as the day lengthened into night, elaborate fantasies about faeries and imps and trolls who came out to dance in the midnight sun. She wanted Joely to phone William on his mobile and tell him that she had seen evidence of faerie infestation in the side yard, but Joely finally convinced the little girl to save up all of her stories to share with her father when he called later that night.

"Will he call us when we're up the hill?" Annabelle asked as she helped Joely prepare the picnic basket of snacks they would take with them later on.

"He'll call us when we get home." Joely washed some cherry tomatoes and dried them on a clean dish towel.

"Why don't we call him?" Annabelle persisted as she swiped one of the tomatoes and rolled it across the countertop. "Then it will be like he's there with us."

"Don't bounce the tomatoes, Annabelle."

Annabelle popped the bounced fruit into her mouth. "I'm not bouncing. I'm eating."

"I saw you bounce it."

"Did not."

Joely bit back a reflexive — and incredibly childish — *did, too.* "Why don't you run upstairs and look for your favorite red plaid blanket," she suggested. "We'll take it with us tonight."

Annabelle's eyes twinkled with delight. "The big soft one with the tickly fringes?"

"Yes, the one my sister made for your birthday."

"Brilliant!" Annabelle darted from the room and clattered up the back staircase. She had taken to wearing clogs that made her sound like a Clydesdale horse.

Joely leaned against the countertop as an unexpected rush of love almost took her legs out from under her. She had never understood the term *unconditional love* until she met Annabelle and every maternal instinct she hadn't believed existed suddenly sprang to life.

The thought of not seeing that precious face every day was unendurable. If she did think about it she would never find the guts to sit down with William and force them to talk about their future.

She had lingered on the edge of a full-on crying jag all day, a combination of that early morning dream and William's e-mail and the rain that had been sputtering on and off for hours. Then again it could be PMS. Whatever it was, she wished it would go away. This weepy nostalgic mood wasn't her style.

The rain came and went all afternoon while Annabelle provided a running commentary on the weather, interspersed with melodramatic laments over the welfare of the faeries who lived in the gardens. Joely, who didn't have a fanciful bone in her body, had to remind herself that these problems were very real to the little girl. Finally she retrieved an umbrella from the stand in the hallway and jury-rigged a way to suspend it over a tiny part of the side garden where Annabelle claimed the faerie children liked to hide.

Her mother would have known exactly how to handle the situation. Mimi hadn't been very good at mundane chores like paying the electric bill or keeping the telephone service on, but she would have known how to shield the faeries from the rainfall, then taken Annabelle on a guided tour of every faerie hiding spot in the Highlands.

Joely winced as she remembered the time she had tried to entertain Annabelle with a double helix made of dried macaroni. The poor child had fallen asleep before the first helix was in the planning stage.

The off-again/on-again rains finally stopped a little before five o'clock, and the sun reappeared. It was in full bloom at eight when they got ready to head up the hill.

"You'll still need a cardi and your Wellies," Joely warned as they finished a light supper. "It's going to get cold to-night."

Not even the prospect of rubber boots was enough to dim Annabelle's enthusiasm and, to her surprise, Joely found her mood much improved by the time they gathered up blankets, extra sweaters, the picnic basket, and an umbrella (just in case) and set out.

"What time is it in Japan?" Annabelle asked as they made their way toward the hill path.

"Much later."

"Is it already tomorrow?"

"Yes, it is."

"So Daddy knows what happened today before we do."

She needed more than a master's in bioengineering to field that question. "Everything is happening at the same time," she said, gripping Annabelle's hand as the child's clogs slipped on the wet grass. "It's just that it's later in Japan than it is here."

"But you said it's already tomorrow."

"Yes, but —"

"If it's already tomorrow, then he knows what happened today."

"No, he doesn't, Annabelle, because it hasn't happened yet."

"But it must have if it's tomorrow."

She stopped and put down the picnic basket, then held out her left wrist toward the child. "What time is it?"

Annabelle peered at the watch. "Half six."

She pulled out the stem, adjusted the time forward three hours, then pushed it back in. "What time is it now?"

"Half nine."

"That's all there is to it, honey. We play with the clocks, but time itself remains constant. It may be tomorrow in Japan, but

51

your father is still living in the same moment as we are."

Annabelle had a quick and curious mind.
She peppered Joely with questions about
the nature of time that would have stumped
her old physics professor at MIT. She was
glad when they reached the top of the hill,
and Annabelle spotted her best friend Louis
and ran off to tell him all about time zones.

Louis's mother Sara motioned her over
to her blanket. "You look like you need a
glass of plonk." Sara had been a Sloane
Ranger in the early 1980s and occasionally
slipped back into the slang of her misbe-
gotten youth.

Joely spread out her own blanket and
settled down next to her friend. "I love
cheap wine," she said, accepting a plastic
cup of red. "William thinks I'm a peasant
at heart." She made Sara laugh with a re-
counting of the rain-soaked garden faeries
and her own struggle to figure out a way to
keep them from drowning.

Sara topped off their cups. "So how are
you coping without Mrs. Macdonald?"

Joely took a long sip of wine, grateful for
the meager warmth it sent into her system.
The sun might still be out, but the temperature was beginning to dip. "We're doing
fine at the moment."

"What about when you go back to work?"

"I'll figure something out."

"Shouldn't that be her father's job?"

"Sara." Her tone held a gentle warning. They had been over this territory a hundred times before. "We both do what's right for Annabelle. She's our first priority."

"Darling, she's not your child."

"I know that."

"Loving her isn't a crime, but —"

"Sara." The warning was less gentle this time.

Sara waved away the warning. "If Hugh and I weren't heading down to London tomorrow, I'd take Annabelle and send you off to Japan right now. What you and our William need is some time alone."

"Don't be ridiculous."

"When was the last time you two went on holiday alone?"

"Never," she said after a moment.

"That's not good."

"It's not bad either. We're a family," she said. "We don't need to escape on holiday."

"Every couple needs to escape."

"Sara, is there a point to this?"

"I'm British, darling. We ease our way

53

slowly toward personal revelations."

"You're wondering why William isn't here tonight." He had, after all, made loud and enthusiastic promises.

"Why isn't he here tonight?" she asked.

Next to Cat, Sara probably knew her as well as anyone on earth, and even Sara knew very little. "No big secret. He's off to Kyoto to fill in for a sick colleague."

"Bugger all." Sara plucked a salmon roll-up from the picnic basket and popped it into her mouth.

She laughed out loud. "Yeah," she said. "Bugger all."

"I meant what I said. You and our William need some time alone. You've never had the chance to be simply the two of you."

She shook her head. "I'm afraid your William and I need more than time alone."

"It's come to that, has it?"

"I think so."

Sara opened her mouth to speak, then closed it again.

"Oh go ahead," Joely said with a wave of her hand. "I can take it."

"I know you're the practical sort, but would you mind awfully if I held a good thought for the three of you?"

It would take much more than a good

thought, but Sara was her friend and she already knew that.

"What was his wife like?" Joely asked as they divided up a piece of cake layered with lemon curd. "I've seen pictures, but they don't really tell you anything."

If the question surprised Sara, she didn't let on. Her brow furrowed ever so slightly as she considered her answer. "Thoughtful. When I think of Natasha, that's the first thing that comes to mind. She knew how to listen."

"Was she funny?"

"Obliquely."

"Obliquely? You'll have to do better than that."

Sara rolled her eyes. "You Americans are so literal." She was silent for a bit. "It's been a very long time, but when Annabelle laughs, it's Natasha I hear."

This was one of those times when Joely longed for the plain talk of her old hometown. Pretty words, but they told her nothing beyond the fact that Annabelle was her mother's daughter. "Where did you meet? How did you all become friends?"

Sara and Natasha met in an obstetrician's office near Kensington Park. They were both there for their first postnatal visit, both accompanied by their husbands and brand-new offspring. The men worked in finance. The women were delighted to be stay-at-home mums. It had been a heady time. They were all young and beautiful and healthy, and the future went on forever.

"How did she die?" Joely asked, making sure Annabelle was out of earshot. "I mean, I know she was sick, but I never asked William for details." Natasha had never seemed real to her, and so she had been content with what little she knew.

"Pancreatic cancer," Sara said. "Forty-five days from diagnosis until her funeral." She met Joely's eyes. "She was buried a week before Annabelle's first birthday."

Once Sara started, she couldn't stop, and Joely listened, first in fascination and then in despair, as William's wife, Annabelle's mother, suddenly became a flesh-and-blood woman.

William and Natasha had had a real marriage. They had formed a real family, and if the fates had been just a little bit kinder, it would have been Natasha sitting here with Sara watching their children play in the heather on the night of the summer solstice.

She had never given much thought to

William's loss. It had happened before they met, and he had made his peace with it. Or so it had seemed to Joely. And if there was one thing she had learned growing up, it was to take things as they presented themselves and not ask questions. She wasn't an explorer. The dark and murky waters of emotion were foreign territory to her and, she had assumed, to William as well.

But maybe that hadn't always been the case. Maybe with Natasha things had been very different.

A skirl of pipes drifted up from the valley below, and Joely shivered. There was something timeless about the Highlands that even she, with her practical mind, couldn't help but acknowledge.

"Nobody back home would believe this," Joely said. "Annabelle says she hears the pipes every morning, echoing in the hills."

Sara laughed. "And Louis claims he saw William Wallace last week coming out of the cinema."

"Are we sure there isn't Scots blood running through their English veins?"

"Speaking as the mother of a seven-year-old, I am most certainly not sure of anything."

Annabelle and Louis finally ran out of energy. They threw themselves on the

57

blankets and lay on their backs, looking up at the soft indigo sky. Before long the kids drifted off into sleep, and after a bit even Joely and Sara found themselves hiding yawns behind their hands, and it wasn't even nine o'clock.

"Safe trip," Joely said as they hugged good-bye at the foot of the hill. "I'll miss you."

"It's only until September, love." Sara hugged her back. "You and William and Annabelle must come down for a weekend. Promise me you will."

She tried to speak, but an onslaught of unwelcome emotion grabbed her by the throat and cut off her words. September was a very long time away, and almost anything could happen. Sara was a good friend and a very wise woman, and she was able to read between the lines of Joely's silence.

"It will work out," Sara said as they all parted company. "I know it will."

The long, eventful day finally caught up with Annabelle, and she clung to Joely like a spider monkey. She smelled of grass and heather as she pressed her face against the side of Joely's neck. Her warm, moist breath was sweet as clover.

"I want to talk to Daddy," Annabelle

said a few minutes later as Joely closed the front door behind them.

Joely slid the lock into position and dimmed the lights. "I think we should get you ready for bed, don't you?"

"Can we call him? Why can't we call him right now?"

"Brush your teeth and change into your pajamas," Joely said. "I'll bet he phones us before you climb into bed."

Annabelle brightened. "Can I sleep in your bed tonight?" she asked as they climbed the stairs to the second-floor bedroom.

"Since when do you ask first?" Joely said, placing a kiss on top of the child's head. "Brush your teeth, and we'll negotiate."

Annabelle dashed into the little bathroom adjacent to her bedroom. A second later the sound of running water drifted through the closed door. Stifling a yawn, Joely walked slowly down the hallway toward the corner room she shared with William. She was exhausted through to her bones, a deep yawning exhaustion that sapped both energy and hope.

The bleat of the phone, followed by Annabelle's squeal of "Daddy!" from the bathroom, almost jolted her out of her shoes. She darted across the room and grabbed the receiver before it could ring again.

"Your timing is perfect, William," she said by way of hello. "We just got in a few minutes ago."

"Honey, it's not William," a familiar voice said in return. "It's Cat, and I've got some bad news."

"Are you okay?"

"It's Mom. I don't have all the details, but she either fell and accidentally set fire to the house or set fire to the house then fell when she was trying to escape."

"Oh, Jesus . . ." She sank onto the bed as hideous images filled her brain. "How bad?"

"I don't know. I was in New York when Karen called to tell me."

"Where are you now?"

She heard the sound of muffled conversation. "Northeastern Connecticut, near Storrs."

"Was she drinking?"

"I don't know."

"Come on, Cat, I think we both know —"

"I told you I was in New York when it happened. I don't know the details."

"Sure you do. We both do. She was drinking and —"

"Daddy!" Annabelle burst into the bedroom. "Let me speak to Daddy!"

Joely placed a hand over the mouthpiece. "Honey, this isn't Daddy. It's my sister."

Annabelle's lower lip trembled. "I want Daddy."

"I know you do, and I'm sure he's going to call as soon as he possibly can."

She patted the bed next to her, and the little girl climbed in, clearly torn between tears and a minor tantrum.

"Sorry," Joely said into the phone. "William's been delayed in Japan, and Annabelle isn't very happy about it."

Cat didn't acknowledge the interruption. "Joely, I need you to come home."

For the second time in less than five minutes, Joely struggled to catch her breath. "I wish I could. I know there's a lot on your shoulders, but I just can't. This isn't a good time." Not now. Not when things were so fragile, so uncertain. Not with Annabelle looking up at her with big weepy eyes. Not with William half a world away. Not with her professional life teetering on the brink. Not with her past tucked away like an old photo album, exactly the way she liked it.

If Cat wanted reasons, she had reasons. She could give her reasons for the next five years why she didn't want to go back to Idle Point now or ever, but her sister's full frontal assault was under way.

"When you left for MIT we made a deal," Cat was saying. "I'd stay here and take care of Mom, while you went out there and grabbed the world by the balls and made us proud. Remember?"

"I'm grateful. You know that." *Everybody in town knows that, so why are we going through this? It's not like she'd even know I was there, Cat. You're the only one who matters.*

"This isn't about gratitude. I promised I would let you go, and you promised you would come home if I asked you to."

"And you're asking."

"I'm asking."

That was the thing about promises. Sooner or later the person you made those promises to expected you to make good on them.

Funny how she had never really believed this day would come.

"I'll see what I can do. William will be home in a week or two. Mrs. Macdonald's not with us anymore and —"

"You're not listening. I need you here now."

"To do what? Hold her hand? Maybe I

62

don't want to hold her hand, Cat. Maybe I wish she'd been there to hold my hand once or twice over the years."

Annabelle was looking up at her with a combination of puzzlement and fear that tore at her heart. This was exactly the kind of thing she would throw herself on her sword to avoid.

She took a deep breath and regrouped. "Listen, I'm sorry about the accident. I want her to be well. I don't want you to have to deal with this on your own, but I have responsibilities here." She laid her hand on Annabelle's shoulder, and the little girl snuggled close. "I'll do what I can, but I can't give you a timetable."

"If that's the best you can do."

It wasn't. She could do better, and they both knew it.

"Call me when you know how Mom is," she said.

No response. Cat was long gone.

"Damn," she whispered, then pressed the disconnect button.

"Where's Daddy?" Annabelle demanded as she tossed the phone down on the bed. "Why didn't he talk to me?"

"Honey, I told you that wasn't your daddy," Joely said. "That was my sister."

"Why are you crying?"

She touched her cheeks. "I didn't know I was." She wasn't a crying kind of woman, and she sure as hell wasn't about to shed a tear for Mimi's self-inflicted troubles.

"Why are you sad?" Annabelle persisted.

"My mother —" She buried her face against the child's bony shoulder. What kind of pathetic loser of a woman fell apart in front of a little girl? "My mother is in the hospital, and I have to go home."

"Silly!" Annabelle squirmed away. "You're home already."

"I know, honey," she said, holding the child tight. "I know I am."

It was the first time she had ever lied to Annabelle, but she knew it wouldn't be the last.

Chapter Four

Everyone who had ever met Mimi Doyle agreed that she was as high-strung as a racehorse at the starting gate. She felt things more keenly than other people. Whatever it was that buffered other hearts from the slings and arrows of real life was missing in Mimi. Her behavior, which had once been labeled harmlessly eccentric, grew more erratic with the years, and by the time Grandma Fran died, Mimi's spells of heavy drinking alternated with spells of angry abstinence and the occasional naked sprint up Main Street.

The line between normal and abnormal had been blurred out of existence. Mimi careened through life like a runaway train while Cat followed behind, minimizing the damage the best she could.

Sometimes Mimi drank. Sometimes she didn't. Sometimes she was lucid and agreeable. Sometimes she shed her past along with her inhibitions and tested the chaos theory of living to its limits. But there was one constant, one North Star that guided everything Mimi did: her belief that one day Mark would come back to her.

It never once occurred to Mimi that maybe this time there wouldn't be a happy ending, that maybe this time the story would end the way all of those old folk songs they had made famous always ended: with the fair maiden pining away for love of the errant knight who would never return.

Mimi was sixty-two years old, and she was still waiting for him to show up at the front door, metaphorical hat in hand, sheepish and contrite. And Cat knew exactly what would happen if he did. Mimi would open her arms wide to him, and he would flash what remained of the wicked grin she had fallen in love with at St. Bernadette's, and it would be like the last twenty-seven years had never happened. No anger. No recriminations. She loved him now the way she had loved him then, and not even the cold hard bite of reality would ever change that.

Cat had believed she was doing a pretty fair job of keeping things under control without sacrificing her own life or her mother's safety until today, when reality turned around and bit her instead.

Cat and Michael crossed from New Hampshire into Maine around five thirty. She had kept up a humorous but brittle commentary on the scenery across four states, and the effort was beginning to take its toll.

"You drive like an old lady," she said as he followed the signs to the tourist center. "I could've cut forty minutes off your time without even trying."

"Assuming you didn't fall asleep and hit a tree."

"I've been wide awake the whole trip."

"The hell you have." He cut a quick look in her direction. "You were snoring."

"I don't snore."

"You did today."

He pulled into a parking spot beneath a stand of fragrant pine trees tall enough to remind you why you believed in God.

"What are we doing here? I don't need a rest stop."

"I do." He switched off the engine and pocketed the keys.

"You're taking my keys?"

"I don't trust you," he said. "You might leave me stranded here in Paul Bunyan country."

He knew her too well. Part of her wanted

to break every speed limit and get home before it was too late, while another, uglier part — the part that was her father's daughter — wanted to grab the wheel and keep on driving until she hit Canada or a major body of water, whichever came first.

But she was a good daughter, and good daughters didn't do that. Good daughters continued doing what they had been doing their whole lives. She flipped open her cell and pressed Redial.

"Idle Point General. How may I direct your call?"

"Terry, it's Cat Doyle. Any news?"

"I hope you're not driving. I hate people who talk on the phone while they're driving." Terry Seaborne had been answering phones at Idle Point General for as long as Cat could remember.

"Don't worry. I'm not driving."

"Where are you?"

"Tourist center parking lot near Kittery."

"Good. You're not too far."

"Terry, please. Have they taken Mimi into surgery yet?"

"She's prepped and ready. Laquita on women's surgical told me they're waiting for Green to finish in the big room, and they'll wheel her in."

Terry launched herself into a long story

about the splenectomy Green was performing on old Mr. Dunaway from Frenchtown. Usually Cat was happy to listen until either Terry ran out of breath or Cat drifted off into a spontaneous siesta, but she didn't have the energy today.

"Terry, I seem to be losing the signal," she said as Michael opened the driver's side door and climbed back in. "I'll talk to you when I get there." She met Michael's curious gaze. "Don't say a word," she warned him.

"You were dragging your ring across the mouthpiece."

"And I'm ashamed of myself. I'll take her for coffee and make up for it later."

He started the engine. "So how's your mother doing?"

"She's still in a holding pattern."

"Good," he said. "Let's get you there in time to see her before surgery."

She was a lousy passenger. Always had been. She only felt comfortable when it was her foot on the gas pedal, her hands on the wheel.

"Pull over," she said, gesturing toward a grassy shoulder near the entrance to the highway.

"You need the bathroom?"

"I need to drive."

"What about the dizziness?"

"Gone."

"Great."

"Are you going to pull over so I can drive?"

"Nope."

"It's my car."

"I know. Mine's better."

"Anyone can lease a fancy car. At least I own this."

He launched into a very funny riff on Beemers and Hummers and the women who loved the men who leased them, and she couldn't help but laugh. He was as transparent as rain on a freshly washed window. He was talking about anything and everything except the reason why she was in the passenger seat and he was behind the wheel, and the two of them — scratch that, the three of them — were headed north to Idle Point.

"This isn't exactly the way I had today planned out," she said.

"Me neither." He had a great smile, a real smile. Not that big fake ear-to-ear baring of the teeth that some men flashed like Get Out of Jail Free cards. "I was planning to take you back to bed for the afternoon."

"I probably would have fallen asleep on you."

"I can think of worse things than watching you sleep."

On any other day she would have volleyed that statement back to him with a self-deprecating laugh and a well-aimed one-liner, but today she couldn't manage to find the words to defuse the longing that suddenly made it difficult to breathe, much less think.

This shouldn't be happening. The whole thing was wrong, about as wrong as it could possibly be. She had tried so hard to keep the two disparate parts of her life separate and distinct, and now they were on a collision course, and there was nothing she could do to stop it.

When a pregnant woman keeled over in a pricey Manhattan restaurant, she couldn't blame the father-to-be for wanting to protect both child and mother. That was why she had chosen him in the first place, wasn't it, because he was a good man and a kind one and he had his priorities straight. And, likewise, you couldn't blame the mother for accepting the protection even if she had spent most of her life denying she needed help of any kind.

But the rules changed when you were

carrying a life deep inside your body. It was all part of nature's insidious little plan for propagating the species. Sooner or later she knew she would have to let him into her world, but not now. Not this way.

She had planned to wait until she was into her second trimester, when she was beginning to show and could no longer blame the size of her breasts and belly on the world's longest case of water retention. She would time it for one of Mimi's up cycles, when her mother loved the world and the world loved her, and even her frequent lapses of judgment and good taste seemed more fey than just plain crazy.

Michael was a writer. He grew up in New York and had a high tolerance for eccentrics. With a little preparation, he might have found three hours with Mimi Doyle fascinating.

Too bad Mimi had her own plan, one that included waiting for the housekeeper to head out to the store, then setting fire to the house.

Don't mind my mother, she would tell Michael. *She's crazy, but she's not dangerous.*

She didn't want to have to explain Mimi to him. She didn't want to see the concern in his eyes turn to pity. She didn't want to hear that angry, defensive tone her voice took on when somebody got too close. Bad enough he had heard her side of that edgy conversation with Joely.

This was her problem, her family. She was here because she wanted to be, because somebody had to be, and she was the one with the right skill set to handle it. She didn't have to explain the situation to anyone in Idle Point. They had been there from the start of the story, back when her parents first locked eyes across a crowded dance floor, and they would be there at the end. She wasn't sure she could say that about Michael.

"Are we there yet?" Michael broke into her thoughts. "I think we're heading for the Canadian border."

She quickly got her bearings. "Next exit. You'll make a right at the stop sign and keep going until you hit water."

"Metaphorically speaking."

"Of course."

"A lot of trees up here," he said in a conversational tone.

"It's Maine," she reminded him. "We're known for our trees."

"Looks like you're known for shopping," he said as they rolled past a half-dozen discount shoe stores, musty antique shops, and factory outlets that wouldn't make the grade in Kittery or Portland.

"It gets more picturesque as we get closer to Idle Point."

"I like it," he said. "It reminds me of Secaucus."

She couldn't help it. She laughed out loud again.

Her stomach knotted when they hit the town limits and rolled past Gas-2-Go and the car wash next to Jiffy Lube. A pounding sensation began behind her eyeballs when she caught sight of Nancy Westgarten and her sister Maureen standing in front of the bank, peering in her direction. Only ninety feet into town, and they had already been spotted by the Idle Point equivalent of Page Six.

"They're probably burning up a month's worth of cell phone minutes," she mumbled into the window.

"What was that?"

"A rude remark you don't need to hear."

He shot her a look but made no comment.

"Next left," she said, "at the corner by Cumberland Farms. That road will take us straight to the hospital."

He made the left and drove past First Presbyterian, Chase Memorial Middle

School, and what used to be Ada's Hairport but was now Video Haven. "So this is where you grew up."

"Sort of. I was almost twelve when we moved here," she said, then instantly regretted saying even that much.

"I thought you were born here." She could almost see the questions starting to spin in his writer's brain.

"My mother was."

"And then she ended up coming back home?"

"Something like that."

"I have a lot of questions," he said.

"I'm sure you do, but you won't ask them now, will you."

"No," he said, "but that doesn't mean I won't ask them later."

Later was good. It was right now that had her worried.

Michael had seen veterinary hospitals that were bigger than Idle Point General.

"Parking's in the back," Cat said as she unfastened her seat belt. "Next to the newspaper office."

She looked ready to bolt. His cool, unflappable Cat was coming apart at the seams.

"Why don't I drop you at the front entrance," he said, pulling over to the curb. "You go in and find your mom."

"But you won't know where I am."

"I don't think there'll be a problem." She was out of the car and moving up the walkway before he could get out and help her. For a woman who had spent most of her life in a town that could fit inside Madison Square Garden with room to spare, she walked like a city girl, quickly and with purpose.

He waited until she disappeared through the front doors, then circled around to the parking lot adjacent to the emergency room, where he had his pick of spots. He pulled in two over from a bright red Mercedes convertible. Top down. No LoJack or wheel lock. Didn't the good people of Idle Point know that auto theft was big business?

He locked Cat's car anyway. He was a New Yorker, and New Yorkers locked the car even when they were in Maine.

"Second floor, Michael." A small woman with black hair that gleamed blue under the fluorescent lighting greeted him as he stepped into the lobby.

He stopped midstride. "Excuse me?"

"Cat said to tell you she's on the second floor."

"Thanks," he said. He tried to imagine the receptionist at Columbia-Presbyterian greeting visitors by name. The mind boggled.

"The elevator's right over there," the woman said. "Near the water fountain."

"Thanks," he said again.

So she read minds, too. Un-freaking-believable. Clearly she didn't know everything, however, because she looked like she was dying to ask what the deal was between Cat and him, and only three hundred years of strict Yankee discipline kept her tongue in check.

The place was so quiet he could hear the sound of his own breathing. It made Temple Beth-El during the High Holy Days sound like Mardi Gras. There was only one elevator, and the light was holding steady at three. He pressed the Up arrow again, waited a few seconds, then ducked into the stairwell, where he bumped into an octogenarian candy striper lugging a basket of magazines and paperbacks.

"Cat's in surgical waiting," the woman said as he held the door for her. "She's trying to see Mimi before they wheel her in."

He blinked like one of those characters

in the old black-and-white cartoons.

They either had an intelligence network the government needed to know about, or he was the first outlander to come to town since Prohibition.

Surgical waiting turned out to be a line of chairs set up in the hallway outside the swinging doors that led to the operating rooms.

Cat was standing near the window looking down at the street. She turned around at the sound of his footsteps. She looked exhausted, drained of energy and joy in a way he hadn't seen before, and it scared him.

"Hey." He draped an arm across her shoulders. She didn't lean into him, but then she never did. "How's your mother doing?"

"I'm still waiting to see her . . ." She shrugged and looked down at her hands. "I'm hoping there's a chance before they wheel her in for surgery."

It was like looking at a marble statue, lovely and unreachable. He couldn't read her. He thought he knew most of her moods, all of her expressions, but she was suddenly terra incognita.

"C'mon," he said, turning her toward the row of chairs. "Sit down. I'll go find you something to eat."

"I'm not hungry."

"Sure you are. You're eating for two, remember?"

"That's not public knowledge yet, Yanovsky."

"I know." He bent down and kissed the top of her head. "Your secret's safe with me."

"I know," she said, and she leaned against him.

She didn't lean against him for long, not his Cat, but he liked to think it was a start.

Chapter Five

Loch Craig

"You're a good friend," Joely said as she started a pot of tea brewing. "It's almost midnight. You should be home with your family."

Sara broke off a piece of scone and popped it into her mouth. "So should you, darling. Your mother needs you."

"Trust me, Sara. My mother doesn't need me. I'm not even sure she remembers my name."

"I'm sure there's a story behind that, but forgive me, darling, if we postpone it for another day." She leaned forward, her dark eyes intent upon Joely. "Have you reached William yet?"

Joely shook her head. "I phoned his cell three times, but he wasn't answering. I asked him to call."

"E-mail?"

"Of course."

"And nothing?"

"Not yet." He was in transit, so she still didn't know the name of the hotel in Kyoto where he would be staying.

The kettle began to whistle, and Joely leaped up to silence it before the din woke Annabelle.

"So what are you going to do?" Sara asked as Joely poured boiling water into the teapot.

"I don't know," Joely said. "I can't reach William. I certainly can't leave Annabelle home alone. There's nothing I can do but stay put."

"Take Annabelle with you."

"To America?"

"I hardly think you have a choice in this, darling. You have a family emergency. William will understand."

"No," she said firmly. "Cat will have to handle things without me."

Sara pushed back her chair and stood up. "Then I think I'll head back home. You've made up your mind, and I have to finish packing for the trip down to London."

"If you knew my sister, you'd understand," Joely said as she walked Sara to the door. "She's the most capable woman on earth. She really doesn't need me there."

"You know best, darling," Sara said.

"But this isn't really about your sister, is it?"

"No," she said, feeling control slipping away from her. "It's not about Cat at all. It's about me." She forced herself to meet her friend's eyes. "It was a car accident . . . a few days before I was set to start school at MIT. I needed Mimi to sign the financial documents that dealt with my scholarships — she'd been putting it off and putting it off, and I was starting to freak out that the whole thing was slipping away from me — so I finally dragged her away from whatever it was she'd been doing, and she drove us over to the bank and got things done. Mimi seemed spacey to me, kind of out of it, although with Mimi it was hard to separate what was normal from what wasn't. I remember telling her she shouldn't be driving, that I'd drive us both home, but she fought me. She hated anyone telling her what to do, absolutely hated it. Finally I managed to get the keys from her. She was pissed as hell at me. She went so crazy that I remember being afraid she was going to reach over and try to grab the keys out of the ignition. I even thought maybe we should walk home or maybe I should ask her to sit in the backseat. Something. Anyway, I was trying to keep one eye on Mimi and one eye on the road, and all I could think about was how I only had to get through seventy-two more hours in that town. Seventy-two hours! It was nothing. The blink of an eye. All I had to do was get through seventy-two hours, and I'd leave, and I was never going to come back. We were about to make a left at the intersection near the post office when I saw Ty Porter's red Camaro shoot across and —" She stopped and shook her head. "The next thing I knew I was in the emergency room having my head X-rayed, and they were saying Ty was dead."

Sara touched her hand. "I am so sorry, love. What a terrible thing to happen."

Ty was his parents' favorite son, the one who was expected to take over the farm and carry on their name. Their pain, the entire town's pain, exploded all over Joely.

"Every time I closed my eyes, the whole thing played out all over again inside my head, but I couldn't change the way it ended," she said as Sara listened quietly. "The cops brought me in for questioning after I was let out of the hospital, and I couldn't stop crying. I kept thinking if only I'd taken the back way home . . . if only I'd made Mimi sit in the backseat . . . if only I hadn't frozen right there in the

83

intersection when I heard his Camaro coming —"

Nothing sounded quite like a '69 Camaro. The whole town knew the sound of Ty Porter's car. She should have moved forward or made the turn. Anything. But she didn't. She couldn't move. She couldn't breathe. All she could do was wait for fate to catch up with her.

Ty had been traveling east on Main Street with his brother Zach in the passenger seat when he ran the stop sign and broadsided Mimi's battered old van. By some miracle of the gods, neither she nor Mimi had been badly injured. However, Ty slammed full force into the steering column of his Camaro and died instantly.

"And you want to know the worst part, Sara? While this whole hideous thing was happening all around me, I could still hear this ugly little voice in the back of my head bargaining with God, promising I'd go to church every day for the rest of my life if He would just let me leave for MIT the way I planned."

"You were young," Sara said. If she thought less of Joely for the admission, she was too dear a friend to let it show. "We're horribly selfish when we're young. When you're that young, you're incapable of understanding mortality."

But it was more than that. She had seen a vision of her future buried in the grave along with Idle Point's favorite son, and that vision overshadowed everything else. The relief she had felt when the autopsy report came back with the news that Ty's blood alcohol level had been more than twice the legal limit still shamed her today, ten years after the fact.

Kyoto, Japan

William Bishop's mobile died somewhere between Tokyo and Kyoto when it fell out of his jacket pocket and bounced off the stainless steel sink in the lav of the Shinkansen and cracked in two.

He wasn't a superstitious man by nature. He wasn't one to knock wood or toss salt over his left shoulder. He would gladly walk under a ladder if that was the shortest route between points A and B, but the sight of the cracked mobile left him unsettled, as if the only thing tying him to home and hearth had been severed, and he was out there alone.

"Bad luck," his coworker, a middle-aged

man named George, said as he reclaimed his seat. "But this is Japan. You'll pick up a new one when we get to Kyoto."

He nodded. George's advice sounded reasonable enough, but the sense of being cut adrift refused to go away. The world was a dangerous place. He had been in Phuket just weeks before the tsunami. He had lost friends in the World Trade Center towers. In the blink of an eye a man could lose everything he loved most, and he wouldn't even know it was happening. He could be walking down a city street thinking about his next meeting or his next meal, not knowing that at that very moment love was slipping away.

Those nightly phone calls might not mean as much to Joely or Annabelle, but they were his lifeline. Knowing they were safe and well made the time spent apart more endurable.

Had he ever told Joely as much? He wasn't sure. He tended to censor things like that with her. She wasn't a sentimental sort, not at all the type of woman who grew teary-eyed over an armful of red roses or treacly greeting cards. Early on he had believed it was her scientific training that made her such a creature of the mind, and she had encouraged that belief. She was a bioengineer whose work centered around finding a way to help paraplegics regain use of their limbs through bypassing the damaged nerves and creating new synthetic pathways for the impulses to travel.

They had met when she attended a seminar on income management for foreign professionals in Glasgow, and he was instantly captivated. She sat in the back of the room, taking notes on a laptop. She was focused, clearly evaluating every word he was saying for merit, and he found himself wanting to impress her. She asked a few questions, and despite her disclaimer that finances left her dazed and confused, her questions were of a higher level than he had been prepared to address.

It wasn't that he didn't know the answers — he was as well-versed in his field as she was in hers — but there was something deeply exciting about the mind that had formed them. She was quietly attractive — brown hair, light eyes, pale skin — and dressed casually in dark trousers and a soft gray jumper, but to William she glittered like the brightest star.

God, how he missed those early days.

"Did you say something?" George looked at him with curious eyes.

He shook his head. "Not a word."

"I'm thinking about a massage," George said as the countryside raced by the window. "Some sake. I need to take the edge off." He grinned at William. "Are you on?"

"Sorry," William said. "I'll order room service and try to get caught up for tomorrow's presentation."

True enough. He needed to bring himself up to speed, but that wasn't the reason. George treated overseas trips as a license to cheat. George's idea of a great night was trolling the bars of whatever city they happened to be in, sampling the women like they were pastries in a breakfast buffet.

All William wanted was a room, a phone that worked. He wanted to hear Joely's voice drifting toward him across the miles and Annabelle's laughter when he told her one of the terrible elephant jokes she loved. He wanted to hear stories about the solstice picnic. He wanted to know that Joely was still there. Not just for Annabelle's sake. Not just from habit or convenience or loneliness, but because she wanted to be there.

In the beginning she had resisted his attempts to bring her together with

Annabelle. He had wanted to drive her up to Loch Craig to see his house, meet his daughter, but she always had an excuse. She claimed she was a city girl and that country living was anathema to her. "If you ever bring Annabelle down to Glasgow, I'd love to have lunch," she had said once, but beyond that it was clear she simply wasn't interested.

Normally that would have been enough to send William packing. He had had a handful of brief flirtations since Natasha's sudden death but nothing that amounted to anything at all. No woman had made him want to take that first step into the future until he met Joely and was overwhelmed by the desire to open up his heart, his family, his life to her.

It took him two months, but she finally agreed to drive up to Loch Craig with him, ostensibly to see the house and, coincidentally, his daughter. She didn't speak much on the drive into the Highlands. The silence was so deep and all-encompassing that he was afraid she could hear the beating of his heart above the low roar of the engine.

He had always considered Americans to be a talkative race, cheerful and big and full of funny anecdotes and endless chat.

She was none of those things. She was a quiet, introspective woman with a doctorate in biomedical engineering who wore sadness the way another woman wore Chanel. He had been quite desperate to break through that wall of reserve, but his own reserve made it difficult to know where to start.

The only thing he knew with certainty was that she belonged at Loch Craig, and he found himself praying to the God who seemed to have deserted him that she would fall in love with the place the way he had fallen in love with her. Not that she had any idea how he felt. That was one of the few blessings inherent in his marrow-deep Englishness.

She was quiet for most of the drive up to the house. Rain lashed the windscreen, and he focused his attentions on the winding, hilly roads. He had warned Mrs. Macdonald, the woman who tended the house and Annabelle when he was in Glasgow, that he would be bringing someone up for the weekend. The fireplaces would be crackling merrily against the wet spring chill. The rooms would be ablaze with light. And, pray God, his little girl would charm the unwilling Yankee into their lives.

"Are we there yet?" she asked and when he looked at her for explanation, laughed. "That's an American joke, William. It's what little kids say when they're on a driving vacation with their parents."

"Two more kilometers," he said, and he noted a tiny muscle underneath her left eye twitch in response.

"I didn't know you lived out in the boonies."

He forced a quick smile. "An Americanism for Highlands?"

"Something like that."

Minutes later he guided the car up the rock-strewn drive, which was lined with overgrown privet hedges and patches of sodden wild thyme that hadn't seen a gardener's touch in years.

The house sat on a small rise overlooking the loch. He tried to see it through her eyes. The shutters hung slightly askew, framing windows that shivered in the punishing wind. The stones were soaked deep gray by the rain, and one glance would tell her that the roof needed repair. A pair of lopsided chimneys rose from either end of the roofline, flanking a satellite dish that always made him smile when he saw it. The front door, a deep barn red faded by time and the elements, was ajar in welcome.

He couldn't hear his heart beating anymore. He was fairly certain it had stopped entirely.

He pulled the Martin up close to the front door. They dashed through the rain and into the warmth of the house, and he saw the moment it happened. The guarded expression in her eyes that he knew so well shifted and changed right in front of him, and for the briefest instant he saw straight through to her heart.

"Pour yourself some brandy," he said, directing her toward the library where the double hearth crackled merrily. "I'll fetch Annabelle."

His daughter was playing upstairs in her room. Mrs. Macdonald had dressed her in a red jumper and blue overalls. Her tiny feet were laced into miniature pink trainers. He tried to see her through Joely's eyes the way he had seen the house, but he couldn't. She was his baby, and he loved her.

"Joely," he said as he and Annabelle walked hand-in-hand into the library, "I want you to meet Annabelle."

She turned, and her glance went from him to his daughter, and that was where it stayed. She bent down in front of his little girl. "Hi, Annabelle," she said softly. "I'm Joely."

Annabelle reached out a baby hand and touched Joely's left earring. "Want," she said, starting to tug. "Want this!"

He started to move his greedy child's hand away, but Joely laughed and slid the earring out and handed it to Annabelle. His daughter cooed with delight and flung herself at Joely with all the force an almost-three-year-old girl could summon. She scooped his daughter up into her arms, and he felt his heart turn over inside his chest. For the first time since Natasha died, he believed he could have a future.

That was four years ago. The blink of an eye. A lifetime.

"We'll be pulling into Kyoto in a few minutes," George in the next seat said. "Push over. I need to have a slash."

"I need to check for messages," William said as he got up to let George through. "Can I use your mobile?"

George tossed it to him and headed down the narrow aisle toward the lav. "Don't expect much, mate. You probably won't be able to connect until we pull into the station."

"I'll give it a try," he said. Somewhere in the world it was still the night of the summer solstice, and he wanted to share it with his girls.

Something was wrong. It had to be. Joely had left five messages on William's voice mail and still hadn't managed to connect with him.

Maybe the sixth time would be the charm.

"William Bishop here. Leave your name and contact information, and I'll return your call."

"William, it's me again. Please phone me immediately. Annabelle's fine. I'm fine. But I need to talk with you."

It wasn't like him to ignore her messages. For that matter, it wasn't like him to let a day go by without phoning home. Kyoto wasn't on another planet. Last she heard they had phones there. The Japanese were the acknowledged masters of electronic communication. There was no excuse for being out of touch unless he wanted to be out of touch.

She didn't blame him for not wanting to speak to her. He probably didn't enjoy their late-night telephonic silences any more than she did. But their problems had nothing to do with Annabelle. He loved his daughter with every fiber of his being, and if he hadn't phoned it wasn't because he didn't want to; it was because he couldn't.

Which didn't automatically mean he was laid up in some foreign hospital unable to communicate with anyone in order to get a message to her. It might just mean that with all the travel and time zone changes he had lost track of things like calling home.

She had to decide whether or not she was going home to Maine, and she needed to decide soon. She wanted to call Cat back and tell her that she didn't owe Mimi anything. Neither one of them did. Maybe Mimi hadn't walked out on them the way their father had, but she might as well have, for all the mothering she had actually provided. Mothers were supposed to shield their children from danger, sacrifice for their children's good. Mothers were supposed to teach their daughters how to navigate the choppy waters of adolescence. When you were trying to make the leap from girl to woman, it was your mother there on the other side of the great divide, holding out her hand to you, encouraging you to jump.

Mimi had done none of those things. Her mother had been weak when Joely needed strong. An embarrassment when she wanted someone who would make her proud.

It was Cat who had helped Joely find her way. Cat who had made the life she was living now possible.

Cat who had never asked one single thing of her in all these years until now.

Annabelle had a passport, and she was a good little traveler. Joely wasn't entirely sure what William would think if she took the child out of the country, but she didn't have a choice. Cat needed her now.

There was some degree of comfort in reaching a decision, and her mind shifted into planning mode. She would book the first flight out of Glasgow tomorrow morning. She would go back to Idle Point for her sister's sake but not for her mother's. She would do whatever she had to do, and then she and Annabelle would fly back to Loch Craig, and it would be like none of this had ever happened.

Kyoto

Unfortunately, George had been dead on. William wasn't able to maintain a mobile connection long enough to either reach Joely or his voice mail messages.

"Let's find someplace we can get a drink," George said as they left the train.

He was nothing if not persistent. "I can't face those meetings without a beer."

"You go," William said. "I'm heading for the hotel."

William believed in traveling light. He slung a garment bag over one shoulder and his laptop bag over the other and set off toward the hotel, which was an easy walk from the rail station. He had only a minor command of Japanese, but that rarely proved problematic. The desk clerk's English was flawless, albeit vaguely American in cadence, and thirty minutes after the Shinkansen pulled into the station, William was listening to the sound of his home phone ringing on the other side of the world.

Six rings and he was transferred to voice mail. His heart slammed hard into his rib cage. Where were Joely and Annabelle? Bloody hell. It had to be after midnight in Scotland. They wouldn't still be up on the hill. He dialed again. Same result.

Something had happened. Solstice or no solstice, you didn't keep a seven-year-old child out until midnight. *Think,* he ordered himself. There had to be a reasonable, benign explanation. One that didn't include blood, broken bones, or worse. Maybe the phone lines were down. That was Scotland, after all. The Highlands. Winds blew hard up there. Weather turned nasty without warning, even on the official start of summer.

Or maybe she had left him.

It would explain a lot. The distance between them. The way she ducked his attempts to sit down and talk about the future. How many times had he approached her with his heart beating right there on his sleeve for the world to see, only to have her retreat behind the wall of glass that kept her just beyond reach?

And how many times had he let her go? Just like now.

So try her mobile number, fuckwit. Like him, she kept her mobile on 24/7 and, unlike him, she didn't drop hers in public lavs. He pressed the numeral one, then Send, and waited.

Loch Craig

"I know this isn't much notice," Joely said for at least the third time in fifteen minutes, "but it's an emergency. I need a car to take me to Glasgow for an eight a.m. flight."

She propped the phone between right ear and shoulder and fixed herself another cup of tea. It was well after midnight. Annabelle was asleep upstairs, blissfully unaware. Joely was trying desperately to keep her mind focused on the Byzantine network of reservations she was piecing together for the trip back to Maine.

"Hold please," the voice on the other end of the line said. "I might be able to call in a favor from one of our drivers."

Of course that was said with the thickest Scottish burr this side of the Spey, and she had to run a simultaneous translation in order to understand what the disembodied voice was saying.

It took another twenty minutes, but by the time she hung up she had her itinerary nailed. In four hours a car would roll up to the front door to take them to the airport in Glasgow, where she and Annabelle would board a plane for Boston. Once they landed at Logan they'd jump on a shuttle and —

She grabbed for the phone before it could ring a second time. "Please don't tell me the driver changed his mind."

Her words were met with silence, but not the kind of silence that meant a dead connection. This silence had some heft.

"It's William, Joely."

She wasn't sure which made her happier:

the fact that it was William or that it wasn't the car service canceling out on her.

"Thank God you got my messages," she said. "Why didn't you call sooner?"

"I've been trying for thirty minutes," he said. "I left three voice mails. You had me worried."

"I was on the phone," she said.

"It must be after midnight there."

"Almost one." They sounded like two strangers waiting for a bus. She drew in a breath and pushed forward. "I was making plane reservations."

She had never realized William's silences could speak louder than his words.

She drew in another breath. "I have to go home for a little while," she said, stumbling over her words. "I shouldn't be gone more than a few days. We'll probably be back before you get home."

"Is there something wrong?"

"No," she said with a quick laugh. "We're fine."

"I mean, at home."

"My sister called. There was a fire at my mother's house, and since we own the property jointly —"

"How is your mother?" he broke in.

She tried to find a way to dodge the question, but there wasn't one. "Hospitalized," she said at last. "She has some broken bones . . ." She let her voice trail off, the international signal for *I don't want to talk about this anymore.*

"I'm sorry I'm not there with you. If you'd like, I can fly home, and we'll go together."

"What for?" she said before she had a chance to censor herself. "What I mean is, I'll go there, sign a few papers, and come right home. No reason to disrupt your schedule."

"You shouldn't have to go through this alone."

"It's no big deal, William. My mother specializes in catastrophes. They're practically daily occurrences."

"We've been together four years," he reminded her, "and this is the first time you've had to fly back to the States because of one."

"Cat called in an old favor," she said. "I don't really have a choice."

"Why don't you call in an old favor and ask Sara to look after Annabelle."

"Sara and Hugh leave for London in the morning."

Another one of those unnerving silences. When had they become part of their intimate language?

"William, please, if you're at all un-comfortable about my taking Annabelle to Maine —"

"No," he said quickly. "It's not that."

He had his reasons, and they all made perfect sense. Annabelle was a handful. Annabelle could be disruptive on a plane. Annabelle was an easy substitute for all the things they couldn't say.

She gave him her itinerary, complete with addresses and phone numbers. He gave her the name of his hotel and his room number. He hoped to be home by the end of the following week. She intended to be back long before.

Finally there was nothing — and every-thing — left to say.

"The car will be here in a few hours, William, and I still have to pack and dig up our passports."

"I'll let you get on with it then," he said. "Kiss Annabelle for me."

"Hurry home."

"You, too."

And just like that, they retreated to their separate corners of the world.

Chapter Six

Idle Point

"We were just about to wheel her in," the nurse said as Cat stepped from the elevator on the second floor. "Mary and I delayed as long as we could."

"Am I too late?" For some crazy reason they had been looking for her in the cafeteria instead of surgical waiting where she had been told to sit.

"Not if we run."

The nurse wasn't kidding. If Cat had been able to run this fast in high school, she would have made the track team.

"She's out cold," the nurse said as she elbowed her way into an anteroom outside the OR. "Once those pre-op meds take hold, they don't know which end is up."

Cat nodded and moved closer to the slight figure on the gurney. It looked like Mimi and it didn't, more like one of those wax figures at Madame Tussauds. A horrible sense of foreboding washed over her.

She bent down close to Mimi's ear, trying very hard not to notice the toll life had exacted from her once-glowing beauty. Mimi looked far older than her sixty-two years, easily a decade or more. Loneliness. Drink. Demons only she could see and hear.

"I'm here, Mom," she whispered. "You're not alone."

The nurse tapped her on the shoulder. "Green is chomping at the bit. I need to get Mrs. Doyle in before Green takes my appendix out with a soup spoon."

"How dangerous is the surgery?"

The nurse made a face as she adjusted the IV drip that fed into Mimi's right arm. "Not very. She'll be fine, honey."

Mimi had never been fine. Their world had always been governed by her mood swings, her fears, her emptiness. She existed in a place only she could find, suspended between the past and some version of the future only she could see.

Cat wanted to feel the things a daughter was supposed to feel for the mother who gave her life, but she didn't. Once, in her early twenties, she spent some time in therapy trying to unlock her heart, but even the therapist had to admit that love wasn't always a given. She cared for Mimi because she was her mother. She believed in the bonds of family. But if you asked her if she loved her mother, if she had the feelings a daughter was supposed to have — well, that was another story.

She waited until her mother disappeared behind the swinging doors, then made her way back to surgical waiting, where she found Michael engrossed in conversation with Karen.

She walked up to where they were standing and gave Karen a quick hug. *Get used to it,* she warned herself. Her worlds were colliding, and there was nothing she could do to stop it.

"I managed to see Mimi just before they wheeled her in," she told them. "They say the repairs are nothing serious, but —" She shivered. The sight of her mother, so tiny and frail, on the gurney had unnerved her deeply. She wasn't one who necessarily believed in omens and portents, but there was little doubt she had taken a look into the future, and what she had seen was terrifying.

She glanced from Karen to Michael. "I take it you introduced yourselves."

"We're very resourceful," Karen said with a wink for Michael. She was ten years younger than Cat and at least a lifetime or two more evolved. One of those old souls who had stepped into the world fully formed and in charge.

"Yeah," he said, draping an arm across Cat's shoulder and giving her a comforting squeeze. "We're old friends now."

She had to remind herself that was a good thing as she studied Michael and Karen for signs of collusion.

Karen, of course, didn't miss a trick. Her dark eyes took in Michael's warmth, the comforting squeeze, her flushed cheeks, but she didn't say a word. Not now anyway. She would save it for when they were alone and she could grill Cat like a porterhouse.

She glanced from Cat to Michael and then checked her watch. "I'll be back," she said, then took off at warp speed for the back staircase.

"I like her," Michael said as the door swung shut after her.

"I like her, too," Cat said. "How much did she tell you?"

"She didn't tell me anything. She was too busy asking questions."

"You didn't tell her anything, did you?"

"I don't know anything."

"You know what I'm talking about."

"Cat, I'm forty-three years old. I think

106

you can trust me to let you decide who to tell and when to tell them."

"I'm being a jerk, aren't I?"

"Yeah," he said, giving her another swift hug, "but you'll grow out of it."

"Quit being so nice to me," she said, ducking out of his embrace. "I might get used to it."

"Cat —"

"Shh." She pressed her forefinger to his lips. "Not now, okay?"

His expression shifted, and she wasn't quite sure what she saw reflected in his eyes. He grabbed a paper bag from the windowsill and handed her a cold bottle of water and a container of strawberry yogurt.

"What's this for?"

"Hydration and calcium. I'm not going to have you passing out again."

"You're worse than a mother." She gave a brittle laugh. "Not my mother, of course. Nutrition was never high up on Mimi's to-do list."

The same man who had stared down a mugger near Columbus Circle flinched at her bad joke, and she was instantly contrite.

"Sorry," she said. "I should've prepared you for reality, but even I didn't see this coming."

He took a chug from his water bottle. "I'm not following."

She cut him a look. "In case you haven't guessed by now, my family isn't exactly Hallmark material."

"And mine is? I don't think they do Hallmark in the *shtetl*."

"I'm not joking." She let out a loud, exasperated breath. "Okay. You want the truth? My family is royally screwed up. We wouldn't know normal if it bit us on the ass. I'd planned to break it to you at our child's high school graduation, but apparently the universe has other ideas."

"You want to tell me about it?"

"No." She must have left her internal censor in Manhattan. The truth was flying out of her like bats from a cave. "I absolutely don't want to tell you anything at all about my screwed-up, crazy childhood, but if you stay here much longer, I'm going to have to, and I really don't want that to happen in front of an audience."

"So you're saying you want me to get out of Dodge."

She linked her fingers with his. "I'm saying I appreciate the fact that you're here with me, but maybe we can take a rain check on the introductions."

"Afraid I might want to sleep over?"

"I know you're tired," she said, "and you probably need a nap."

"But you'd rather I picked a Motel 6 somewhere between here and Florida."

"I didn't say that."

"You didn't have to."

She hated the hurt look in his eyes. "I know you have to fly out to California tomorrow night. I don't want you to miss your meetings."

"Cut the crap, Cat," he said. "We know each other too well for that. You want me out of here, preferably ten minutes ago."

"Yes," she said, almost daring him to argue. "I told you I didn't want you to come up here, and I meant it. This isn't the way I wanted it to happen."

"Tough. Life happens. You can't put it on a time schedule."

"I'm not trying to shut you out."

"Aren't you?"

"No," she said. "I'm trying to keep you." And the only way she could do that was to push him away.

He was a smart man and a talented screenwriter. He knew when it was time to make his exit, and less than fifteen minutes later he was on his way to the airport to catch a commuter hop down to New York. For a moment she had thought he was going to push the issue and stay right where he was, but to her intense relief he opted instead for a quick good-bye and her promise to call him on his cell as soon as she knew her mother's prognosis.

He was angry and he was hurt, and there was nothing she could do to make it right.

He still had some kind of *Ozzie and Harriet* family fantasy going on about her relationship with Mimi, but that was okay. Up until today she had done little to dissuade him of that fact. The truth was complicated, and it was sad and ugly and all things in between. If she had trouble picking her way through the land mines that were scattered through her family history, she could only imagine how Michael would feel.

He had grown up in a classic nuclear family, and despite his veneer of native New Yorker cynicism, a streak of innocence that both charmed and puzzled her still remained. He believed adults took care of children, not the other way around. He believed parents sacrificed for their kids, celebrated their successes, put their kids' welfare ahead of their own. A wellspring of optimism forty-three years on the planet hadn't managed to eradicate.

He had screwed up a time or two along

the way, but he loved his parents, his sisters, his lot in life, and she knew he would love his child. He wasn't like her father. He wouldn't walk out without saying good-bye.

She couldn't have chosen a better father for her baby, but there was more to the equation than a positive pregnancy test and morning sickness. Sooner or later she would have to let him into her life. Her real life. Not just the one she lived a few days a month in New York City.

"A cab," Michael said to the woman behind the information desk. "I need a cab to take me to the airport."

Take it down a notch, Yanovsky. She didn't do anything to you.

The woman turned to her colleague next to her. "Where's Jackie?" she asked.

"Jackie went up to Bangor for the day," the colleague said.

"You're going to the airport?" the woman said. "I thought you just got here."

He felt like a wide receiver trying to field a bad pass. "Look," he said, tamping down his New York agitation, "I have to get to the airport, and I don't have a car, so I need a cab. Can you help me?"

"Why don't you drive Cat's car?" the colleague chimed in.

"That's a good idea," the woman said, nodding her lacquered head. "You drove it up here, so you're familiar with it."

No wonder they didn't lock their cars. They were community property. He was about to try one more time when he felt a tap on his shoulder and turned around to see Cat's partner Karen looking up at him.

"Come with me," she said.

He didn't see where he had much choice, so he fell into step with her.

"Where are we going?"

"First, we're getting you away from Scylla and Charybdis in there."

He laughed out loud, very loud, and Karen grinned.

"Then what?" he asked as he followed her out the main exit into the parking lot.

"I'll take you to Jackie's myself."

What was it the two women had said? "Jackie's up in Bangor for the day," he repeated.

"Damn." For a tiny woman Karen Porter mustered up a mighty scowl. "Okay. Then we'll drop down to Ogunquit. I know we can find you a cab in Ogunquit."

"You don't have to do this," he said, amazed by her offhanded generosity.

"Sure I do. How else can I get you alone so I can ask nosy questions?"

He grinned at her as a late-model Toyota minivan beeped a welcome a few feet away from them. "Name, rank, and serial number, ma'am," he said in a fake good ol' boy accent. "That's all you'll get from me."

"I have three kids," she warned him as they climbed into the minivan and buckled up. "I know how to get answers."

"How far away is Ogunquit anyway?" he asked, and she laughed in response.

"Far enough to get a few answers."

"Fire away," he said, "but don't expect the truth."

At least not the whole truth and definitely not all the time.

"Okay," she said as she exited the parking lot then made a right turn at Cumberland Farms, "I'll understand if you don't want to answer, but I'd never forgive myself if I didn't ask the question." She paused for dramatic effect, and he wondered how many nice ways there were to say *Mind your own business.* "So what is Brad Pitt really like?"

The good thing about small towns was that you didn't have to explain yourself.

Or your family, for that matter.

Everyone knew all they needed to know to make a judgment about you, your past, your present, and your future. No matter how crazy, dysfunctional, or downright weird your family tree might be, it was all right out there for everyone in town to see, cluck over, then file away for future reference.

She hadn't realized how tightly wound she was until Michael left, and her shoulders dropped back down to their normal position. At least now she didn't have to make excuses for Mimi's behavior or try to pretty it up to make the craziness more palatable. It was what it was, and the whole town knew it. The only thing that surprised anyone in Idle Point was that Mimi hadn't done something like this a long, long time ago.

Cat had been waiting all afternoon for the accident to actually register with her in some meaningful way, but she was still keeping the whole thing at a distance, much the same way she kept Michael. The assessment wasn't flattering, but it was painfully true. The look on his face when she finally convinced him to go back to New York had made her feel like a rat and now, almost an hour later, she still felt like a rat.

"Sorry it took me so long," Karen said as she exited the elevator and joined Cat in surgical waiting. "I took your boyfriend to Ogunquit."

"You did what?"

"I took him down to Ogunquit because those two idiots at the information desk couldn't figure out how to get the poor guy a cab to the airport."

"So you drove him down to Ogunquit to find him a cab?"

"Exactly." She gave Cat a sly look. "And yes, I tried pumping him for personal information, but the man's a sphinx. I couldn't even ferret a good Brad Pitt anecdote out of him."

"Probably because he doesn't know Brad Pitt."

"George Clooney. Jude Law. Give me something. The man's in show business, and he doesn't know anybody."

"He's a writer. He's not out there on the party circuit. He sits home and writes."

"I tried to get the four-one-one on the two of you, by the way, but he didn't seem to know much about that either."

She hoped she didn't look half as relieved as she felt. That would be a dead giveaway.

"Any news on Mimi?" Karen asked.

"One of the nurses popped out about a half hour ago. They ran into some trouble repairing her tibia. It might take another hour."

Karen stood up and slung her bag across her chest. "Let's hit the cafeteria. I need a good caffeine buzz."

So did Cat, but she grabbed a bottle of water instead when they got there.

"What's with the water?" Karen asked as they walked back to surgical waiting. "You're usually the coffee bean queen."

Cat shrugged and sidestepped the question. "Have you seen the house?"

"You've got yourself some problems, kid."

"Totaled?"

"No, not totaled, but it's on the hairy edge."

"She wasn't drunk," Cat said, then took a pull on her water bottle. "Can you believe it? She was stone-cold sober when it happened."

Karen frowned over her plastic mug of coffee. "Are you sure? I'm positive Randy said she was way over the limit when they brought her in."

"Pauline in Admitting told me there was no alcohol in her blood work." She took another swallow of water. "They think she had a small stroke and knocked over the candles when she fell."

Karen reached over and squeezed her hand. "She's a strong woman. She'll be okay."

Cat let the statement lie there unattended. Even if Mimi came through the surgery with flying colors, she wouldn't be okay. That much was certain. The house may or may not be salvageable, but even if it was, Mimi couldn't live there without twenty-four-hour-a-day care. And that was the best of the scenarios rattling around inside her brain.

Time to change the subject.

"I spoke to Joely."

Karen muttered something unprintable. "She's not coming back, is she?" Karen's husband Danny and Joely had been an item in high school, something that still bothered Karen ten years after the fact.

"I don't know. She's trying to arrange her schedule but . . ." Fade-out. The conversation with her sister still rankled.

"Zach came in yesterday morning."

And there was the downside of living in a small town. If you weren't related to a guy, chances were you had dated him somewhere along the way. Over the years your paths crossed and recrossed, reminding you of all the many roads not taken.

Zach was Karen's brother-in-law and Cat's first boyfriend. They had dated briefly in high school, then found each other in college. Away from the constraints of home they discovered they did better as friends than romantic partners.

"How long will he be in town?" Cat asked. "I'd planned to have him over for dinner, but now with Mom, I don't know what's going to happen."

"He'll be here until the first, and then he's heading back to California."

"So he's going to the big golden anniversary party?" The Porters, Karen's in-laws, were one of the oldest and most prosperous families in Idle Point, a small-town version of the Kennedys if the Kennedys had been farmers.

Karen shrugged. "Who knows? I asked Danny what was going on, but men are lousy when it comes to emotional detail. Zach says he came back to look into some business thing and that the anniversary party is coincidental, but I'm not sure I'm buying it."

"He never gives up, does he? I can't believe he's still trying to get their approval." Sometimes she thought the world was filled with aging children like herself in search of a thumbs-up from Mommy and Daddy.

"See?" Karen looked triumphant. "You figured it out immediately. Danny doesn't have a clue. Men are incredibly dense when it comes to families."

The swinging doors squeaked, and both women looked up as a painfully young nurse poked her head out, glanced around, then ducked back inside.

"What do you think that meant?" Cat asked as the doors swung to a stop.

"Who knows?" Karen said with a shrug. "She didn't look old enough to drive."

"Am I crazy, or are there a lot of new people on staff? I've been here three hours, and I've only seen one nurse I know."

"Danny told me they hosted six job fairs last year down in New York and D.C."

"I know we're supposed to be thrilled that the town's growing, but we're going to turn into Village of the Townhouse if we're not careful."

"Run for mayor," Karen said. "We need a benevolent despot to keep things under control."

That led to a spirited discussion of the latest ordinances designed to keep a rein on home-based businesses, a topic near and dear to their hearts. From there it was an easy leap to Karen's favorite topic — and real love — the twelve sheep and four alpacas that were the core of the business they were building together, much to the dismay of the elder Porters, who had yet to become believers in the profitability of natural fibers over dairy products.

Cat had been away less than two days, but apparently there had been a great deal of activity with Bess and Mamie, their two nursing alpacas, and a minor skirmish between two of their male Romneys.

"The shearing will probably be next weekend," Karen said as she polished off the last of her coffee. "I finally got the confirmation e-mail. Jack and his crew are driving down from Nova Scotia. They'll hit three farms before they reach us, so it probably won't happen until Sunday." She rolled her eyes. "Or Monday, the latest."

That led to a discussion of ferry service, which led to a secondary discussion of their choice of fiber processors, which finally led to the question Cat had been dreading.

"So who is he?"

"Michael Yanovsky."

Karen waved her hand in annoyance. "I already know that. I mean, who *is* he? Where did you meet him?"

"I met him at the HBO office."

"That's not good enough. I spend my days making PBJ sandwiches and tending sheep. Some mercy details, please."

The last thing she wanted to do was lie to her friend, but this didn't feel like the right time to break the news of her pregnancy.

Cat cast around for neutral ground. "I guess I got a little lightheaded after we hung up. He didn't think it was safe for me to drive back alone, so he volunteered."

"You expect me to believe that some stranger you met at the HBO office volunteered to drive you all the way back to Maine?"

"He's not a stranger. We've known each other a couple of years."

"I figured that when I saw the way he looks at you. So how come I never heard you talk about him before?"

"I know lots of people you've never heard me talk about."

"Details please. What does he write?"

"Screenplays."

"For *Pink Slip*?"

"No. He writes for —" Good grief. What was wrong with her? She couldn't even remember the name of the series he had created. "Did I tell you we were having lunch together at Aquavit when you called?"

Bless Karen's name-dropping heart. "Aquavit? Ohmigod! Isn't that the restaurant they featured on the Food Network last week?"

Michael was forgotten as Karen peppered her with questions about the chef, the waitstaff, the décor, the cuisine, the ladies' lounges. Cat described the table linens, the plates, the presentation, the Swedish meatballs she had barely touched. It didn't occur to her until the bright red swinging doors opened once again and the surgeon emerged that her friend had cleverly managed to divert her attention away from the endless waiting.

The doctor's paper booties made soft shuffling noises on the shiny tile floor as she approached.

"Which one of you is Mrs. Doyle's daughter?"

Clearly the doctor had missed a few classes in bedside manner during med school. Cat put down her knitting bag and empty water bottle and stood up. The only advantage she had in situations like this was her height, and she didn't hesitate to use it. "I am."

"Mrs. Doyle came through the procedure without incident." She offered a few cut-and-dried details about Mimi's pelvis and leg, then turned to leave.

"When can I see her?"

Green glanced up at the wall clock at the opposite end of the hall. "Two, maybe three hours. She'll be in ICU until at least tomorrow afternoon. A neurologist will be in to see her tomorrow and make a further evaluation."

"Was it a stroke?"

"Yes, a stroke was involved but, as I said, without further testing, a more detailed diagnosis is impossible." She glanced down at the pager hooked to the waistband of her pants. "I have to take this." She vanished behind the swinging doors before Cat could say another word.

"Good thing her patients are unconscious when she sees them," Karen remarked. "That girl needs to learn how to smile."

"Didn't she operate on your father-in-law earlier this year?"

"I didn't say she wasn't a good surgeon. It's her bedside manner that sucks." Karen picked up her bag from the seat next to her and stood up. "It's almost nine o'clock. Why don't you come home with me? I made lentil soup this afternoon. You can eat, be reminded why you're glad you don't have children, then come back and see Mimi."

"I'll come if you don't make me eat lentil soup."

Or tell you that I'm pregnant.

123

Somewhere Over the Atlantic

Annabelle fell asleep seconds after Joely fastened the seat belt around her tiny frame.

"No jitters there," the flight attendant remarked as she did her final preflight walk-through to make sure everyone was securely buckled up.

"She's a good traveler," Joely said with a smile. "She'll probably sleep all the way to Boston."

Minutes later they were airborne, climbing through the thin cloud cover into the early morning sky. They reached cruising altitude in no time at all, and the seat belt sign clicked off. She loosened Annabelle's belt a tad, then draped the sleeping child with one of the blankets the flight attendant had been kind enough to slip to her just before takeoff. Annabelle murmured something and dug deeper into her dreams.

"She's adorable." A different flight attendant paused next to her midstride. "Looks just like you."

She started to demur and offer up the standard two-line explanation she kept on file for occasions like this when it occurred to her that they were hurtling through the air in a tin can some thirty thousand feet above the ground where calories didn't count and real life was suspended for the length of time it took to get from here to there. She could be anything she wanted, even Annabelle's mother.

"Thanks," she said. "I think so, too."

Idle Point

Cat spent time in the barn checking on Bess and Mamie while Karen put supper on the table. Danny was working late at the computer shop, and Zach was down in Boston for the night, but the three Porter children saw to it that conversation never lagged.

"Admit it," Karen said as she walked Cat out to her car. "You've never been happier to be single in your life."

"You know I love them," Cat said.

"They're noisy as hell."

"I won't argue that. But they're great kids."

"You have to say that. You're their god-mother."

Cat hid a yawn behind her hand. "Sorry. It's not the company."

"Listen, do you want me to drive? I'll

drop the kids at the shop with their father, and we'll go see Mimi together."

"I'm fine," she said.

Karen wasn't convinced. "You haven't been looking very good," she said. "I'm worried."

"My mother just set fire to her house," Cat said. "How good would you look under the circumstances?"

"Not just now," Karen said. "I mean the last few weeks."

"Thanks a lot. If this is your way of telling me I need Botox —"

"You've been looking tired."

"I'm thirty-eight," she said. "Looking tired comes with the territory."

"How about the morning sickness? Does that come with the territory, too?"

"I'd better sit down."

Karen shoved a milking stool under her and Cat sank down onto it.

"So what did the doctor say?"

"How did you know I went to see a doctor?"

"You gave the studio number instead of your cell, and they called to confirm."

"I was going to tell you," she said, "but I wanted to wait until I was past the first trimester."

"You don't owe me an explanation."

"Michael's the father, by the way." She gave Karen a tired grin. "Not that you asked."

"I didn't have to ask," Karen said. "All I had to do was see the way you looked at him."

"Don't go reading too much into things," she warned her friend. "We both have our own lives."

"Good," Karen said. "I'm glad to hear it. Just tell me you're not moving, and I don't care if you and Michael have triplets."

"I'm not moving."

"Are you having triplets?"

She laughed and gave Karen a playful kick with the toe of her sandal. "I hope not."

"You're happy?" Karen asked, growing suddenly serious. "I mean, this is something you want?"

"Yes to both," Cat said. "I'm very happy, and this baby is very wanted."

Karen's eyes swam with tears.

"Why are you crying?" Cat demanded. "This is good news."

"I know," Karen said. "That's why I'm crying."

What was it about babies that turned levelheaded women into complete marshmallows? She had seen Karen broker deals that would make Donald Trump whimper, without batting an eye, but the merest mention of a baby on its way, and she was sobbing into the sleeve of her shirt.

"I'm the one who's supposed to be hormonal," she teased.

"Sorry. I'm just so happy for you."

"This isn't at all the reaction I'd expected from you."

Karen sniffed and used her sleeve again. "I'm a pushover for babies and small children who aren't mine," she said. "Promise you won't use it against me in seven months."

"No promises. I hear the labor room can get pretty scary."

Karen made a face. "Piece of cake. I'd be happy to walk you through it."

She couldn't imagine a better coach. "Be warned. I just might take you up on it."

"I hope you do," Karen said, giving her a hug. "That first moment when a new person suddenly enters the world is indescribable. I'd love to be there for it but without the stretch marks this time." She hugged Cat again. "I'm glad you finally told me. I was getting tired of biting my tongue every time you disappeared into the bathroom."

Fifteen minutes later she was standing at the nurses' station in ICU. Laquita Chase was the nurse in charge, which instantly put her at ease. She and Laquita had gone through high school together. Laquita had been the "bad girl," the one everyone figured would end up coming to a sad end far away from Idle Point, but she had fooled everyone and turned her life around. Mimi was definitely in good hands.

"I thought you were on the surgical unit today," Cat said after they exchanged friendly greetings.

"Mary Ann called in sick, so I took her shift." She quickly glanced at her computer terminal, then back up at Cat. Her smile was warm and reassuring. "She's still out, but her vitals are rock solid."

"How long do you think she'll be unconscious?"

"Hard to say. You're dealing with a number of different circumstances here, and each one brings its own set of complications."

Cat started to feel lightheaded, and she forced herself to breathe deeply. "Like what?"

Laquita's shoulders rose and fell. "I can't say, Cat. You really should try to corral Green for a few minutes and get the answers you need."

Another nurse joined them. "Do you mind if I use the terminal?" she asked Laquita.

"Be my guest. I have to check on 12A." She motioned for Cat to follow her across the room to Mimi's cubicle, where she began speaking in a warm, conversational tone of voice. "Hello, Mimi. It's Laquita. I'm going to hang a new bag, but it won't take long. Cat's here to see you."

Mimi was much the same as she had been prior to surgery. The area under her left eye was badly bruised, as were her left cheekbone and jaw. A diagonal swath of hair had been shaved away from her hairline and in its place was a network of eight railroad-track stitches. A system of weights and pulleys supported her right leg at an angle necessary to accommodate her fractured pelvis. She was attached to an array of electronic machines that served as silent monitors.

It was everything she had feared would one day happen to her mother, in one hideous package.

She was her mother, and yet she wasn't. Whatever made Mimi the contradictory, troublesome, exasperating, charming, heartbreakingly sad woman she was had been lost, and the woman who had taken her place was a stranger.

"Go ahead," Laquita said as she worked. "You're not in the way."

She felt awkward and deeply inadequate to the task. How little she knew the woman who had given birth to her.

"Hello, Mom." She touched Mimi's arm, then drew her hand back quickly. "There's a full moon tonight, and I made a wish for you." When she was very little, long before Joely was born, Mark and Mimi used to take her outside each month on the night of the full moon to make a wish. A silly thing, ridiculous really if you stopped to think about it, but the memory was still clear, still sweet, despite the years.

Her eyes met Laquita's, and she hesitated.

"Go on," Laquita urged. "Tell her the same things you would tell her if she were conscious."

"Trixie is fine. Remember Matt from the fire department? He found her in the apple tree in the side yard and got her down. Karen told me she's not too thrilled sharing my house with Cosmo and Newman, but a plate of white meat chicken should do the trick."

131

Mimi made a low sound from deep in her throat, a cross beneath a cough and a groan. Laquita moved into action.

"Mimi." She placed her stethoscope against the woman's chest. "Can you cough for me?"

Mimi made that noise again, half cough and half groan.

"Did she hear you, or was that a coincidence?" Cat asked.

"The anesthesia's wearing off."

"Is she in pain?"

"We're regulating her pain the best we can, but without her input it's imperfect at best." Laquita straightened up and cast a swift glance at the monitor adjacent to the bed. "Sit with her while I get a new bag. I think she's coming around."

Cat grabbed a chair from one of the unoccupied cubicles and pushed it next to her mother's bed. Was this going to be the new normal? The thought made her deeply sad.

She had done the best she could to keep Mimi safe, but it hadn't been enough. How did you figure out where the boundaries should be or when it was time for your mother's independence to take second place to your need to protect her from herself?

"I should have figured it out," she said to this shadow of her mother lying on the bed. "I wish I'd paid more attention."

She felt awkward and sad and deeply inadequate to the tasks that lay ahead, and she wished with all her heart that she had someone to share this burden with her. Not to make the decisions or pay the bills. Just someone to sit with her and hold her hand and tell her everything was going to be all right, even if they both knew it wasn't.

Michael would come if you asked him to.

No questions. No hesitation. He would be there by her side for as long as she needed him. He didn't know Mimi. He didn't owe Mimi anything at all. He would do it for Cat, and he would do it out of something too close to love to be ignored. No wonder she had pushed him away with both hands, all the way back to New York.

Joely was the one who should be here with her, if not for Mimi's sake then for her own. At least Cat knew she had issues. Joely still believed the ocean between them was wide enough to protect her from the past.

Mimi's eyes opened for a moment then closed again. Cat leaned forward and again briefly touched her mother's rail-thin forearm.

"Mom, I'm here with you. You're in the hospital, and you're doing fine."

Mimi's eyes opened again. She looked directly at Cat, but there wasn't even a glimmer of recognition.

Nothing had changed.

Chapter Seven

The Next Morning — Somewhere in Massachusetts

Joely had barely left Logan Airport traffic behind when Annabelle stopped being a good traveler and started being a seven-year-old in need of a bathroom.

"Honey, we just stopped five minutes ago," Joely pointed out as the Next Exit — 27 Miles sign flipped past. "We won't see another rest stop for another half hour or so."

"I have to wee," Annabelle said, her tone veering dangerously close to a whine. "I have to go *now!*"

Joely glanced at the speedometer and did a quick calculation. "Twenty minutes, honey, that's all. Can't you hold it for twenty minutes until we reach the next rest stop?" The kind with clean bathrooms, lots of toilet paper, and hot soapy water.

"I don't think so." Annabelle turned big

woeful eyes in Joely's direction. "I really really have to wee now."

She flipped on her right turn signal and moved into the slow lane, then slowed down even more as she eased the car onto the shoulder and came to a stop.

"This is the best I can do," she said by way of both apology and explanation. "We'll have to duck behind those bushes."

Annabelle's face was the perfect picture of horror. "No!" she shrieked. "I want a loo!"

"There isn't a loo for another twenty miles," Joely explained. "We can't even get off the highway until then to go looking for one someplace else." She reached into the huge carryall bag on the seat between them and pulled out a stack of paper towels she'd cribbed from the last rest stop visit. "I'll make sure you're fine, honey. Let's go."

Annabelle's soft brown eyes flooded with tears. "I don't have to wee anymore," she said in a very tiny voice.

"I think you do, honey. You'll be fine. I'll show you how."

Annabelle shook her head. "I don't have to."

She's only seven, Joely reminded herself. *She went to sleep in Scotland and woke up on the Mass Turnpike. Cut her a little slack.*

"You're sure?"

Annabelle nodded.

She eased back into traffic, then moved into the left-hand lane where, if she remembered correctly, speeding was almost mandatory in the Bay State. Annabelle's knees were pressed tightly together, and her little face was contorted into a grimace worthy of a 1940s B-movie actress. She prayed their insurance covered flood damage to the car's upholstery, because the odds of making it to the rest area in time were growing slimmer by the second.

Idle Point

Cat made it to the telephone on the sixth ring.

"Good thing you picked up." Michael's voice, rich and warm with concern, greeted her. "Next call was to the police department."

"Hold on," she managed. "I —" Finishing your sentences was a luxury pregnant women in their first trimester didn't always enjoy before noon. She darted back into the bathroom.

Minutes later she reached for the phone again. "I'm sorry," she managed, trying to sound upbeat. "Are you still there?"

"I'm here. How are you?"

"Steady as she goes." She tried to laugh, but her stomach threatened another mutiny. "They say morning sickness is a sign the pregnancy is proceeding normally, but I'll be extremely happy to kiss the first trimester good-bye."

"Drink some ginger ale," he suggested. "And what about those soda crackers?"

"They're on my shopping list."

"The doctor said they'd help settle your stomach."

"Michael, I was there in the office. I remember what he said."

"Hey, I'm the one who got his ass kicked back to New York. If anyone should be pissed, it's me."

Great going, Cat. First you kick him all the way back to Manhattan, then you snipe at him.

"Are you?" she asked. "Pissed, that is."

"I was," he admitted.

"Are you still?"

"I don't hold a grudge," he said. "It's one of my best traits."

"I'll file that away for future reference."

"How about you? Any grudge-holding genes in your background?"

Under normal circumstances she wouldn't have had any trouble coming up with a properly witty comeback, but this morning she was too raw emotionally to play.

"Okay," he said as the silence deepened. "I'll try again. How's everything in Mayberry?"

"No change." She had brought him up to speed late last night in a brief flurry of e-mails that had been long on information and short on sentiment. "I spoke to the nurse in ICU, but I haven't made it to the hospital yet."

"Any news from your sister?"

She made a sound that was unladylike by even the most generous standards. "She's not coming. Her life is in Scotland."

"She said that?"

"Not in so many words, but I know what she meant."

"She might still surprise you."

"Not going to happen. William is in Japan on business, and she's taking care of Annabelle. She's not about to leave her with strangers."

"Kids are portable."

"Not when they don't belong to you."

"You lost me. I thought —"

"Nope," she said. "They're not married."

"And Annabelle isn't —"

"Nope again."

"We really need to sit down and talk about your family tree."

"I don't think you're ready for that yet, Michael." She wasn't entirely sure *she* was ready.

"Speaking of ready, I'd better get rolling. I'm taking an earlier flight." An unexpected business dinner with a producer who had expressed interest in doing a feature film of one of his short stories.

"Poor you." He wasn't a West Coast kind of guy, not by any stretch of the imagination. "How long will you be gone?"

"Two days. I'll be home Friday night."

"You lead a glamorous life, Yanovsky. Caviar . . . movie stars . . ."

"I'd trade it for a weekend up there with you."

A surge of emotion took her by surprise. "After things settle down with my mother."

"Real life doesn't scare me, Cat. It never has."

"I was terrible to you yesterday," she said. "I'm used to being in control."

140

"Tell me something I don't know."

"You deserved better than the bum's rush I gave you."

"A glass of water and a nap might've been nice."

"Oh, Michael, I —"

"I'm kidding, Doyle."

"I think my sense of humor is missing in action."

"It'll come back."

"I meant what I said about after my mother's situation is stabilized. I want you to come back up for a weekend."

"I'm going to hold you to that, Doyle."

She knew he would. If there was one thing she knew for sure about Michael Yanovsky, it was that he was a man of his word.

Just Outside of Town

"I'm hungry." Annabelle's normally sweet voice was beginning to sound like an air raid siren at maximum volume. "I want a hamburger."

"We're almost there," Joely said. "See the lighthouse?" She pointed out the window. "I used to play on the beach right there at its feet." She played there alone, but that was another story. Nerdy geek girls who saw poetry in physics and heard music in higher math hadn't been in great demand when she was growing up.

"Did you go to McDonald's when you were little?"

"We didn't have a McDonald's in town when I was little. Mostly we stopped at Patsy's in town when we wanted something to eat."

The road wound past the high school on the outskirts of town, then curved around the lighthouse.

"Can we go to the beach?" Annabelle asked.

"Maybe tomorrow, honey."

"I want to go now."

"I thought you wanted a hamburger."

Annabelle's expression downshifted into a scowl. "I don't like it here. I want to go home."

So do I, honey. So do I.

Five years ago Cat bought the old Haynes house, a small ranch with a huge two-car garage on the northern edge of town near the lighthouse. Even Meg, the Realtor, thought she was crazy to pay asking price for something so clearly in need of renovation, but Cat had a vision, and she wasn't about to risk losing the house of her dreams to save a few dollars.

At the time she purchased it, she was just at the beginning of her association with *Pink Slip*, and her private label of hand-dyed, hand-spun yarns had yet to get off the ground. She wasn't sure if she was a total lunatic or a cockeyed optimist, but she took a leap of faith anyway and sank her savings into her future.

The house still looked pretty much as it had when she dragged in her boxes and bags of stuff. There had only been so much money to work with, and her focus, to be honest, had been on creating the perfect studio from a very imperfect garage. Through a convoluted series of loans, barters, and old-fashioned sweat equity, she had succeeded beyond her wildest hopes.

Walking into her airy, light-filled studio was the best part of her day. She loved everything about it, the shiny bleached oak floor, the pure lemon yellow walls, the skylights, the worktables piled high with roving waiting to be spun then plied, baskets of yarn in sapphire and ruby and emerald ready for the needles.

Her spinning wheels were set up near the window wall, adjacent to the huge work flowchart she had pinned above her drafting table. Not that she did much work at the drafting table. More often than not she found inspiration curled up in her oversized easy chair near the window that overlooked her herb garden. They all teased her about the chair, another roadside reject she had saved from destruction and rehabilitated over a period of time, but she didn't mind. Family was allowed to tease family. It was in the bylaws.

And they were all family. The women who worked with her had become like sisters. In a small town like Idle Point, opportunities for stay-at-home moms were limited to opening a day care facility in your house or taking in typing for the three or four people in the world who hadn't mastered keyboard skills.

When Cat posted a sign on the community bulletin board at Barney's Food Emporium, she had been overwhelmed by the enthusiastic response from the town's population of closeted knitters, and within a week they were off and running. By the time the costume designers of *Pink Slip* discovered her work, she was ready to grab the opportunity and run with it.

It was nearly noon when she dragged herself across the yard to the studio. Jeannie and Bev were spinning some gorgeous New Zealand roving she planned to ply with merino and then hand-paint in a beach-at-dawn palette that had been teasing her for months. Denise was carding some Romney at one of the worktables while Nicki and Taylor were mixing vats of dye near the sinks.

Jeannie was the first one to spot her standing near the door. She leaped up from the wheel and ran over, followed by Bev and the rest of them. Within seconds Cat was enveloped in hugs and questions.

"You do whatever you have to do," Nicki said as Cat extricated herself from a bear hug. "We can keep things humming along here without you."

Bev gave Nicki a sharp elbow to the ribs. "She doesn't mean it the way it sounds, Cat. It's just that we can —"

"I know exactly what you both mean. I don't know what I'd do without all of you."

"Stay up nights knitting," Taylor, the practical one of the group, said. "Not that that's exactly a hardship."

"That's what she does anyway," Bev said.

"Oh really?" Jeannie shot her a big theatrical wink. "That's not what I heard."

Further proof that gossip was alive and well in Idle Point.

"So who is he?" Nicki demanded.

"Who's who?" Denise chimed in.

"The guy who drove her up from New York."

"His name is Michael," Cat said. "He's a screenwriter."

"Is it serious?" Denise asked.

Now was as good a time as any to take the first step toward full disclosure. "Yes," she said. "He's a great guy."

"So where is he?" Jeannie pretended to peer under one of the worktables. "Don't make me ransack your house, because I'll do it."

Cat laughed out loud. "He's on his way to L.A. for a meeting."

"Whoa!" Taylor fanned herself with her hand. "So we're not talking starving artist here."

"No, we're not."

"Well, good for you," Denise said. "We've been wondering when you were finally going to — ouch!" She rubbed her arm and glared at Jeannie. "Hey, it's nothing bad," she said to Cat. "We love you, and we want you to be happy."

Which to them meant happy in the way they were happy: married and with children.

"Listen," she said, "I have to go over to

the hospital and see how Mimi's doing, and then I'm going to meet Frank at the house and inspect the damage."

"Oh, honey," Taylor said, eyes wide with concern. "You haven't seen the house yet?"

"It's that bad?"

"Your mother's a lucky woman," Taylor said. "At least she has you to help sort things out."

It was that bad.

"Is Joely coming back to help out?" Denise asked. She and Joely had been in the same high school graduating class.

"I'm not sure," Cat said, beginning to inch her way toward the door. She loved these women, but she loved her sister more. A discussion of Joely's shortcomings, real or imagined, wasn't on her agenda. "She's in Scotland, you know, and —"

"I think I hear the UPS guy," Jeannie said as the low rumble of a car's engine floated through the open windows. "Maybe it's that shipment of Silk Garden we've been waiting for."

"That doesn't sound like a truck," Denise said. "It sounds more like a car."

"It's probably Karen," Cat said, then a minute later, when nobody popped up in the doorway added, "Maybe it isn't. I'd better go check."

She rounded the side of the garage. A Nissan with Massachusetts plates was parked in front of her house, and she noted that her front door was wide open. Not a good sign. She had relatives in Massachusetts, but in times of trouble they were more inclined toward annoying phone calls than on-site visits.

"Whoever you are, you have five seconds to show yourself," she stated as she stepped into the tiny foyer, "or I'm calling the police."

"Cat?" A familiar voice sounded from the back of the house. "Is that you?"

Oh God . . . it couldn't be . . . Joely was in Scotland . . . she had responsibilities . . . Joely couldn't possibly be standing there in the kitchen doorway with a little girl clinging to the hem of her sweater, shrieking at the top of her lungs that she needed to go to the loo.

The two sisters locked eyes, and Joely nodded. First things first.

"You must be Annabelle," Cat said as she walked toward them. "I'm Cat." She crouched down in front of the little girl, whose face was pressed against the fabric of Joely's black trousers. "Would you like me to take you to the loo?"

"No!" Annabelle's voice was muffled.

"She's shy," Joely said, her hand resting on top of the child's head. "If you'd just point me in the right direction, I'll take her."

She pointed toward the hallway. "Second door on the right. You can't miss it."

Joely's smile was tentative. "Thanks. We'll be right back."

Joely whispered in Annabelle's ear, then the two of them walked down the hall to the bathroom. Cat experienced an odd sense of envy, something she had never felt before with her sister.

The difference between knowing of Annabelle's presence in her sister's life and actually seeing the two of them together was overwhelming. Joely looked so . . . maternal. That was the only word that fit. Her brittle, hard-edged younger sister, the one who had always lived in her head and kept her heart under lock and key, had clearly given her heart to William Bishop's little girl.

"Annabelle, please stop crying!" Joely pleaded with the child in the privacy of her sister's sparkling white and yellow bathroom. "Everything's going to be fine."

"I want to go home!" Annabelle howled as Joely lifted her up so she could reach the high sink. "I want my daddy!"

"I know you do, honey, but your daddy is in Japan, remember?"

What kind of woman would attempt to reason with a tired, hungry, homesick seven-year-old when bribery was a viable option?

"I have a great idea," she said as she helped Annabelle dry her hands. "Let's go have a real American hamburger with the works."

Annabelle's scowl began to show signs of cracking. "You said we couldn't go to McDonald's."

"I know someplace even better," Joely said. "I know a place just like the malt shop in *Grease.*" *Grease* was right up there with *The Princess Bride* and *Sound of Music* on Annabelle's top-ten list of favorites.

"May I have a cheeseburger?"

"Sure," Joely said. "And a milk shake, too, if you want."

Annabelle considered her options. "I don't want her to go with us."

"Do you mean Cat?"

"Yes," Annabelle said firmly. "Just us."

She chose to bypass the statement. Sometimes cowardice was a woman's only way out.

Cat's back was to them as they entered the kitchen. "Why don't you bring your bags in?" she tossed over her shoulder. "I'll put them in the spare room for you."

"I don't want you to go to any trouble," Joely said. "I was planning to stay at the Motel 6."

"Don't be silly. I have room. You'll stay here."

"No!"

Hurricane Annabelle struck again.

Cat spun around. "You don't want to stay here?" she asked her.

Annabelle glared up at Cat. What had happened to the fey faerie child Joely knew and loved?

"No," Annabelle said. "I don't like it here. I want to go home."

Joely wanted to crawl under the kitchen table and stay there. She had been counting on Annabelle to charm them over the rough spots, but Annabelle had another agenda entirely.

"She's hungry," she said to Cat with an apologetic smile. "I told her I'd take her to Patsy's for a cheeseburger and shake."

"Patsy's gone vegan," Cat said. "You could get a great soy-veggie burger."

"No!" Another outburst from Annabelle. Thank God this one was directed her way.

151

"I want a real cheeseburger. You promised!"

Joely met her sister's eyes and mouthed the word "Help!"

Cat leaned back against the sink and regarded Annabelle. "I've been told I make the best cheeseburgers in Idle Point."

Annabelle's scowl was alive and well. She looked up at Joely, who nodded her agreement. "Cat's a great cook, Annabelle. She made me cheeseburgers all the time when I was your age." And chili and spaghetti and meatballs and fish sticks — God, how would she have survived without Cat watching out for her? "I know I'd love a cheeseburger if it's not too much trouble."

"No trouble." Cat was already in motion, pulling items from the fridge at the speed of light. "Why don't you bring in your bags, and I'll have your lunch ready before you're unpacked." She glanced over at Annabelle who, judging by the expression on her face, was considering a mutiny. "I hope you like cats, Annabelle."

Cats, dogs, kittens, puppies, faerie children who hid beneath the heather.

Annabelle glanced around the kitchen. "I don't see any cats."

Cat wiped her hands on a snowy white

dish towel. "Oh, there be cats." She held out her hand to Annabelle, but her girl refused to take the bait. Instead they followed Cat down the short hallway to the guest room. The door was closed, and Cat paused, hand on the doorknob, and met Annabelle's eyes.

"Her name is Trixie," she said solemnly, "and she's very scared and lonely."

"Why is she lonely?" Annabelle asked, her tender heart beginning to overcome her resistance.

"She was up a tree," Cat said, "and a fireman rescued her."

Joely's eyes widened. "You don't mean Mom's Trixie?"

Cat nodded. "The same."

"I can't believe she's still around!"

"I don't know if you like cats very much, Annabelle," Cat said, "but I do know that Trixie could really use a friend."

She opened the door, and Annabelle squealed when she saw poor old Trixie asleep in the middle of the bed.

"Go nice and slow, Annabelle." Cat led her over to the bed. "Trixie's very old. Her eyes and ears aren't what they used to be."

"I'll be real quiet," Annabelle whispered. "She'll like me."

"I know she will." Cat met Joely's eyes

and smiled. "I think you're exactly what Trixie needs."

"Trixie," Annabelle crooned. "Can I scratch your ear, Trixie, can I?"

Trixie looked up and took Annabelle's measure, then nudged Annabelle's hand with her nose.

"That was a stroke of genius," Joely said as she followed Cat back into the kitchen. "She was maybe ten seconds away from a major meltdown."

"She's tired and hungry. She'll be fine once she eats."

"I think I'm the one who's supposed to say that."

Their eyes met, and years of history rose up between them. The nights Mimi didn't come home. The many times it was just the two of them huddled together in bed praying for the sound of their mother's footsteps. The way her sister had been there for her every single day.

"Oh, Cat —"

Their hug was clumsy, more than a little awkward, but it felt so right to be there in her sister's kitchen.

"Sorry." She tried to pull away, but Cat wouldn't let go. "I absolutely refuse to cry."

"Me, too." Cat's own eyes looked suspiciously damp. "I'd rather eat dirt."

"Nature or nurture," Joely said with an embarrassed laugh. "Someone should study us and figure it out once and for all."

Stupid nonsensical talk. What was wrong with her? She hadn't seen her sister in five years, and she was shifting a warm, honest moment into a discussion of genetics versus environment.

"We've been studied before, baby," Cat reminded her as they finally drew apart, "except it was by *Rolling Stone*, not the *New England Journal of Medicine*."

"Before my time," she said lightly. *Rolling Stone* belonged to a life the Doyle family had led long before she came along.

Cat fixed her with one of those speculative looks that had always made her feel painfully exposed and vulnerable.

"I'm glad you're here," Cat said. "I didn't think you would come."

"Neither did I. I guess I didn't realize how good you are at wielding the guilt card."

"That's not what I was trying to do."

"Don't be modest, Cat. Of course it was."

"Well, looks like it worked. I'll have to figure out how I did it for future reference."

"So how is she?" Joely asked as Cat pulled a grill out from under the sink and placed it on the stove.

"She came through surgery fine," Cat said, "but she's still not fully conscious." Cat went on to explain — a little defensively, Joely thought — that she hadn't been to the hospital to see Mimi yet today.

Joely was proud of herself for biting back a bitter comment, but Cat knew her too well. "Go ahead," Cat said, ripping into a package of ground beef. "Say whatever you were going to say. Don't censor yourself around me."

"I don't feel anything." The words sounded cold and ugly, but she couldn't stop them. "I know I should be feeling something — I mean, she's my mother, for God's sake — but —" She shrugged. "Nothing. I feel nothing."

Cat, who was up to her wrists in forming burger patties, didn't seem shocked at all. "There's no law that says you have to. You're here. That's the important thing."

"I didn't come here for her," Joely said.

"I know that," Cat said, "and it doesn't matter. The point is, you're here, and I'm very glad."

Nothing was going quite the way Joely had expected it would. She had been expecting a battle. She had been primed to go on the defensive, but there was no need. The sense of unity, of shared purpose, surprised her and left her slightly off balance.

Cat filled her in on the nitty-gritty details of their mother's condition while she heated the grill pan and started the hamburgers cooking. She put Joely to work toasting buns, cutting slices of cheddar from a foil-wrapped block. Cat had always been a multitasker, but those skills had been refined into a daunting display of competence.

"We'll need lettuce, tomatoes, and pickles," Cat said, gesturing toward a wicker basket of produce on the far end of the counter. "Slice them up and arrange them on a platter. We'll serve ourselves."

"When did you turn into the Martha Stewart of Idle Point?"

"You've been gone a long time," her sister said. "A lot's changed."

Joely rinsed a pair of tomatoes under the faucet, then dried them with a dish towel. "Annabelle is usually a very well-behaved child. I hope you won't hold her outburst against her."

Cat lowered the flame under the burgers. "She's seven years old. It comes with the territory."

"She's just upset," Joely went on. "I wish

157

you could see her at home. She —"

"She's *seven,*" Cat repeated. "You don't need to apologize for a seven-year-old acting like a seven-year-old."

She relaxed for the first time since the plane landed at Logan. "How did you do it?" she asked. "I mean, how did you know what to do when I was her age? You were only seventeen yourself."

"You made it easy," Cat said, flipping the burgers onto the toasted buns. "You were like a middle-aged woman in *Little House on the Prairie* pajamas. All I had to do was make up a list or post a schedule, and you jumped on board."

"You make me sound like a nerd."

"You were a nerd," Cat said affectionately. "Our brilliant little nerd. Grandma Fran and I used to look at each other sometimes when you were doing your homework and wonder where in hell you came from. You were scary smart, honey. We were in awe of you."

"And I was in awe of your artistic ability. I'd give anything to be able to draw or paint or do any of the things you do."

"Right," Cat said with an eye roll for good measure. "You're out there helping people walk again. There isn't much that compares to that."

You wouldn't be so proud of me if you knew I haven't worked in almost six months, Cat, or that sometimes I don't think I care if I ever work again.

The fancy education, the freedom to go out and meet her destiny head-on that Cat had sacrificed to make possible for her — it had stopped mattering a long time ago. She felt ashamed and looked away.

Cat, however, had moved on to another topic.

"Tell me about Annabelle," she urged. "Is she a logical type or more fanciful?"

"Fanciful," she said as she helped carry the platters over to the table. "She has the most amazing imagination. She believes there are faerie children living in our side garden."

"Maybe there are," Cat said with a wink. "Just because you can't see them doesn't mean they aren't there."

"You should have seen me yesterday — was it just yesterday? She had me out there trying to hang umbrellas over the heather so the faerie children wouldn't get wet."

"Saran Wrap," Cat said. "That's what I always used when I was a kid. All you have to do is drape it over the tops of the plants, and the faerie children will be just fine."

"You're scaring me," Joely said, only half

teasing. "Don't tell me you believed in faeries when you were little. I thought we both had trouble believing in things we couldn't see."

"Faeries, leprechauns, trolls under Old Man Willis's front porch. The things I couldn't see were never a problem. It was the things I could see that gave me trouble."

"Like Mimi?"

"Yeah," said Cat with a wry smile. "Like Mimi."

They were back on common ground.

Chapter Eight

"Four," Annabelle said, holding up the correct number of fingers.

"Me, too!" Cat wrinkled her brow and pretended to think deeply. "Your favorite color."

"Red!" Annabelle cried. "Red! Red!"

"Nope," Cat said, shaking her head. "Yellow."

"Nobody likes yellow best."

"I do," Cat said. "My workroom is yellow."

"Can I see it?"

"Sure you can," Cat said. "After lunch."

"But I want to see it now."

"Not now," Cat said, winking at Joely, "but we'll definitely see it after lunch."

Joely held her breath. Annabelle was a good child, but she was most definitely mercurial. Her reaction could be anything from an eruption of giggles to a flood of tears.

"Okay," Annabelle said then reached for the rest of her burger.

Cat definitely had a way with kids. Joely had been watching with undisguised admiration as her sister and Annabelle got to know each other over an all-American lunch of burgers with the works and cold glasses of milk. Joely bypassed the milk, but Cat didn't. She was bending over backward to make Annabelle comfortable, and Joely found herself wondering why she had waited so long to bring the two of them together.

Clearly they were soul mates. Annabelle regaled her sister with tales of the faerie world in the garden, while Cat kept up her side of the conversation with a long and very funny story about the tiny troll who had lived under their front porch in Pennsylvania a million years ago.

She had always known her sister was good with kids — after all, it was Cat who had raised her — but she had never known it from the perspective of a grown woman. Annabelle was a mercurial little creature, and Joely had worried all the way across the Atlantic that she was making a terrible mistake. What if her sister looked at Annabelle and saw nothing more than a seven-year-old girl with an accent?

She wanted Cat to fall in love with Annabelle the same way she had. She wanted Cat to see all the wonderful things that she saw in that remarkable little girl. She wanted her sister to understand the choices she had made along the way, and Annabelle was the key.

Cat didn't have children of her own. She had never shown the slightest interest in domestic entanglements. She had forged a supremely independent life for herself, if you didn't count Mimi, one that seemed to suit her down to the ground. It was as if her maternal instincts had had a good enough workout when Joely was growing up and could now be set aside so Cat could get on with her life.

"I have a bit over," Annabelle said, holding up a bite-sized piece of burger. "May I share with Trixie?"

"I think you should ask Cat," Joely said.

Annabelle turned to Cat. "May I?"

"Oh, honey," Cat said, "I know Trixie would just love to share your lunch with you, but she's an old girl now, and she feels better when she eats simpler food."

Joely's heart swelled with pride as the child nodded sagely then suggested a soft-boiled egg and buttered toast to tempt Trixie's palate. Cat's eyes twinkled with delight, and the look the two sisters exchanged over the child's head made Joely feel the entire trip had been worthwhile.

You see how special she is, don't you, Cat? She really is wonderful, isn't she!

"Come on, Annabelle," she said. "Cat was nice enough to make this delicious lunch for us. Why don't we clear the table and do the dishes?"

Annabelle proudly carried her dinner plate over to the dishwasher, then went back to fetch her drinking glass. William would be so proud of his daughter. She found herself wishing she could share this moment with the one person on earth who would really understand.

"I'm going to head out to the hospital in a few minutes," Cat said as she pressed the Start button on the dishwasher. "I should have been there a few hours ago. Do you want to come with me?"

Every cell in Joely's body was urging her to flee, but she stayed put. "Is Mimi conscious yet?"

"I don't know. She wasn't when I called this morning."

"Maybe I'll skip it this time," she said. "Annabelle's going to crash any minute, and I'm not sure the hospital is the place I want it to happen."

A perfectly reasonable, logical excuse to everyone but her big sister.

"You're going to have to see Mimi sooner or later. You might as well do it now."

"I'm not here for Mimi." She wanted there to be no doubt about her position.

"If you're worried about bringing Annabelle with us, we could ask Karen Porter to watch her while we're gone."

"Karen as in Karen and Danny?"

Cat nodded. "Karen homeschools her kids. Annabelle would fit right in. Besides, it would only be for a couple of hours. It might even be fun for her."

"A couple of hours?" Joely felt like her scalp was on too tight. "I thought visitors were moved in and out of ICU pretty quickly." She could manage fifteen minutes. Sixteen if she had to.

"So don't go," Cat said. "We can meet up at Grandma Fran's later to take a look at the damage."

"How bad do you think it is?"

"Karen said it's pretty bad but . . ." Cat's words trailed off into a shrug.

She wasn't sure if it was a trick of the lighting or a shift in perception, but her strong, indomitable big sister suddenly looked fragile. Her blue eyes were ringed with shadows so dark they seemed almost violet. Worry lines creased her forehead. She looked like what she was: a woman of almost forty who had the weight of the world on her shoulders, the same weight she had carried since she was ten years old and their father walked out the door.

This is why you came home, isn't it? She needs help. Are you going to make her beg for it?

"Karen never liked me," she said bluntly. "I don't want Annabelle playing with her kids if she's going to bad-mouth me."

Cat looked at her and started to laugh. "You're not in high school any longer, Joely. She's married with three kids. I don't think the fact that Danny took you to the prom instead of her matters anymore."

"You're right. I sound like an idiot."

"I know what you're really worried about." Cat laid a gentle hand on her arm. "Nobody blames you for the accident, honey. I promise you the whole thing was put to rest years ago."

"It's just —"

"I know," Cat said again. "But it's time you put it to rest, too. You were in the wrong place at the wrong time. There's nothing you can do to change the past. It's over. Move on."

She thought she had, but there she was in Idle Point once again looking for a way out.

★ ★ ★

"I'll stay here," Joely said as Cat shifted the car into Park at the top of Karen's drive. "It'll be faster that way." She was still reeling from the raucous reception she had received from the co-op of craftswomen who worked in Cat's studio. Any hopes she might have entertained of slipping in and out of town quietly had flown out the window.

"Don't be ridiculous," Cat said. "Come in. Say hello. Karen knows we're in a rush. We'll be out in three seconds."

"It's hardly worth it for three seconds," she pointed out.

"Then do it for Annabelle. This is all new for her. It will be easier if you introduce her."

Her sister's words hit home, and she felt the heat of embarrassment burn her cheeks a nice bright red. This wasn't like her at all. Annabelle was always, *always,* her number one priority.

"You're right," she said as she unbuckled her seat belt. "Of course you're right. I should have thought of that myself."

"Oh, shut up," Cat said with a good-natured laugh. "You didn't commit a crime."

But it felt like it to Joely as she unfastened Annabelle and helped her out of the backseat.

"Do they have kittens here?" Annabelle asked as they crunched their way up the rocky path to Karen's kitchen door.

Joely met Cat's eyes, and her sister shook her head. "No kittens," Joely said, "but they have baby lambs."

"Do they have puppies?" Annabelle asked, clearly unimpressed at the prospect of lambs.

"No puppies," Cat said, "but they have two great big fluffy dogs named Simon and Garfunkel."

Joely started to laugh. "Simon and Garfunkel? Tell me you're kidding."

"Just wait until you meet Peter, Paul, and Mary."

"I can't wait," she said, adding an eye roll for emphasis.

Karen wasn't in the kitchen or the office.

"The barn," Cat said. "That's where she usually is."

They walked around the side of the house and were halfway across the yard when two dogs the size of Shetland ponies galloped toward them and knocked Joely flat on her butt. Annabelle shrieked with laughter as the dogs licked Joely's face and danced around her. And Cat wasn't any better. She was doubled over with laughter herself.

"Would somebody please do something?" she pleaded as the furry assault continued. "I'm drowning in dog spit!"

"Simon!" a sharp voice called out. "Garfunkel! Get off her this minute!"

Oh God. It was Karen. She wanted to crawl under the dirt and disappear. The girl voted Most Likely to Succeed was not supposed to end up trapped beneath two hundred pounds of crazy dog fur in front of the girl voted Most Likely to Run Away and Join the Circus. Joely had two master's degrees and was halfway toward a doctorate. Karen raised sheep. This couldn't be happening.

"This minute, guys!" that sharp, unmistakable voice called out again. "I mean it."

Simon and Garfunkel jumped away from Joely and tore off, leaving Joely struggling to pull down her sweater, find her left shoe, and recover her dignity.

"It's been a long time." Karen, neat and clean in jeans and a bright blue T-shirt, stood over her. "I'll help you up."

She flashed her sister a quick *Some help you are* look, then took Karen's hand and stood up.

"Herding's in their blood," Karen said, clearly trying not to laugh. "They were just trying to keep you in line."

Cat and Annabelle started laughing all over again, and Joely couldn't help but join in. She introduced Karen to Annabelle.

"Hey, Annabelle!" Karen turned to the little girl whose attention had wandered toward the barn. "How would you like to hold a baby lamb?"

"I guess," Annabelle said and suddenly clamped herself to the side of Joely's leg.

"Maybe you could help us," Karen said, bending down to meet the child's eyes. "We have some kittens who —"

That did it. Annabelle headed full-speed toward the barn.

"Kittens?" Cat asked. "Where did you get kittens?"

"I forgot to tell you! It happened three days ago. A little surprise, courtesy of Mr. Big and Samantha." Karen turned to include Joely in the conversation. "We brought her in to Gracie so she could put her out of the kitten business and found out she was going into labor."

A squeal followed by loud whoops of laughter floated toward them from the barn.

"Uh-oh," Karen said. "I'd better see what's happening."

"Maybe I'd better come, too," Joely said.

"She'll be fine. Believe me, I can handle one more with my ovaries tied behind my back."

A mind-blowing metaphor that knocked the words right out of Joely for a moment.

"We'll be back in two hours," Cat said, leaping into the discussion. "Thanks for helping out." She flashed Joely a *Let's go* look.

"Yes," Joely said finally. "Thanks a lot for watching Annabelle."

"No problem," Karen said. "Good to see you again."

She disappeared into the barn.

"See?" Cat said when they climbed back into the car. "That wasn't so bad."

"At least the dogs didn't bite me."

"You should see Karen with her kids. She's one of those great earth mother types. I don't know how she manages to homeschool them and keep up with work at the same time."

"What about Danny?" she asked as they drove past the old high school. "What's he up to these days?"

"He owns a computer shop in town. He buys, sells, repairs, builds." Cat eased to a stop at a traffic light. "Now he's building

Web sites for some pretty big concerns."

"Sounds like he's doing well."

"He's doing great," Cat went on. "They both are. They're a terrific team. Everybody says —" She glanced over at Joely. "This doesn't bother you, does it? I mean, you haven't been carrying a torch for Danny all these years, have you?"

"God, no!" She started to laugh. "To be honest, I was afraid he might have been carrying a torch for me."

"If he is, it's the best-kept secret in town, and you know this town isn't good at keeping secrets."

"Phew!" She pretended to wipe sweat from her brow. "That's a relief."

"She has three kids, honey. Annabelle's in good hands."

How easily they had slipped back into their old ways.

"You always could see right through me."

"Not always," Cat said, "but this time it's easy."

"I've never left Annabelle with a stranger before."

"What about that Mrs. Macdonald of yours?"

"She wasn't a stranger. She'd been with William's family for years."

"How feudal of them."

"Mrs. Macdonald was like a grandmother to Annabelle."

"Karen's not a stranger," Cat reminded her. "She sat behind you in French."

"She's a stranger to Annabelle."

"You're right," Cat said. "I should have realized that."

"The place has changed so much," she said as they drove down Main Street. "What's with all the condos? We're starting to look like the suburbs."

"You don't know the half of it. The town council is thinking of making part of the beach private."

"Get out! That's terrible."

"Tell me about it. Suddenly we're attracting a well-heeled crowd, and they're demanding their privacy."

"It's like that back home, too," she said. "So many of the big houses are being bought up or rented by —" She started to laugh. "Well, by people like William to be honest. The old families aren't taking it well at all."

"I thought he *was* one of the old families."

"Not an old Scottish family," she said. "Believe me, that makes a big difference."

"Is it like the difference between

Kennebunkport and Bangor?"

"Worse." She thought for a second. "Like the difference between the QE II and that rowboat Grandma Fran kept in the backyard."

"Your Down East accent is gone," Cat observed. "You're starting to sound very English."

"The butcher back home thought I was from Brooklyn." They both laughed. "He thinks every American is from Brooklyn."

Cat pulled into a spot and turned off the engine. "Ever been homesick?"

"What a crazy question," she said, forcing a little laugh. "Have you?"

"Sure," Cat said. "Every single day when I was in college."

"You commuted to Bowdoin. You slept every night in your own bed. When did you have time to be homesick?"

"What can I say? This is where I'm meant to be."

"Or maybe it's just where you ended up."

"All I can tell you is that the second Mimi rounded the curve near the light-house and I saw the sign Welcome to Idle Point for the first time, I knew I was home."

Loch Craig — Four Years Earlier

"Tell me the truth," Joely said as they neared Loch Craig. "How badly are bipeds outnumbered around here?"

William's laugh always surprised her. William was a successful, sophisticated financial planner with clients in every part of the globe. His suits were Savile Row and Armani. His shoes were handmade for him by a cobbler in Rome. Very few English business types of her acquaintance knew how to really laugh, but William would have been right at home at a Three Stooges revival.

"I think the sheep-to-human ratio is fifty to one," he said, then laughed again at her gasp of surprise. "They're nonviolent, Joely. You're not in danger."

Which of course made her laugh despite the growing awareness that he knew nothing at all about the kind of woman she was. She hadn't a bucolic inclination in her entire body. She thrived on noise and crowds and exhaust fumes. Her heartbeat was synched to city rhythms. Despite the fact that she had grown up in a nowhere town in Maine, you could take everything she knew about country living, multiply it by five, and still end up with nothing at all.

Why on earth had he rented this ramshackle accumulation of stones and timber in the middle of nowhere when he could have easily leased a beautiful flat in town with access to all the things a man in his position needed to do business?

The kid, she thought, spirits sinking even lower. When you had a child you were supposed to give up your old ways and say good-bye to city life and hello to horses and hounds.

"Here we are," he said as they reached the end of the drive.

"Do you always keep your front door open?"

"Mrs. Macdonald's expecting us. She thinks it seems more welcoming this way."

Grandma Fran had believed in an open-door policy, too. Cats, dogs, neighbors, and her daughter Mimi came and went at whim. If it hadn't been for Grandma Fran, Joely and Cat would have ended up living in the back of a Volkswagen bus until they were old enough to strike out on their own. That little house had been their haven, and her sister had been her protector for as far back as she could remember. Cat claimed she could hear the house's heartbeat deep inside its walls, but Joely knew it was only the sound of bad plumbing.

She was a scientist by training and by temperament. She knew that houses were inanimate objects built to provide shelter, and families were groups of people thrown together by an accident of genetic timing. To romanticize either one was simply asking for trouble.

The world of emotions was as alien to her as a Pillsbury Bake-Off. She believed in what she could see and touch and quantify. You couldn't see happiness. You couldn't gather up dreams and arrange them in neat columns in a lab notebook. You couldn't reach back into yesterday and make things turn out the way they did in children's storybooks.

Joely knew who she was, what she wanted, and how to achieve it. She always had. She wasn't afraid of hard work or failure. The choices she had made along the way weren't always popular, but they were the right ones for her. She had her future mapped out by the time she was ten years old, and after all the years of schooling and struggle, she was finally in full control of her destiny.

And then she stepped into the foyer of William's rented house on that rainy springtime afternoon, and all of her most cherished assumptions about life, and about herself, flew up the chimney like woodsmoke. The sense of recognition struck her like a physical blow. An emptiness inside her heart, an emptiness she hadn't been aware of, was suddenly filled to overflowing. It was as close to love at first sight as she had ever come, and it took her breath away.

She loved everything about William's house, from the worn Turkey carpets underfoot to the smells of heather and thyme and dampness that seeped through the walls. The overstuffed leather couches, the polished wooden balustrades, the portraits of somebody else's ancestors that lined the hallways — it was all exactly the way it should be.

The drafty old house with the leaky roof and an ancient Aga as temperamental as an aging tenor felt like home to her, a home she had never known before, never even wanted, but one that had been waiting for her, right there at the edge of her consciousness from the day she was born, and she found herself wanting to hang on to the illusion for as long as possible.

"So how about you?" Cat asked as they waited for the hospital elevator to take them up to ICU. "I still want to know. When was the last time you were homesick?"

"Now," she said as the doors slid open. "Right now."

Chapter Nine

"I need chocolate," Cat said as they exited the elevator two hours later, "and I need it now."

"I need a vodka martini," Joely said, "but I'll settle for a hot fudge sundae."

"The Ice Cream Cottage," they said together, and then they started to laugh.

"Why are we laughing?" Joely asked as they almost ran across the hospital lobby toward the exit. "It was horrible up there."

"You won't get an argument from me." Cat hit the exit like a Patriots linebacker on Super Bowl Sunday. "It was pretty bad."

"She asked for him," Joely said as she pushed through the door after her sister. "She opened her eyes, looked straight through me, and she asked for him."

"At least she's coming out of the coma," Cat said. "That's something."

"Doesn't it bother you at all?" Joely asked. "I mean, I wasn't expecting miracles here, but she's our mother. You would think she'd —"

"It is what it is," Cat said. "It only hurts if you expect anything else."

"But why him?" Joely persisted. "The son of a bitch walked out on us before I was out of diapers. He walked out on *her*. Why should he be the first one she thinks about?"

Cat pulled out her car keys, and a second later her car beeped hello from the other side of the small lot. "What do you want me to say? I was there, too, Joely. She didn't do handsprings when she saw me either." *And I'm the one who's been here year after endless year.*

"Yes, but you're used to it." Joely seemed to hear what she had said, and the tips of her ears reddened. "Sorry. I didn't mean that the way it sounded."

"The hell you didn't," Cat said as she swung open the driver's side door. "And in case you're wondering, yes I am used to it, but that doesn't mean I like it."

Joely slid into the seat next to her and closed the door. "She's crazy, isn't she? I mean, why else would she still be carrying a torch for a guy who split over twenty-five years ago."

"She thinks he'll be back one day," Cat said.

"That's nuts."

181

"No argument here." Cat started the engine and checked her mirrors. "And why the surprise? You grew up with it. Remember the way she used to leave the door unlocked for him until Grandma Fran threatened to make her live in the VW? She was like a kid leaving cookies out for Santa, except she was forty years old, and it was a bottle of Johnny Walker on the kitchen table instead of chocolate chips."

Cat pulled in a breath, but the words kept on coming. "Why would you think anything had changed? I really want to know, because it doesn't make any sense. You're the logical one in the family, aren't you? You're the scientist. What did you see that I didn't that would make you believe there was a chance in hell that Mimi was going to change?"

Joely said nothing. She turned her head away and feigned interest in the Toyota Highlander parked next to them.

"Sorry," Cat said, resting her forehead against the steering wheel. "It's hormones."

"You're pulling the premenstrual card on me?" Her words were as perfectly articulated as always, but Cat could hear the emotion behind them. "I think I deserve better than that."

"I'm not premenstrual, honey; I'm pregnant."

"Not funny." Joely spun around in her seat and aimed her anger right between her eyes. "I can't tell you how not funny that is."

"I'm pregnant," Cat said again. "I was seeing an ob-gyn in New York when Mimi had the accident, and if you don't think I'm feeling like a guilty shit right now, then you don't know me half as well as I thought you did."

Joely continued to stare at her, eyes wide, mouth open in shock.

Cat had the feeling she would be seeing that look a lot over the next few weeks as the news spread.

"I'm due the end of January, in case you're wondering."

"You're really pregnant?"

"So you *can* talk," Cat joked, aware of the little twitch in the corner of her right eye. "I thought maybe I'd struck you dumb with my news flash."

"Who?" Joely asked. "I never thought — I mean, you're the last person I —" She stopped cold, cheeks a bright fire-engine red. "You never said you wanted children. I mean, I didn't even know you were seeing anyone."

"You never asked."

"Would you have told me if I had?"

"I don't know."

Joely's expression shifted slightly. "I'll give you points for honesty."

"I'm not trying to hurt you, honey. We're not as close as we used to be. I'm sure there's a lot about you and William that I don't know." How could she tell her sister that one of the best parts of being with Michael was the fact that those hours with him happened beneath the radar of family and friends?

"It's Zach Porter, isn't it," Joely said. "You said he was back in town. I always thought you'd end up with Zach."

"No, it's not Zach. His name is Michael Yanovsky," Cat said.

"Don't tell me he's some new guy who lives in one of those condos they put up near the lighthouse."

"He lives in Manhattan," she said. "I met him at HBO two years ago. He's a screenwriter."

"So that's why you go down there so often. I knew it had to be more than business."

"No, I go down there for business," she said quickly. "He just happens to be a very nice fringe benefit while I'm there."

"Does Mimi know you're pregnant?"

"It's early days," she reminded her sister. "I wasn't planning to tell anyone for at least another month." Now she wasn't sure how much Mimi would even understand when, or if, the time came to share the good news.

"Does Karen know?"

"I told her yesterday."

"How did she take it?"

"She burst into tears."

"Karen?" Joely looked skeptical. "She was the only girl in biology who could dissect a frog and eat a candy bar at the same time."

"Karen's really a softie," Cat said, "but don't tell her I said so. She has a reputation to protect."

It was meant to be a joke, but Joely wasn't laughing.

"I'm sorry," Cat said. "If I'd known you were on your way, I would have waited so I could tell you first."

"Don't be ridiculous," Joely said, but once again Cat was surprised by the depth of emotion hidden away inside such a logical heart. "It's no big deal."

"You're going to be an aunt."

"That should shock the hell out of Idle Point."

"You know what? The whole town will

just have to get over it." Cat started to back out of her parking spot. "Now come on, Auntie Joely, let's get those hot fudge sundaes while we can."

There wasn't enough chocolate in the world to prepare either Joely or Cat for the sight of Grandma Fran's house.

"Oh God," Cat breathed as she parked at the curb. "This is so much worse than I expected."

"She's lucky she's alive," Joely said.

Yellow tape crisscrossed the front door, courtesy of the police department. Not to be outdone, the firefighters had boarded up the shattered windows. Grandma Fran's favorite chair, an old orange La-Z-Boy, lay sodden and abandoned in the front yard next to three torn sofa cushions and what remained of an old pine coffee table.

A middle-aged man with a paunch and receding hairline rounded the corner of the house as they made their way up the walk.

"Sorry we're late, Frank," Cat called out. "We were at the hospital."

The man gave Cat a kiss on the cheek. "Chocolate," he said with a wink as he pointed to the corner of her mouth. "Can't say I blame you."

"Frank, you remember my sister Joely."

She extended her hand politely, but he leaned forward and placed a dry peck on her right cheek. "You won the New England Young Scientists award three years running. You were the toast of I.P. High."

"I'd forgotten all about that," Joely said, amazed.

"You beat my kid brother Adam. My father ended up sinking two thou into self-esteem therapy for him. Believe me, my family hasn't forgotten."

She flipped through her mental file cabinet and pulled out a tall red-haired boy who blushed even more than she did. "So how's Adam doing these days?"

"Heading a research team at Stanford." He waited for the obligatory nod of respectful approval. "How about you? Rumor has it you're some big muckety-muck doing big stuff in England."

"Scotland," Cat jumped in, "and yes, Joely's doing very important work in bioengineering research."

That was a big sister for you. Cat couldn't help protecting her from troubles both real and imagined and, in true younger sister fashion, Joely found herself letting her do it. There was no sense bringing up the fact that she hadn't actually done any bioengineering research in almost a year.

"How long are you here for?"

"Not very," she said, wishing she had stayed in the car. "I'll be heading home as soon as Mimi's situation has stabilized."

He gave her an odd look, but Cat, bless her, stepped in again.

"You've probably had a long day already, Frank. We don't want to keep you any longer than necessary." Offered up with a wide and friendly smile. "Anything we need to know before we go inside?"

"Only that someone was watching over your mother. It could've been a whole lot worse."

Which didn't prepare either of them for just how bad it was.

The police had given them permission to do a walk-through as long as they didn't disturb anything. The fire marshals had already done a preliminary investigation and confirmed there were no signs of arson, but they hadn't signed off officially on it yet.

Frank pulled down the yellow tape that ran across the doorway while Cat fumbled in her pocket for Mimi's keys.

"They forgot to lock up," she said as the door swung open at her touch. "I'm going to give Henry a piece of my mind for this."

Joely understood why he hadn't bothered when she stepped inside.

"Oh, God," Cat breathed, leaning against the wall for support. "I had no idea."

Joely touched her arm. "Are you okay? Why don't you wait outside."

The place stank of smoke, chemicals, and charred wood. Their mother's chairs were turned upside down. The water-soaked cushions leaned up against the outside wall. Broken glass littered the floor. And that was only the front room.

"I told you it was bad," Frank said as he scribbled notes.

"How about upstairs?"

"Depends which room. The staircase is shot, so you can't check it out. The attic's okay."

"How did the attic escape damage?"

"Who the hell knows. Fires do what they do. We clean up after them."

"Can you clean up after something like this?" Joely asked, glancing around at the wreckage of the house where she grew up. "It doesn't look very promising."

"It's not. You want the truth?"

"I'm not sure," Cat said.

"I think the best thing you can do is sell the place. The land is worth more than the structure, and frankly I'd be surprised if your mother can live alone after this."

Cat looked pale and shaky. Joely stepped closer to her just in case. "I've already thought of that. I'm going to look into a live-in for her."

"Look," Frank said, "it's not my business, but the three of us go back a long way. I'm no doctor, but I don't think Mimi's coming back here either way. I think you're going to have to see about assisted living."

"I know we're probably facing a long period of rehabilitation, but I don't think —"

"Nobody ever does," he said kindly. "Amanda and I had to put her mother into assisted living last year, and she's not even sixty yet."

Cat's right hand moved toward her belly, and Frank's eyes followed the movement. She quickly tugged at the hem of her sweater, but he was already connecting the dots.

"Will you look at all this stuff?" Joely picked her way through the mess, trying not to focus on the artifacts of their mother's life scattered across the floor. A vein in her right temple began to throb, but she ignored it. "How many *Gone with the Wind* plates does one woman need?" Perhaps the comment wasn't in the best of taste, but if it took Frank's mind off Cat's

190

belly, she would take the risk.

"You're white as a sheet," Frank said to Cat. "It stinks from smoke in here. Let's go outside."

"I'm fine," Cat said. "Really."

"I think you'd better go outside," Joely whispered in her ear. "You look like you're going to hit the floor."

Cat nodded. They headed for the door and not a moment too soon. "Distract Frank," Cat whispered. "I think I'm about to lose the hot fudge sundae."

"I shouldn't have let you two go in there," Frank berated himself as Cat disappeared around the side of the house. "You grew up here. She's your mother. I should've taken pictures instead and showed them to you." A strangled sound drifted toward them. "Do you think you should go check on her? That doesn't sound too good."

"It's all that smoke on an empty stomach," Joely lied. "She'll be fine."

His left eyebrow twitched, but he didn't argue with her. "Listen, about what I said in there. I mean, like I said, I'm not a doctor. Just because Amanda's mother needed assisted living after her stroke doesn't mean it's going to work that way for Mimi."

"I'm not sure it's been confirmed that she had a stroke."

"Well, whatever it was," Frank amended, "you just need to figure out what you want to do with the house and let me know."

They both turned as Cat approached.

"Jeez, Cat," Frank began, "I'm sorry I —"

"No apologies." Cat joined them, cutting him off mid–mea culpa. "It's just —" She gestured in the direction of the house. "Her whole life is in there. I wouldn't know where to start if she decides to sell. I guess I got overwhelmed."

"One step at a time," Frank said, flipping his notebook closed. "Go home. Take a nap. I'll work up a report and put a rush on it with District. Then you two can figure out the next step."

"He knows," Cat said as they watched him drive away.

"You think?"

"Did you see the way he looked at me when I touched my stomach?"

"You might want to stop doing that until you're ready to break the news." She grinned at her older sister. "Not to mention the barfing."

Cat feigned a quick left hook. "I feel like I've been run over by an eighteen-wheeler."

"I don't know what I was expecting, but it wasn't this."

Cat's eyes, a grayer shade of blue than her own, swam with tears as she glanced around the yard. "She deserves better than this."

"Her choice," Joely said. "It didn't have to be this way."

"Everyone's not as strong as you are, Joely. She did the best she could with what she had to work with."

"Awfully forgiving of you." She was almost thirty years old, yet the bitterness felt fresh and new.

"I wish you could have seen them together," Cat said, taking her hand in hers. "If you had, then you'd understand."

"I've read their clippings. That's enough."

"The clippings only got half the story. They really were like that, Joely. When they looked at each other, the rest of the world fell away, and it was just the two of them."

"And that would be a swell story if there hadn't been four of us at the time."

"I know you don't believe me, but there were good times, too." Cat squeezed her hand. "A lot of them."

Joely was trying to frame a persuasive argument that would prove her thesis when

Cat swayed on her feet. "Come on," she said, putting her arm around her sister's shoulders. "I'll drive us home."

"Clearly I'm on the decline," Cat said as she flipped Joely the keys. "I used to be the one who drove everybody else home."

"That was before you were driving for two."

"We have to swing past Karen's to get Annabelle."

"We'll drop you off, then I'll go for Annabelle."

"I'd fight you, but I'm too tired."

"And I'm wired." Considering the time difference and her lack of sleep, she should be falling over with exhaustion, but instead she felt like she had been mainlining espresso.

They walked down the pathway to Cat's car, and Joely helped her sister into the passenger seat.

"Get in," she ordered, "and don't forget to buckle up."

Cat laughed out loud. "I'm glad you're here, Joely."

She didn't have the heart to tell her sister that *here* was the last place on earth she wanted to be.

Chapter Ten

Funny how the things a woman couldn't say echoed louder than the words she managed to say out loud.

Cat hadn't seemed to notice when Joely swiftly changed the topic from sisterly affection to the shortest route from Cat's house to Karen's farm. Or, if she had, she didn't let on, which was almost as good.

She let Cat out in front of her house, nodded a few times while her sister repeated directions to Karen's place, then headed for the town limits. She tried to empty her mind of everything but the road, the car, and the fact that Annabelle was waiting for her, but the past kept tugging at her, trying to drag her down.

She would rather think about Annabelle. She couldn't wait to scoop her up into her arms, breathe the sweet clover smell of her hair, listen to her clear, high voice. Longing for home tore through her like a summer storm. She longed for Scotland, for the house with the wonky roof, the enormous mahogany bed that sometimes seemed too small to hold her heart.

Karen and Danny lived five miles outside of town on one-quarter of the Porters' dairy farm. According to Cat, the Porters had decided to move to Arizona, and since neither Danny nor Zach were interested in becoming dairy farmers, they divided the farm into four separate parcels that set them up for a very nice retirement far from Idle Point.

The back door was open when Joely arrived, and she rapped on the jamb and called out, "Hello! Anybody here?" to no response.

Okay. Don't let your imagination run away with you. Karen's not about to kidnap Annabelle and hold her for ransom. Maybe they were out in the pasture tending sheep or doing whatever it was you did with the alpacas once you found out exactly what they were in the first place.

"Joe-leeeee!" Annabelle's shriek made her jump. "Come see!"

She spun around in time to see Annabelle dart back into the barn. Her batteries were beginning to wind down, and the thought of making pleasant conversation over livestock made her want to jump back in the car and run away, but that wasn't the way adult women acted. No matter how tempting the thought was.

Annabelle's back was to Joely. She was kneeling on a pile of straw, cooing over something small and furry. But it was the man next to her, who was neither small nor furry, who caught her attention. Danny Porter was the same age she was. He couldn't possibly have a full head of gray hair. Then again, he was married to Karen . . .

"Sorry I'm late," she said, crackling her way toward them across a carpet of straw. "Things took longer than we'd figured, and I —"

He turned around, and she stopped midsentence.

"Zach?"

"It's the gray hair," he said. "Better than going into the witness protection plan."

Neither one of them pretended they didn't remember the last time they had seen each other. A young man's funeral wasn't something you could forget.

"You look great, Joely. Being an expat agrees with you."

"You look good, too," she said as she struggled to push the past behind her where it belonged. "I like the gray hair."

"Karen left a box of that five-minute hair

color on my pillow. She thinks I need a makeover."

"Don't," she said, tugging at her own dyed-and-highlighted locks. "Too high-maintenance. Take it from a woman with a lot of experience."

He really did look terrific. Tall. Lean. A pair of wire-framed glasses on his strong, straight nose. He looked like what he was: a grown man who was comfortable in his own skin. Adulthood suited him.

She glanced around the barn. Karen and the kids were nowhere in sight. "Where is everyone?"

"Dinah cut her foot on a nail. When Will heard his sister was going on a trip to the emergency room, he decided he wanted to go, too, so he stepped on a piece of glass. And Kerry went along for the ride."

"Are they okay?"

"Karen phoned from the hospital. Danny's meeting them there. Dinah's getting a tetanus shot, and Will needs two stitches."

"And Kerry?"

"She's waiting for them to start passing out lollipops."

"Thanks for staying here with Annabelle. You should have phoned me. I would have come right over and taken her off your hands."

"No biggie," he said, and she almost laughed at the thought of William using that expression. "She's something, your Annabelle. I think she'll be asking you for a cria of her own."

"Cria?"

"Baby alpaca. If you spend five minutes with Karen, you'll know everything there is to know about them. One of the mothers has a problem with her milk, and they've been hand-feeding her cria. Annabelle took to it like an old hand."

"She's just like William. They both love animals."

"William's her father?"

Joely nodded.

"She calls you Joely."

"That's my name, Zach, isn't it?"

"Very progressive."

"Not really." There was no point to dancing around the truth. "I'm —" Why was it so hard to say? "I'm not her mother."

"So you and this William aren't — ?"

"No," she said. "We aren't."

This was the place where you normally inserted one of those hideously awkward silences that made you question every personal decision you'd ever made about your life, but Zach hadn't read the instruction manual.

"How long have you been together?"

"Over four years." She sounded defensive. What was that all about, anyway? She had nothing to feel defensive about. Her life was her life. She didn't have to explain it to anyone.

"You look happy," he said, considering her. "Are you?"

She wasn't sure. She couldn't even remember the last time she'd felt happy. Lately she had managed moments of happiness, but that pure thread of joy that used to run through her early days with William and Annabelle had been missing for a long time. Uncertainty had replaced it. A sense that every day brought them closer to saying good-bye.

"Uh-oh," Annabelle called out. "The bottle's empty! May we have more please, Zach?"

"Zach?" Joely's eyebrows shot skyward. "When we were her age, everyone was Mr. and Mrs."

"You're home, Doyle. We don't stand on formalities around here."

"I think we'd better go," she said to Annabelle. "It's been a long day."

"But the cria needs more milk."

"Your new friend Zach will take care of it. It's almost suppertime."

"Have supper with us," Zach offered. "Karen and Danny should be home in a little while."

"Now there's a great idea for you," Joely said. "The poor woman comes home from the ER and finds two strangers sitting here waiting to be fed."

"You're not strangers."

"You know what I mean. The woman has three kids. She doesn't need company for dinner." She took Annabelle's hand. "Besides, Cat's waiting for us. We should go home."

Annabelle frowned. "Do you mean home to our real home or home to Aunt Cat's house?"

First it was "Zach." Now it was "Aunt Cat." Where was this coming from?

Zach walked them out to the car. "I was really sorry to hear about Mimi's accident."

Joely nodded. "Thanks."

"How is she?"

"Not good." She glanced pointedly at Annabelle, then back at Zach. "The house is pretty much of a write-off."

"I hate hearing that," he said. "Mimi's always been special to me."

It took a second, but the memories came flooding back. "That's right," she said.

"You liked all those old folk songs, didn't you?"

"You're looking at the last of The Doyles groupies," he said with a rueful laugh. "Cat claimed I dated her so I could sit there and listen to Mimi Doyle's stories."

Annabelle tugged on her sweater. "What stories?"

"Great stories," he said, crouching down to be on level with the child. "Stories about kings and queens and movie stars and princesses and the sweetest, most beautiful music you've ever heard in your life."

Annabelle's eyes widened. The man was speaking her language. "Like a fairy princess?"

"Yes," he said, "except the fairy princess was real, and she had two beautiful daughters."

"He's talking about my mother, Annabelle," she cut in before they veered too far off Reality Road. "She was a singer a long time ago."

"When you were a little girl?"

"Long before," Joely said.

"She was a great singer," Zach said. "So was your dad. The Doyles were right up there with Peter, Paul, and Mary."

"How old are you really?" she asked with

202

a bit more bite than she intended. "Their music was over by the time you could afford to buy your first eight-track."

"So was Mozart's," he said, "but that doesn't mean I can't appreciate it." He gave her a funny look. "Don't tell me you don't like their music?"

"I don't like their music."

"Come on. They were great."

"Your opinion. Their music was a tad too . . . sentimental for me."

Annabelle poked her in the left hip. "What does 'sentimental' mean?"

"Cheaply emotional," she said, then chuckled at the frown on the little girl's face. "Like too much sugar in your tea."

Annabelle thought for a second. "Like the Barney song."

Zach started to laugh. "How old are *you*, Annabelle? Forty-three?"

"Seven," Annabelle said in her most British voice. "I am seven."

"Call me crazy, but she looks like you," Zach said.

Okay. Now it really was time to go.

She helped Annabelle into the backseat and buckled her in.

"Good to see you, Zach," she said, jingling her sister's car keys for emphasis. "Thanks again for watching Annabelle."

"I didn't say good-bye to Mamie," Annabelle piped up from the backseat. "The babies need another bottle! Don't forget to give them another bottle."

"Don't worry, Annabelle," Zach called through the open window. "I'm on the job."

They waved good-bye to Zach and the livestock and hit the road.

"Did my sister tell you to call her aunt Cat?" Joely asked as they drove to Geno's Pizza to pick up a large pepperoni for supper.

Annabelle yawned.

"Honey, did Cat tell you to call her aunt Cat, or did you decide all on your own?"

A shrug of tiny shoulders and another yawn. "I forget."

Joely knew better, but she didn't push. Cat would have run it by her first. This idea was pure Annabelle. Like most little English girls, Annabelle understood familial relationships. Maybe they hadn't said she could call Joely "Mommy," but the fact remained that Joely was the only mother she had ever known, and everything else she understood derived from that. If Cat was Joely's sister, then it would follow that she was also Annabelle's aunt.

"Can I have Pepsi with my pizza?" Annabelle asked.

"You know how I feel about fizzy drinks."

"In America you drink Pepsi with pizza."

"Okay, but just this once." Annabelle squealed with excitement, and Joely laughed. "Tomorrow it's back to milk."

"Can I have ice cream after the pizza?"

"I think the Pepsi's enough for one day."

"But I love ice cream." Annabelle's feathery brows knotted over her tiny nose as she stared at Joely. "Dinah has ice cream every single day."

"And when Dinah's all grown up, she'll wish she'd eaten more broccoli."

"I hate broccoli. I only like ice cream. If we lived in America, I could eat ice cream every day."

Less than twelve hours on U.S. soil, and her beloved English rosebud was turning into a pint-sized American beauty.

William was in for an earful when they finally connected.

There was tired and then there was first-trimester tired.

"Please tell me I didn't fall asleep with my head in the pizza," Cat said as she dragged herself up from the kitchen table.

"You snored!" Annabelle said with a giggle. "I heard you."

"I seem to be doing a lot of that lately." She pretended to tickle the little girl. "Ladies, feel free to watch TV or do jumping jacks in the living room, but I'm going to call it a night."

Annabelle's giggling grew louder. "That's silly. You're too old to go to bed so early."

"Annabelle!" Joely's cheeks blazed with embarrassment. "Apologize right now."

"For what?" Cat said as she slid her plate into the dishwasher. "She's right. Not too many thirty-eight-year-old women go to bed at seven o'clock at night."

"Are you okay?" Joely asked. "Is this normal?"

"That's what they say. Supposedly I'm going to wake up on day one of trimester number two and feel like a nineteen-year-old cheerleader."

"Too bad I won't be here to see that," Joely said, laughing. "That might be worth hanging around for."

"You can hang around for as long as you'd like," Cat said. "Both of you."

Joely shook her head. "No, we need to get home. William will be back from Japan and —"

206

Cat raised her hand to stop the stream of words. "You don't have to explain, honey. She's his daughter. I understand." *I understand more than you think, Joely. You haven't even been here a full day yet. Is it time to run already?*

Cosmo and Newman were curled up in the middle of Cat's bed, dark heads pressed close together.

"Shove over, guys," she said, collapsing next to them.

Cosmo opened one eye and meowed.

"I'll shower in the morning," she promised, curling around the aging tuxedo cats. "I'm too tired to think."

Except she wasn't.

The second she rested her head on the pillow and closed her eyes, the entire crazy-quilt day rushed toward her at supersonic speed, and there wasn't time to duck. It hit her full force, and all she could do was lie there and stare up at the ceiling until her heart slowed down to something close to normal. *Too much,* she thought. The whole thing was way too much. She was still trying to adjust to the fact that she was thirty-eight years old and pregnant for the first time. That alone would be enough to send a woman into emotional overdrive, but add Mimi's accident into the mix, and you had trouble.

She was accustomed to being in control of her life. Her organizational skills, honed during childhood, were her safety net. Most creative types sailed through their days on a whim and a wish, but not Cat. She believed in being prepared, and the fact that Mimi's accident had so totally broadsided her had shaken her faith in her own judgment and ability to cope.

Grandma Fran's house was a total loss. Anyone could see that. It would cost more to rebuild than it was worth and, besides, what was the point? Mimi wouldn't be living there again. That much was certain. Her mother would need full-time, live-in help, and that cost money. Better they sold the house and land to the highest bidder and used the proceeds to settle Mimi comfortably in an assisted living facility or, God forbid, an actual nursing home.

She was glad Joely was there. They might have chosen separate paths as adults, but their shared childhood was a bond that could never be broken. She wished Joely could have known their mother before the bad times came to stay, but more than that she wished Joely could have known their father. A few weeks ago she'd caught the scent of cherry pipe tobacco, and it awakened memories that had lain dormant for over twenty-five years.

It was nice to be reminded that it hadn't all been bad.

They say a girl never forgot her first love, and there was bittersweet truth to that. Her father had been Cat's first love. She had adored Mark Doyle with every fiber of her little girl's heart, and when he walked out the door that October morning in search of a guitar string, a part of her heart had stopped beating.

Maybe she was more like Mimi than she had ever realized. The ten-year-old child she had once been was still waiting for him at the front door of the Pennsylvania cottage if only for the chance to say good-bye.

Joely sat in the middle of the sofa in the middle of Cat's living room and listened to . . . nothing. It was nine-thirty eastern daylight time, and she was the only one awake in the entire house. Cat was sound asleep on top of her bed with two very large, very protective felines wrapped around her. Annabelle had fallen asleep on the sofa, and Joely had quickly settled her in for the night in the guest bedroom. Mimi's beloved Trixie had scooched over to make room for the child, then reclaimed part of the pillow.

That was all fine and good for those involved, but it left Joely wide-awake, wired, and alone with her thoughts, which was her least favorite place to be.

No, scratch that. It was her second least favorite place to be, the first being her old hometown of Idle Point.

She was more than ten years gone from Idle Point, but the need to escape felt as urgent as it had when she was a teenager. Grandma Fran's wrecked house. Her mother's wrecked life. The memory of Ty Porter's wrecked future.

No, she wasn't going to think about that. The town had grown up since the accident. The old landmarks were long gone. There was a four-way traffic light where the blown stop sign had been, but she could see the ghosts just the same.

She had tried phoning William's cell twice. Both times she had left voice mail messages behind, and her disappointment had been surprisingly intense. She wasn't a "sound of your voice" kind of woman, but the sound of his voice would have been nice.

She wandered into Cat's kitchen in search of leftover pizza. There was something irresistible about cold pizza washed down with a can of beer. Not that Cat would have any beer in the house. Cat was more Beaujolais sipped from a fabulous wineglass she'd found at some yard sale or the front porch of a down-on-its-luck antique shop.

Joely settled for Pepsi straight from the can. She ate standing over the sink, watching the pizza crumbs fall into the drain.

"Now what?" she asked the appliances when she finished. It was ten minutes to ten, and instead of being sound asleep the way any normal jet-lagged westward-bound traveler would be, she was more wired than ever. The thought of forcing herself into bed — and deeper into her own head — made her feel like the walls were closing in on her.

She used to feel that way all the time when she was growing up. There were nights when she could almost see the house, her family, her future, closing in on her, and she'd practically explode from the house and head for the beach by the lighthouse where she could breathe.

Wasn't it just last night that she had been looking up at the Scottish sky and longing for the inky blackness of a Maine summer night? The one thing, besides her sister, that she remembered with fondness, and she wasn't out there enjoying it.

She checked on Annabelle, who was out like a light, then scribbled a note for Cat, which she left propped up on the kitchen table. A long walk under a Maine night sky was exactly what she needed. Maybe then she'd be able to sleep.

Chapter Eleven

The squeak of her door pulled Cat up from sleep. Who needed a burglar alarm when you had a door that squealed like a stuck pig every time it opened or closed? She was reasonably certain it was just Joely heading out on one of her midnight rambles, but she knew herself well enough to know she wouldn't fall back to sleep until she knew for sure.

She extricated herself from her spot between Cosmo and Newman and tugged her clothes back into place. Yawning, she stepped out into the hallway and quickly checked the guest room. Annabelle was sleeping soundly, her arm around Trixie. No sign of Joely in the living room. She popped her head into the kitchen and found a note propped up against the sugar bowl.

"Gone beachcombing," the note read. "Be back soon. Please keep an ear open for Annabelle."

She smiled and tossed the note down

onto the table. It was nice to know some things never changed. Her sister might not share her love for the town of Idle Point, but that crescent stretch of beach cradling the lighthouse was something else again.

For a second she considered joining Joely on her nocturnal ramble, but then she remembered there was a sleeping child in her guest bedroom.

"Better get used to it," she said to the empty kitchen as she grabbed a bottle of water from the fridge. This time next year there would be a sleeping child in her guest bedroom every night. Except it wouldn't be a guest bedroom any longer. It would be a nursery.

And the child would be hers.

The realization was better than caffeine and a cold shower. She was wide awake now and likely to remain so for awhile. Before sperm met egg, she had been nocturnal by nature. Her most creative and productive hours began after the sun went down, but pregnancy had turned her body clock on its ear. This was the first time in weeks that she had been alert after dark.

She had maybe twenty rows left to finish the sparkly leg warmers she'd been working on in the doctor's office. If she finished that up tonight, then she would be free to cast on the elaborate lace shawl she'd promised Nona at HBO for the series finale and at least get the establishing rows in place.

Then again, maybe she'd fire up her laptop and do a little Web surfing. This really was the golden age of information. Everything she could possibly want to know about pregnancy was only a click away — and more than a few things she didn't want to know as well. She wasn't a group kind of woman, but she'd been toying with the idea of joining a few e-mail lists for pregnant women of a certain age. She had even gone so far as to request information on how to join.

Maybe they'd sent her the secret password. It might be waiting in her in-box right now. And if she happened to stumble across a note from Michael, that wouldn't be so bad either. Not that she was expecting an e-mail. Unlike every other writer she had ever met, Michael didn't travel with his laptop, so unless he stopped in at an Internet café in L.A., there wouldn't be any mail from him until he returned to New York.

She curled up in the corner of her sofa with her laptop balanced on the arm and clicked on the e-mail icon. Spam. Spam.

Really ugly spam. A note from one of the actresses on *Pink Slip* about commissioning a sweater for her real-life daughter.

And one from Michael.

TO: cat@wickedsplitty.com
FROM: movieman@soho.net
SUBJECT: YOU

I wanted to call but figured you have your hands full right now. L.A. is L.A. Took a meeting. Did the dinner thing. Counting the hours until I'm back in civilization.

I'm at the Bev Wilshire. Room 1299. Brought the cell and my PowerBook and proved the thesis that both actually work west of the Hudson. Rumor has it they work in Maine too but further testing necessary.

Please advise. — Yanovsky

He knew her too well. Full-on sentiment wasn't their style, even if she sometimes had the feeling he was a closeted hearts-and-flowers type who was tempering his own romantic enthusiasm out of respect for her sensibilities.

She didn't put a whole lot of stock in the

idea of soul mates or the outdated notion of one Mr. Right in a sea of Mr. Wrongs. Or at least she hadn't until she met Michael. Who knew it could be so easy? They fell into step with each other as if they'd been together all their lives. The heat was there — lots of heat — but there was more to what they had than sexual chemistry.

When she met him she saw her future, doors swinging open, wide open, to possibilities she had never let herself consider. Under normal circumstances that would have scared her back up to Idle Point permanently, but not even the strongest woman could fight her own destiny.

TO: moievman@soho.net
FROM: cat@wickedsplitty.com
SUBJECT: not me, YOU

So guess who showed up at lunchtime? Yes! The prodigal sister has returned and she brought Annabelle with her. She looks wonderful, very sophisticated, and Annabelle's a little dream. I may get in some parenting practice while she's here.

Looks like my mother had a small stroke. We're waiting for more particulars but I think we're heading

217

down a very rocky road. The house is a disaster. We met with Frank the insurance guy this afternoon. He thinks we should sell it for land and move on. Easy for him to say etc. etc.

BTW you were right about those meatballs. I wish I hadn't left the doggie bag at Aquavit.

Safe trip home. Love from your friend in Maine

She pressed Send and was about to shut down the laptop when the phone rang.

"Now that's fast," she said, laughing into the receiver. "Are you using speed dial?"

A slight pause then a very British, "Pardon?"

"Oh." She switched ears. "You're not Michael Yanovsky, are you?"

Another slight pause. "Cat, it's William Bishop."

"William, hello." What was it about men with accents that turned American women immediately into goofy thirteen-year-olds with bad skin and braces? "How are you?" *Great, Cat. Even a thirteen-year-old would come up with something more original.*

He inquired about Mimi, and she gave him a truncated version of the facts as she knew them. She had expected him to move quickly past the obligatory health check to the real reason he'd called, but he surprised her by asking follow-up questions. He surprised her even more by listening to her answers.

William had always been a shadowy figure to her. She knew the vital statistics — widowed, a father, thirty-five years old, and successful — but Joely had never given her much of an idea of the man behind the data. She liked what she was hearing from the man himself.

"Listen, I know this is costing you a fortune," she said, ever the thrifty Yankee, "so I'd better tell you that Joely isn't here."

Silence.

"William? Are you there?"

"I am." A shorter pause this time. "Will she be back soon?"

"She went down to the beach for a walk. Annabelle's asleep, but if you'd like me to wake her —"

"No, no. Let her sleep. I'm sure she had a big day."

Cat told him quickly about Trixie and the baby alpaca, and he laughed. "She's a wonderful child, William. You must be very proud."

"I can take some credit for genetics, but

the rest belongs to Joely. She's brilliant with Annabelle."

Brilliant with her. Warning bells went off. He had sounded warm and engaged when he inquired after Mimi's health, but the moment the conversation shifted to Joely, he became politely guarded and distant.

Cat had to dig her fingernails into the palm of her hand to keep from asking something she shouldn't. They exchanged a few more meaningless pleasantries, and then he rang off to catch his plane.

"Damn," she said as she hung up. She had forgotten to ask him where he was flying off to and where he would be staying when he got there.

Then again, maybe William Bishop had chosen not to volunteer the information.

Joely had presented the Bishop-Doyle household as a family unit, a tightly knit trinity of souls who were in it together for the long haul. She didn't get that sense from William. She wasn't sure if she was mistaking a natural reserve for lack of interest, but the conversation left her feeling unsettled and vaguely sad for all of them, but especially for Annabelle.

Women made mistakes all the time in the name of love, and they lived to tell the tale. Broken hearts mended and were stronger for the experience. It was part of life.

But a little girl's heart was more fragile. When a little girl's heart broke, it broke into a thousand pieces, and no matter how hard you tried to make it whole again, you were destined to fail. Their hearts just weren't made that way.

She hoped her sister remembered that.

"Why do we have to see a social worker?" Joely asked as she and Cat waited for the elevator to take them down to the hospital basement the next morning. "We're not asking for public assistance for Mimi."

"It's the way things are done these days." Cat's voice vibrated with tension.

"I don't see why we have to sit there with some stranger and answer personal questions about our family."

"Neither do I," Cat said, "but sometimes you have to pick your battles. Let's save the heavy artillery for when we need it."

And there was little doubt that they would need it soon.

Dr. Green's office had called earlier that morning and confirmed that Mimi had suffered a serious stroke and that there would not be a full recovery. Neither Joely nor Cat were surprised, but the news affected each of them deeply, although in different ways.

A few days from now Joely would board a plane and head back to Scotland. There would be an ocean between her and her mother's needs. Cat wasn't so lucky. Mimi's life was intertwined with hers. Every decision they made about Mimi's future would have a powerful impact on Cat's future as well.

"I can't believe they have offices in the basement," Joely muttered as they wound their way through a maze of corridors. "Don't these people believe in windows?"

"They've run out of room," Cat said as they followed the signs marked Social Services. "The township's thinking about floating a bond to help fund an expansion."

"I'm glad we left Annabelle at Karen's again. This would have been a disaster."

"Why put her through this?" Cat said. "She doesn't need these memories."

"Neither do we." Joely bristled at the sharp look her sister aimed her way. "You told me not to hold back, didn't you? That's the way I feel."

"You might want to hold back with the comments around the social worker."

"Good point."

The social worker's office was at the end of the corridor, a small, windowless, airless room with a metal desk, two file cabinets, and a pair of metal folding chairs for visitors. The fluorescent lighting overhead only added to the stark ugliness of the situation.

"I'm Emilie Weaver," she said, shaking hands with each of them. "Please sit down and make yourselves comfortable."

Joely made a point of avoiding Cat's eyes. Emilie Weaver was either a master of irony or the most clueless individual on the planet. Nobody short of a masochist with a thing for painted metal could get comfortable in that office.

Emilie was new to Idle Point. Maybe that explained the faintly judgmental way her eyebrow lifted as she scanned the police report and the rest of Mimi's voluminous file.

"Your mother lives alone?" She directed the question toward Cat.

"She has someone in during the day to help out," Cat said. "And I live less than a mile away."

Joely cringed at the apologetic tone of her voice.

"She's been under psychiatric care for quite awhile." Clearly Emilie Weaver was just getting started.

"She's been under a medical doctor's care for manic depression," Cat corrected her. "She's been on medication, and it's helped enormously." It had been at least a year since Mimi pulled one of her crazy stunts.

"The inference here is that she also has substance abuse issues," Emilie noted.

"She's been known to drink too much in the past," Cat said.

Joely's anger rose as her sister slid lower in her chair.

"Mrs. Doyle lives alone," Emilie Weaver continued. "You aren't with her twenty-four hours a day to know her habits."

Joely had never seen her sister look so vulnerable or more alone.

"I know what goes into her trash," Cat said with remarkable restraint. "I see the soda cans in her recycling bin. I balance her checkbook. I think I have a pretty fair idea about her daily habits, Ms. Weaver."

"You're not with her all day."

"No, I'm not. That's why I hired a housekeeper for her."

"A live-in housekeeper?"

"She's there from eight until four."

"The fire happened at ten in the morning." Emilie Weaver leaned back in her chair. "Your mother was alone."

And my sister was alone from the time she was ten years old, Joely wanted to scream. *She doesn't owe Mimi anything.*

She leaned forward in her ratty folding chair and locked eyes with the social worker. "I'm afraid I don't see the relevance of Mimi's alcohol consumption, Ms. Weaver. The stroke takes that issue off the table."

Emilie Weaver was prone to high color. She looked down at the sheaf of papers on her desk and spent a few moments shuffling them around. Joely wasn't above relishing her discomfort.

"After careful review, I think it's clear Mrs. Doyle will no longer be able to live alone."

Both she and Cat nodded their agreement, but neither said a word.

The look on Emilie's face made it clear that the woman didn't believe they understood much of anything where Mimi was concerned.

"You both live in town?" Emilie Weaver asked.

"I do," Cat said. "My sister lives in Scotland."

The social worker focused in on Cat. "If you choose to bring your mother into your home, you'll have to make considerable

225

changes to your life, but it can be done."

"I intend to look into an assisted-living situation."

Emilie favored her with a chilly smile. "Most elderly patients thrive in a familial environment."

"I think assisted living is a better option in this case."

"I disagree, Ms. Doyle. Research has proven that —"

"I'm pregnant."

"I see."

"I'm not sure you do," Cat said pleasantly, "but I don't think I could handle her care and a new baby simultaneously."

"Have you read that file, Ms. Weaver?" Joely demanded. "Do you have any idea how we grew up? It's a miracle either one of us made it through to adulthood."

"Joely." Cat placed a hand on her wrist. "It's okay."

"No, it's not okay. We would have thrived in a familial environment, too, but I didn't see anyone offering us one."

"You seem to have some unresolved issues," Emilie observed.

"And your point is?" She had gone too far to back down now.

"Perhaps you should speak with someone about them."

"Perhaps I should have spoken to my mother about them," Joely shot back, "but I think we'll all agree that ship has sailed. Cat is here because she wants to do what's right for our mother, and I'm here because my sister is the best woman I've ever known, and I love her. The rest is none of your business."

That was the difference between the movies and real life. In the movies a statement like that would end with wild applause and an exit worthy of Meryl Streep in her prime. Too bad real life wasn't anything like that.

There was no applause, no sweeping stage-left exit. They all sat there, still as stones, on their cheap metal folding chairs and stared at each other.

Joely was glad the office was in the basement because if there had been a window available, she would have thrown herself through it.

What had she been thinking? Grand gestures had their place, and this wasn't it. She had meant every word she said in defense of her sister, but this hadn't been the way to go about it. This was the equivalent of tossing a ticking time bomb into somebody's house and setting it to explode when you were long gone. In another day or two she would be back in Scotland, far away from the everyday reality of Mimi's life, but Cat would still be here picking up the pieces.

She turned to her sister. "I'm so sorry," she whispered. "I didn't mean to —"

"My sister is right," Cat said, and Joely felt like cheering. "Those papers of yours can't possibly tell you what it was like to grow up with Mimi for a mother, and I'm not going to try. Now let's talk about what we need to do to provide the best possible care for Mimi. As Joely said, the rest is nobody else's business."

The silence was deep and wide. Emilie Weaver looked at them. They looked back at Emilie Weaver. The silence between them stretched. The social worker didn't know what she was up against. Nobody could stretch a silence like a Doyle woman on a mission.

"All right then," Emilie said, flipping through the papers one last time. "Now, about your options for assisted living . . ."

"You were great in there," Cat said as they waited for the elevator. "I was a heartbeat away from a meltdown, but you stepped in there and saved the day."

"Officious bitch," Joely said, glaring in

the general direction of Social Services. "She should mind her own business."

"She was," Cat reminded her. "Patient welfare is her business."

"She had no business putting you on the defensive."

"I wasn't on the defensive."

"Yes, you were. She was trying to make you feel guilty."

The elevator doors glided open, and they stepped inside.

"She didn't have to try to make me feel guilty," Cat said as the doors slid shut. "I do a pretty good job of that myself."

Joely made a dismissive gesture and pressed L for Lobby. "You have nothing to feel guilty about."

"If Mimi hadn't been alone yesterday morning, none of this would have happened."

"Come on, Cat. You can't believe that. That stroke would have happened when it did even if Mimi had had a houseful of company with her."

"I know that, but somehow it doesn't seem to matter."

"So why don't I feel guilty?" Joely challenged her. "She aimed a few of her arrows in my direction, too."

"That's a good question," Cat said as the

elevator shimmied to a stop. "Not that I think you should, but why don't you feel guilty?"

"I don't know," Joely said as the doors opened. "Just lucky?"

Every now and then God handed a woman exactly the right thing to say at the right moment. The haunted expression in Cat's eyes vanished, and the two of them started to laugh.

"Now, I'm the last one to object to laughter, but are you girls in or out?" Roxanne from Radiology was holding the door open.

"Out," said Joely.

"In," said Cat.

"Make up your mind, ladies. I have a hot left shoulder waiting for me upstairs."

"I need to check for messages," Joely said, "and make sure Annabelle's okay." She also wanted to see if William had phoned again with new contact information. They had never gone so long without speaking, and it made her feel disoriented and unsettled.

"I'm going upstairs to see Mimi."

"I'll meet you in ten," Joely said as the door slid shut behind her.

How did Cat do it? Didn't she ever feel like saying to hell with everything and walking away from Idle Point and the endless cycle of responsibility? All Joely could think about was how quickly she could get from the elevator to the exit. She felt like a prisoner on a jailbreak, tunneling her way to freedom.

She didn't want to make pleasant conversation with the receptionists or chat with the aging candy stripers who knew her way back when. Ten more steps . . . seven . . . three . . . freedom!

God, the air smelled wonderful. All fresh and scrubbed clean with pine and sea salt. Last night's walk on the beach had reminded her of all the things she had loved about the town where she grew up. She sank down onto the stone bench to the left of the door and let it all wash over her in blissful solitude and silence.

The solitude didn't last long. She heard footsteps coming up the walk, and in a town the size of Idle Point, odds were she knew who they belonged to. She closed her eyes and pretended to be deep in meditation but — big surprise — it didn't work.

"Hey, Joely."

She squinted up into the sun at Zach Porter and her heartbeat lurched forward. "Is Annabelle okay?" *Please God please.*

"Why wouldn't she be?"

"Sorry," she said, placing a hand over the center of her chest in an attempt to keep her heart inside where it belonged. He wouldn't be carrying an explosion of flowers if he'd come to deliver bad news. "When I saw you, I —" She attempted a laugh. "I guess Annabelle isn't the only one with a vivid imagination." *It's called separation anxiety, Doyle, and if you think this is bad, what will you do when you and William say good-bye?*

"Everything's fine," he said, dropping down onto the bench next to her. "Karen had them all learning Spanish when I left."

Relief tasted better than chocolate.

"So what's with the flowers?" she asked. "Are you picking up some spending money running deliveries for Becky's Blooms?"

"Actually they're for Mimi."

"Who are they really for?"

"Mimi," he said again. "She's out of ICU. I figured she could use some cheering up."

"She had a stroke, Zach. She won't even know the flowers are there." Joely was too embarrassed to say this was the first she'd heard that her mother was no longer in intensive care.

"I'll know."

"Isn't this carrying fandom a little far?"

232

"She's a friend," he said. "I care what happens to her."

He strode off toward the entrance before she could think of something suitable to say. Zach Porter had left Idle Point long before she went off to MIT, and as far as she knew, his trips home had been infrequent at best. When had he found time to forge a friendship with Mimi? Not that it was any of her business. Her mother had never lacked for friends. Mimi could be funny and charming and all sorts of wonderful things when she was of a mind to be. The one thing she couldn't seem to manage was being a parent.

It wasn't hard to see how, on a good day, she might have dazzled Zach. If you didn't have to depend on her for things like food and shelter, she was great company. She was beautiful and mercurial, and she had known everybody who was anybody way back in the sixties and seventies. If you cared about that sort of thing, the stories were worth the price of admission, which, in Zach Porter's case, was an armful of flowers.

Apparently the tired old legend of Mark and Mimi Doyle still had some juice.

Like she said to Zach last night, that was way before her time.

Chapter Twelve

Idle Point

"It was spur of the moment," Cat said again as she and Joely set the table for supper later that day. "If you'd seen him with Mimi, you would have done the same thing."

Joely made a face. "If I'd seen him with Mimi, I would have lost my lunch."

"That's my area of expertise."

"I always was competitive," Joely said. "What's the deal with him and Mimi? I knew he'd had a big case of idol worship but I never heard they were such good friends."

"You never asked."

"Your point is well taken, but it seems an unlikely pairing if you ask me."

"You were a baby when it started," Cat said as she swapped out the bright yellow place mats for the poppy red ones. "When we first moved here, he was on Grandma Fran's doorstep every day, waiting to see Mimi."

Joely feigned an enormous shudder. "Sounds like an adolescent stalker to me."

"He loved their music," Cat said. "He had every album and tape Mark and Mimi ever made. He knew their work inside out, backward and forward. He could tell you where they were when Mark wrote a certain song. He knew what Mimi wore at Newport in 1965. He had shoe boxes filled with clippings from *Rolling Stone* and the *Village Voice* —"

"Now wait a minute." Joely leaned against the table and fixed her with a look. "You want me to believe a kid from Idle Point was reading the *Village Voice*?"

Cat threw a yellow place mat in her sister's direction. "This is your heritage we're talking about, little sister. It might not hurt you to learn something about it."

Although she didn't say it to Cat, there had been times when Joely would rather say she'd been raised by wolves than lay claim to Mark and Mimi Doyle.

"Just tell me he's not going to bring his albums with him and force us to have a hootenanny in the living room."

The idea made Cat laugh out loud. "Don't worry. The man lives in the Napa Valley. I doubt he travels with his old eight-tracks."

"He probably has an iPod," Joely muttered.

"I heard that."

They went back into the kitchen, where Cat gathered up the dishes while Joely collected the glassware.

"Is it true he sold his software company for eight figures?" Joely asked as she followed her sister back to the dining area.

"Karen said it was high eight figures. That's how he bought the vineyard. He still owns the hardware side of the enterprise."

"Looks like you missed out on a real winner, Cat. You should've stuck with your old high school sweetheart. You'd be rolling in Cabernet and Manolos."

"Right."

"No, I mean it. You two were great together. Everybody said so. I can't believe you never think about what might have been."

Cat stopped what she was doing. "You really don't know."

"Know what?"

"I can't believe you never realized that Zach's gay."

"Gay?" Her voice rose a full octave. "When did that happen?"

"No cheap jokes, please, but he figured

it out while we were dating in high school."

"But you were crazy about him."

"Just my luck, huh? I can't believe you never guessed."

"I was ten years old when you two were dating," Joely said in her own defense. "I was still playing with my Barbies." She set a glass down at each of the four places. "What about college? I thought you two got back together."

"As friends," Cat said. "We both had a tough time settling in, and it was nice to have someone you could trust on your side."

"I always wondered why the Porters hung all their hopes on Ty instead of Zach."

"The future," Cat said simply. "If they wanted grandchildren to take over the farm, they knew they weren't going to get them from Zach, so they turned to the next in line."

"Pushing Zach out into the cold."

"Pretty much."

"Why didn't they turn to Danny after Ty . . . after the accident?"

"Danny told them he didn't want any part of being a dairy farmer. He was estranged from them for awhile, but they've worked it out."

"Apparently so. He and Karen are living on the north forty."

"And that could've been you," Cat teased.

"Maybe in an alternate universe."

"Do you ever think about it?"

"Alternate universes?"

"Marriage. Family. A house in the suburbs. You know what I'm talking about."

"Do you?" Joely countered.

"Sometimes," Cat admitted, "but I think I might be missing the wife gene."

"No plans to marry the mysterious Michael?"

"We like things the way they are." Her expression grew more serious. "How about you? Are you happy with your arrangement?"

"Arrangement?" Joely bristled. "We're not an arrangement. We're a family."

She was determined not to flinch under her sister's scrutiny, but it wasn't easy.

"Do you love him?"

"What kind of question is that?"

"You never talk about him."

"We've had a few other things to talk about since I got here, Cat."

Her sister shook her head. "Not just now," she said. "You've been like this practically since you met William. You never mention him, Joely. Not on the phone, not in your e-mails. Sometimes I forgot he was even living with you and Annabelle. I'm glad I got to speak to him last night. I was beginning to think he was a figment of your imagination."

"You never mentioned Michael to me," she pointed out. "If Mimi hadn't had this accident, I still wouldn't know about him." She paused for dramatic effect. "Or about the baby, for that matter."

"That's because I was keeping him a secret."

"I rest my case."

"It's not the same thing. You never tried to keep William a secret."

She tried to come up with a logical reason for her behavior, but everything she thought of sounded lame, even to her. "It's easier to talk about Annabelle," she finally admitted. "It's less complicated."

Cat sighed deeply. "That's what I was afraid of."

"It's nothing," Joely protested. "Really. Things have just been a bit off balance since my contract ended. Once I'm back in the lab, things will fall back into place."

"I can't believe someone with your background would have trouble finding a position." She narrowed her eyes in Joely's direction. "You have been looking, haven't you?"

So this was what that legendary deer in the headlights felt like.

"My old team is reforming," she said, "and there might be another opening down the line. It's not like I'm in a rush."

"You're not?" Cat sounded skeptical. "I thought you loved your work."

"You know I do," she said, "but now that Mrs. Macdonald has retired, I need to be there for Annabelle."

"Mrs. Macdonald is the only nanny in Scotland?"

"We trusted her. She was with William's family for years."

"You're not a nanny, Joely. You're not his wife. You're not Annabelle's mother."

"Thanks," Joely said. "I appreciate the clarification of my status." She didn't need to be reminded that nothing in life lasted.

"Oh, honey." Cat rested a hand on her shoulder. "Be careful."

"Don't worry," Joely said lightly. "I'm not in danger of a broken heart, if that's what you're thinking."

"It's not your heart I'm worried about," Cat said. "It's Annabelle's."

★ ★ ★

Maybe dinner wasn't such a good idea after all.

First Annabelle didn't like the salad. The "green bits" were prickly and scratched the back of her throat. Joely, red-faced with embarrassment, quickly substituted Cat's lovely mix of baby greens with a small wedge of iceberg.

Cat leaned forward and smiled across the table at her sister and Zach. "So tell us more about this big IPO you're working on, Zach."

"Is that what they're saying around here?" Zach laughed and poured himself some more wine. "No IPO." He swirled the Merlot he'd brought with him and inhaled the aroma. "BJT Industries in Boston made me an offer for my hardware enterprise, and I think I'm going to take it."

"What?" Cat shrieked. "I can't believe it. I thought —"

"I'm hungry," Annabelle stated. "When are we going to eat?"

"We are eating," Joely said in a measured tone of voice. "Finish your lettuce, then we'll have the next course."

"But I don't want lettuce," Annabelle said. "I want food."

"Annabelle," she warned. "You interrupted a conversation."

"I don't care."

Cat saw that they were sailing perilously close to a full-fledged mutiny. "It's just spaghetti," she said. "Why don't I fix Annabelle's right now."

"No," Joely said. "I'm not going to reward her for bad behavior."

"She's not so bad," Zach said, trying to be helpful. "You should see Danny's kids when they —"

He never had the chance to finish his sentence because Annabelle erupted into an impressive display of red-faced, clenched-fisted tears.

Joely placed her napkin on the table and rose from her seat. "I'm sorry," she said to Cat. "I'll be back."

"She's overtired," Cat said as the door to the guest bedroom shut behind Joely and a shrieking Annabelle.

"And confused, no doubt." Zach looked amused.

Cat speared a tomato with her fork. "Why should Annabelle be any different?"

"Joely's good with her."

"She loves her," Cat said.

"You say it like that's a problem."

"It could be." She stopped and shook her head. "Forget I said anything."

"She's wound pretty tight."

"She's seven, and she's homesick. What do you expect?"

"I mean Joely."

"How about we change the subject?" She wasn't going to gossip about her sister . . . at least not with her sister just three rooms away. "So tell me more about this IPO that isn't."

"It's pretty basic stuff," he said. "Business one-oh-one. I have something they want, and they're willing to pay me big bucks to get it."

"I thought you loved your company. I can't believe you'd let the rest of it go."

" 'Loved' being the operative word. It hasn't been the same since Lloyd . . ." His words trailed away.

Tears sprang to her eyes. "Oh, Zach!" She leaned across the table and took his hand. "I'm so sorry. I had no idea. My God, he was younger than we are."

"He didn't die, Cat — not that I haven't thought about killing the son of a bitch." He looked away but not before she saw the pain beneath the fast talk. "If I'd known he was going to walk out, I wouldn't have stopped smoking."

"The bastard," she said. "Are you saying he left you *and* the company?"

"He didn't pull a Mark Doyle, if that's what you're asking. He asked me to buy him out. He said he wanted to start his new relationship without any baggage from the past."

"And here I thought you were the one who'd have the Hollywood happy ending."

"It could still happen."

"Not another dreamer." She made a face as she gathered up the salad plates to take them into the kitchen. "Just don't end up like Mimi."

"You sound bitter," he remarked as he followed her into the kitchen. "I don't remember you sounding that way before."

She slid the salad plates into the dishwasher, then turned to face Zach. "You saw her today. The woman's almost sixty-three years old, and she's still waiting for the knight on a white charger to come along and make it all better again. There's not one other damn thing in her life but Mark Doyle, and there never has been." She wagged a finger at him. "And don't go telling me it's the stroke, because she's been that way as long as you've known her which, I might point out, is almost as long as I've known her."

"I didn't say she was perfect. But you got to see the real thing up close and personal. You know it can happen."

"And your parents are about to celebrate their fiftieth anniversary. I'd trade you intensity for longevity any day."

"Let's make a pact," he said, draping his arm around her shoulders. "If we're still alone when we turn sixty-five, we'll buy a house together and take in stray cats."

"Zach," she said, "I have something to tell you, and I think you'd better sit down."

Annabelle was inconsolable.

Joely's embarrassment over her outburst vanished as she held the little girl in her arms and tried to make sense of the jumble of words pouring from her.

"I know you miss Daddy, honey. He misses us, too, but he's very far away, and sometimes the telephones don't work the way they're supposed to."

"But he always calls us," Annabelle said between heart-wrenching sobs. "Please call him! Please, Joely, please!"

She had never felt so helpless in her life. She couldn't let Annabelle see that her own worry level was rising with every hour that passed without a call from William.

"I have an idea," she said, desperate to

stop Annabelle's tears. "Maybe Daddy left us a message on the computer."

"Oh yes!" Annabelle brightened immediately. "Maybe Daddy's wondering why we didn't write back."

It was a long shot, but she couldn't think of anything else to do. She pulled her laptop out of its carrying case and set it up in the middle of the bed.

"Wait a second," she said, hunting around for an outlet. "We'll be up and running before you know it."

Bless Cat for thinking of everything. The telephone on the nightstand had a working data port, and less than two minutes later she had a connection.

"Okay," she said, fingers flying across the keyboard, "let me access our e-mail, and we'll see if there's anything from Daddy."

Come on, William, she silently pleaded. *Maybe you're done with me, but come through for Annabelle . . .*

"It's taking a long time," Annabelle said, bouncing up and down on the bed, her tears forgotten. "Why is it so slow?"

"Okay, here we go." They watched as the screen filled up with notes and messages about Viagra, school reunions, real estate opportunities, two notes from Sara, and —

thank God a million times — one from William.

"Here's a note for us from your daddy," she said, moving over so Annabelle could see the screen. "Looks like he sent it this morning."

TO: jdoyle@clendenning-bio.uk
FROM: w.bishop@globalfinance.uk
DATE: 22 june
SUBJECT: re: itinerary
ATTACHMENT: hokkaido.doc

J and A, miss your voices. I'm v. busy and it's hard to know when I'll be at a phone. Mobile broken but v. probably wouldn't have worked here anyway. See attachment for hotel info, room #, etc. Call if you can.
A's Sinclair grandparents expect her next week for holiday visit. If problem, let me know soonest.

L,
W

Oh God. She had totally forgotten about the Sinclairs' annual holiday trek to Loch Craig to fetch Annabelle for a weeklong visit touring the Highlands. She quickly closed the e-mail before Annabelle reached that part.

"Can we ring him?" Annabelle begged.

Joely did a few quick calculations. "He's probably giving a lecture or something, honey. It's midmorning in Japan."

"Please try, Joely, please!"

She couldn't come up with a good reason not to pick up the phone and place a call. She grabbed her cell phone, punched in the long string of access codes, area codes, and numbers, then waited while the impulses sped through thousands of miles of fiber optic cable lacing the oceans. The modern world was filled with small miracles every moment of the day.

The connection was crisp and clear. The operator spoke English. Even better, she understood it.

The only problem was, there was no William Bishop registered there.

Somewhere Over the Pacific

The flight attendant stopped in the aisle next to him. "I spoke to the captain, Mr. Bishop, and we're running ahead of schedule. You should make your connection to Boston with no difficulty."

He thanked her for her trouble, then leaned back and closed his eyes. Normally he slept well on overseas flights. He had trained himself to use the time spent in transit to recharge his batteries. Unfortunately, that ability seemed to have gone suddenly missing along with the cancelled series of seminars in Hokkaido. George had opted to stay on in Japan for the weekend while William headed for the train station straightaway to begin the journey home.

He tried to phone Joely from the airport lounge in Tokyo with no luck. The phone at Cat's house rang through, and the voice mail on Joely's mobile was full. This ongoing game of phone tag only added to the sense of isolation that had been building between them. The only avenue he hadn't pursued was leaving a message on their machine at home.

He glanced at the clock. They wouldn't be boarding for another fifteen minutes. Why not give it a try? He dialed home, listened to the standard-issue far-off ring, but instead of the standard-issue outgoing message, he heard the four tones that meant he needed to delete some incoming messages before he could leave one himself.

He dialed again, pressed the star sign to

access the box, chose the wrong PIN number and then the right one, and the messages — a startling nineteen of them — started to play. He deleted one from his tailor. He deleted another from the roofer apologizing for yet another delay. One from Natasha's parents for Annabelle, reminding her to pack tights for the drive north. He was about to hit the pound sign when a plummy voice said, "Joely Doyle, this is Richard Straitharn from Clendenning. We spoke a few weeks ago about staffing for the new unit we're putting together for our facility in Surrey. I'm impressed — very impressed — with the new ideas you presented, and it's our consensus that you would be a natural team leader. We're looking to open in early September, if that's good for you, but you're welcome to start any time. I look forward to pursuing this with you at your earliest convenience."

He'd heard wrong. He must have. He replayed the message, but the same words spilled out. Thirty minutes later his credit card was suitably scorched, but he had a first-class ticket to Boston in his hand.

"Mr. Bishop." He opened his eyes and smiled up at the flight attendant. "Would you like something to drink?"

"No," he said. "I'm fine."

"Please don't hesitate to ring if you need anything."

Joely, he thought as he turned toward the window. He needed Joely, but he was afraid it was too late.

Chapter Thirteen

Idle Point

"You can relax now," Joely said after she'd tucked Annabelle in for the night. "She's asleep."

Zach had a great grin. Funny the things you don't notice until you're ready for them. No wonder Cat had been dizzy with delight when they were first dating. "You're good with her," he said. "I wouldn't have figured you as a natural, but you are."

She tilted her head in Cat's direction. "I had a good teacher."

"You did," he said, lifting the remains of his third glass of Merlot in the general direction of her sister. "To the next generation."

Joely's eyes widened, and she turned to Cat. "You told him."

"I can't seem to keep my mouth shut."

"I've been sworn to secrecy," Zach said.

Cat stretched out on the sofa with a

glass of decaf iced tea. "I didn't plan on telling any of you for at least another month, but apparently I'm not that good at keeping a secret."

"Oh please," Joely said with a Merlot-tinged snort. "You had no trouble keeping Michael Whatever-His-Name-Is a secret."

Zach settled back at the other end of the couch and fixed Cat with an amused look. "The kid's right," he said. "If you hadn't decided to procreate, we wouldn't know anything about your secret life."

"I operate on a strictly need-to-know basis," Cat said, "and neither one of you needed to know what I didn't want to tell you."

"That's not the way it's supposed to be," Joely said, her tongue loosened by wine and worry. "Don't you people watch television up here? Happy families share everything. We should be living side-by-side in cute little Cape Cods so our kids can grow up together while their loving grandparents shower them with toys and cookies."

"The Von Doyle Family Singers," Cat said, "with Daddy Von Doyle there to lead us over the mountains to safety."

"Yes!" Joely exclaimed. "That's exactly the way it's supposed to be."

"There is no 'supposed to be,'" Zach said. "There's only the way it is."

The two women looked at him, then each other.

"You just put three thousand self-help authors out of business," Cat said.

"Not to mention the therapists," Joely added.

"Nobody's life is perfect," Zach went on, "and sure as hell nobody's family is either. I'm not going to say things couldn't have gone easier for you two, but your heritage is something to be proud of."

"Give me a break," Joely muttered. "A pair of broken-down old folkies who flipped out when parenthood raised its ugly head. Yeah, there's something to be proud of."

"You're missing the big picture." Zach wasn't about to be put off by either sarcasm or scorn. "Your parents have a place in the history of American music. There was nobody like them before, and there's been nobody like them since. I don't give a damn what they were like as parents; it doesn't take away from what they gave to our culture."

Joely clapped her hands together slowly. "Bravo," she drawled. "I'll trade you a star on the Walk of Fame for five minutes with two parents who actually knew I was alive."

"What about you?" Zach zeroed in on Cat, who had been watching them closely. "Can you separate the bad parents from the great musicians?"

"I wish I could," Cat said. "I know they were great — I mean, you can't listen to their old albums and not know they were special — but it's like listening to Elvis or The Beatles or Frank Sinatra. The music's terrific, but it has nothing to do with my life."

"She tried to make it your life," Joely said. "Remember that summer she dragged us all over New England, trying to turn you into a singer?"

Cat groaned and covered her eyes with her hands. "Thanks for reminding me. I spent good money with a therapist trying to put that fiasco behind me."

Zach laughed out loud. "You weren't bad, Cat."

"I threw up every time I had to go on-stage!"

"Good practice for motherhood," Joely offered, then ducked as her sister aimed a pillow at her.

"I convinced Mimi that she needed to take me along to be her roadie," Zach said, "but I ended up babysitting the kid instead."

"I haven't thought about any of this in years," Joely said, shaking her head. Quick flashes of listening to Mimi and Cat singing their way down the Mass Turnpike, lobster shack suppers in a Rhode Island shore town, playing Go Fish backstage with Zach. "It wasn't all bad, was it?"

"No, it wasn't," Cat said. "That's what I've been trying to tell you."

"But it was you she was interested in."

"Not really," Cat said with that easy acceptance of their mother's flaws that had always left Joely baffled and somehow humbled. "I was just the closest she could get to Mark."

Zach nodded. "That's why she went out on all those gigs. She hoped he'd hear about them and show up."

"So did I," Cat admitted. "I'd see a tall man with dark brown hair standing in the shadows, and my heart would start beating so hard I couldn't sing."

"How could I not have known this?" Joely asked.

"You were a kid," Cat said. "You were Annabelle's age. Our life was strange enough. I wanted you to have as much of a childhood as you could. You didn't need to be scanning a crowd for your father, too."

"See?" She turned to Zach. "That's the way you love a child. Mimi should have taken lessons from her own daughter."

"She did pretty well the day of the accident."

Everything inside Joely froze at his words. He was the one other person on earth, besides herself and Mimi, who had been there. "Not funny, Zach."

"I'm not trying to be."

She looked into his eyes for signs of sarcasm but saw nothing but compassion.

"I couldn't imagine my mother doing what she did," he said.

"I'm not following."

Frowning, he glanced at Cat, who shrugged her shoulders.

"I'm not following either," she said.

"After —" His voice cracked, and he cleared his throat. She was reminded forcefully of the fact that he had lost his brother in that accident. "It was clear — I mean, there was no doubt that Ty was . . . gone. I was pinned inside the Camaro . . . the seat belt saved my life." He glanced at Joely, his pain clearly visible, and she looked away. "You had been thrown clear and were lying on the ground next to the van. Mimi was —" He stopped, searching for the right words to convey whatever it was he saw in his mind's eye. "She was crazy. That's the only way I can put it. She ran to the Camaro . . . to my side of the car . . . and kept saying, 'It wasn't her fault! It wasn't her fault! I was driving!' She kept saying it over and over when the cops came, telling them how smart you were, what a great future you had, how you were all set to go to MIT in a few days, and how proud she was." He stopped for a moment to catch his breath. "She was terrified you would be charged for Ty's stupidity, and your future would be lost."

"I never heard this before," Joely said.

"Neither have I," Cat added.

"The cops never questioned you?" he asked Joely.

"Sure they did. Over and over. They —" She stopped as memories of that hideous time resurfaced. "Oh God. That explains it. I thought they were trying to trick me into something when they said Mimi had been driving drunk. I wondered why they were pretending not to believe me when I said I was the one who'd been behind the wheel."

"And you argued with them," Cat said. "I remember you in the ER. You were fighting with one of the cops, trying to make him understand that you were the one who'd been driving, not Mimi."

Joely turned to Zach. "She really did that?"

"I'll never forget it," he said. "Your mother tried to protect you. My mother blamed me for killing my brother."

"Oh God, Zach —" Cat leaned forward and touched his arm.

"She wasn't entirely wrong," he said. "I shouldn't have let him drive."

"You didn't know he was high," Cat said.

He shot her a look. "I knew something wasn't right. We all knew he was heading for trouble. Everyone in this town knew that. I've spent ten years trying to figure out what I could have done differently."

"So have I," Joely said quietly. "If I'd taken another road home, if I'd made the turn more quickly." She closed her eyes. "You know how it goes."

"You somehow always end up with the same bad ending."

"Always."

"I know you don't believe me yet," he said to Joely, "but she loves you. It may not be in the way you needed, but I saw it that day."

"You think you saw it."

He raised a hand to stop her. "I saw it. I know what happened."

She looked toward Cat and saw the same hopeful confusion she was feeling reflected in her sister's eyes.

"It doesn't change anything," she said to Cat. "One moment doesn't make up for twenty-eight years."

"No, it doesn't," Cat agreed. "But it's one more moment than you had before."

She had never been good with raw emotion. Neither was Cat. She liked to step back and let her feelings mellow for a day or two, if only so she could regain perspective and a degree of control. Being in the moment was dangerous. That was when you said and did things that could change your life forever.

"I don't know about the two of you," she said, "but I feel like I'm trapped in a *Lifetime* movie for women. Two sisters, their wildly successful gay friend — tell me that's not the stuff ratings are made of."

Cat suddenly leaped up from the sofa. "Oh, damn!" she said. "I meant to watch *Entertainment Tonight*. They told me Janna from *Pink Slip* was going to be featured tonight, and she gave me a big plug."

"I hope she wore that gorgeous lavender cashmere tank top," Joely said.

"I think it's the felted bag with the Swarovski crystals knitted in."

She found the remote under a stack of *Vogue Knitting* and clicked on the television.

"I keep telling you to get TiVo," Zach said as she started clicking madly around the dial. "It'll change your life."

"It'll turn me into a total hermit," Cat said as she landed on Mary Hart. "I watch too much as it is."

"Shh!" Joely ordered. "Let's hear what she's saying."

"Get well wishes go out to Mimi Doyle, one-half of the classic sixties folk-rock duo The Doyles. Sources in Idle Point, Maine, say Mimi Doyle suffered a stroke yesterday morning and is in intensive care at a local hospital. The Doyles stopped performing in 1978 when Mark Doyle disappeared. It was believed at the time of the disappearance that Doyle was heading down to Appalachia to tape some mountain music for an album he and Mimi were working on. Coming up next on *Entertainment Tonight*, we roll out the red carpet for the premiere of —"

"Appalachia!" Joely and Cat said simultaneously.

"I knew that," Zach said, clearly delighted by the mention on *Entertainment Tonight*. "Mark's passion was bluegrass and mountain music. In 1968 he told an interviewer from *Time* that the roots of all American music could be found in the mountains of Appalachia."

"How do you know this stuff?" Joely asked, shaking her head.

"You should know this stuff," he countered. "It's important. Mark was trying to compile an aural time line of the progression of American music from the time of the first settlers until the present day. Mimi said she had his notebooks and tapes hidden away."

Joely and Cat exchanged glances.

"If they were put away in her attic," Joely said, "then they're lost for good. The house is a total disaster."

"Not if she put them in some kind of fireproof safe."

Cat laughed. "Mimi put something in a fireproof safe? You're lucky if she didn't just stick them under her mattress."

"We should take a look."

"No, thanks," Joely said. "One visit to that place was enough for me."

"How important would those papers be?" Cat asked Zach.

"Very." His tone of voice was deadly serious. "This would be Smithsonian type of material."

"Unless they're a figment of her imagination," Joely said.

"I don't think so," Zach said. "I believe she has them."

"She's never said a word about them to me," Cat said, "and I never saw anything interesting in her attic."

"We're not talking the crown jewels here," Zach said. "You'd see a box of papers and some reel-to-reel tapes, maybe a cassette or two. Would you have paid much attention to that?"

"No," Cat said. "I wouldn't even have noticed them."

"This is ridiculous," Joely said. "Even if she had anything of value, it would be lost now." There was fire and water damage everywhere in Grandma Fran's old house.

"It wouldn't hurt to look," Zach urged.

"Why bother?" The conversation was starting to get on Joely's nerves. It smacked of the kind of romanticism that made a sixty-something-year-old woman believe her man would come back one day. "If it's there, you'll find it when they empty the house to sell the property."

"When 'they' empty the house?" Cat

gave her a look. "Try when 'we' empty the house."

Joely drew in a breath. "When are you planning to start?"

"When are you planning to go home?"

"This weekend," she said. "Annabelle misses her father."

"I thought her father was in Japan." Cat kept her voice free from inflection, but the words carried a punch just the same.

"She's got you there," Zach observed.

Very sorry, but there is no William Bishop registered here, miss.

She pushed the thought away. "I don't see why we can't hire somebody to go through Mimi's things."

"Who would we hire?" Cat shot back. "She would hate knowing some town busybodies were pawing through her things."

"If I understood the extent of the stroke's damage correctly, she won't understand enough to care."

"I care," Cat said. "If you don't want to help, fine. That's up to you."

"I'm not doing anything tomorrow," Zach spoke up. "If you need some manual labor, I'm yours."

Cat turned all her attention away from Joely and directed it toward her old friend. "That's great, Zach, but you might change your mind when you see what you're in for."

"We're not planning to knock down any load-bearing walls, are we?"

"I doubt it," Cat said with a laugh, "since I'm not sure I know what a load-bearing wall is."

"Then count me in."

"Don't we have to check with the police before we do anything?" Joely asked. "And with the insurance company?"

"She's right," Zach said. "You'd better get the okay before you start sifting through things."

"Thanks," Cat said to Joely with a stiff nod of her head.

"You're welcome," Joely said with an equally stiff nod of her head in return.

"The Olsen twins wouldn't behave like this," Zach observed dryly, and the three of them burst into air-clearing laughter.

"We need chocolate," Cat said, getting up from the couch. "Lots of chocolate."

"Screw the chocolate," Zach said. "I could use more Merlot."

"You've already had too much," Cat shot back. "You're either spending the night on my sofa, or I'm driving you home."

"I doubt that, since I live in Napa."

She tossed a throw pillow his way. He

ducked, and it slid across the floor toward poor Newman, who was napping in his bed near the window. "Your parents' place, Karen and Danny's, wherever you're hanging your hat these days."

Their bond was so vital, so strong, that Joely found herself awash in unexpected envy. She had always held herself apart from deep friendships, unwilling to let down her guard long enough to let anyone see the woman behind the facade. Even with Sara, her closest friend, she withheld much more than she revealed. The night of the solstice — was it really only two days ago? — she had revealed more of herself in a few hours than she had in the four years that had come before.

"It's too bad you're gay," she said as they followed Cat into the kitchen on a chocolate hunt. "You and Cat would be perfect together."

"You sound like my mother," Zach said. "Ever hopeful."

"I didn't mean that the way it sounded," Joely persisted. "I'm talking about the way you two get along. You get each other's jokes. You really care about each other. Except for the sex thing, it's the perfect relationship."

"The sex thing is pretty hard to ignore,"

Cat said as she pretended to pat a nine-months' belly.

"I know what you're saying, though." Zach held open the freezer door while Cat rummaged around for the chocolate fudge ripple. "When the fireworks stop going off every night, there has to be something more to keep you there."

"Exactly!" Joely grabbed three big white bowls from the cupboard and put them on the counter. "You two talk to each other. You listen. You know each other's secrets."

"What secrets?" Cat and Zach said simultaneously.

"See? You two are in perfect harmony."

"We're both Libras," Zach said. "It's in our nature."

Very sorry, but there is no William Bishop registered here, miss.

"I don't think you're talking about Zach and me," Cat said as she dug the ice cream scoop out of the junk drawer. "This is about you and William, isn't it?"

Very sorry . . . very sorry . . . very sorry . . .

"I think it's over between us."

The silence in the room had a physical presence.

"Don't look at me that way," she said to them. "I swear I'm not going to fall

267

apart on you. I'm just stating a fact."

"He *told* you it's over?" Cat asked.

"He hasn't told me anything," she said. "We've been playing phone tag for the last two days."

"You're jumping to conclusions," Cat said, looking toward Zach for support. "You're mistaking crossed wires for trouble."

"I phoned the hotel in Hokkaido where he said he'd be staying. They told me he wasn't registered."

"Shit," Zach murmured. "That's not good."

"Zach!" Cat glared in his direction.

"Don't jump Zach," Joely said. "I *know* it's not good."

"Maybe he switched to another hotel," Cat offered. "Reservations get screwed up all the time."

She shook her head. "I don't think so."

"It's crossed wires," Cat persisted. "I'm telling you that's all it is."

"Oh, Cat, it's more than crossed wires. Things haven't been right for months. We tiptoe around the house like there's a dormant volcano in the middle of the drawing room and we're afraid a little noise will set it off."

"Great analogy," Zach said. "Lloyd

didn't even give me that much warning."

"Zach," Cat warned again. "I don't think this is the time."

"Don't listen to her," Joely said. "I'll bet you knew, didn't you, Zach? Tell the truth. Deep down in your gut, you *knew* things were changing with Lloyd."

He glanced over at Cat, who was glaring at him down the length of the couch. "Sorry," he said to his old friend, "but she deserves the truth." He met Joely's eyes. "We started being very polite to each other. Please this and thank you that. Excuse me, pardon me — we were sickening."

"That's no help. William's English," she said. "He thanked the OB for delivering him."

"You and William need to sit down and talk about things," Cat said. "You can't go on this way. Not with a child involved."

"It didn't seem so urgent when Annabelle was younger, but she asks questions now. We want to be honest with her, but there's just so much adult baggage you can allow a child to carry. She wants a real family, and I'm not sure we can give that to her."

Cat glanced away, and she knew exactly what her sister was thinking. They had both carried more than their fair share of their parents' baggage. Especially Cat.

"She's started calling me Aunt Cat."

"I know." She buried her face in her hands. "She wants to call me Mummy, but William and I —" She shook her head sadly. "What am I going to do?"

"Talk to him," Zach said. "The two of you need to sit down and talk it out."

"He's right," Cat agreed. "You can't go on like this any longer. If for no other reason than the fact that Annabelle deserves more from both of you."

She looked up at her sister. "They used to say I was the smart one, but I'm not. You're the smart one, Cat. You have your own house, your own life, your own baby. Nobody can swoop in and take any of it away from you."

"Wait a minute! I'm not doing this alone. Michael is going to be a full partner in our child's life."

"But on your terms," Joely persisted. "You're not in love with him. You're not planning to marry him. You're not a visitor in your own life. I was supposed to be the smart one. I was supposed to be the one who thought things through before she jumped, who made logical decisions."

"And who told you there was anything logical about love?" Zach asked.

Cat's gaze was direct and uncompromising. "Are you with William because you love him, or are you with him because you love his daughter?"

"I'm not a hearts-and-flowers type, but the second I walked into his house, I knew I belonged there. That has to mean something, doesn't it?"

"I wish I knew the right thing to say, honey, but I'm at a loss here."

Joely shook her head and looked down at the plain polish on her fingernails. "Do you love Michael What's-His-Name?"

"We're talking about you."

"You didn't answer the question, Cat."

"Neither did you."

Joely looked at her sister and sighed. "Mr. Spock found it easier to admit to human feelings than we do. What's wrong with us?"

Cat plunged the scoop deep into the tub of chocolate fudge ripple. "Do you really have to ask?"

Chapter Fourteen

The phone shrieked them awake a little after seven the next morning.

Zach was out to the world on the back porch, and Cat was wrapped around the john in her bathroom, so Joely leaped from bed to answer it. It was probably for her anyway. Who else but William would call at such a crazy hour? She dashed down the hallway and pounced on the phone before the third ring.

"William!" she cried into the phone. "I'm so glad you —"

"You'd better get over to Mimi's," a vaguely familiar female voice interrupted her. "There's trouble."

"What?" she said, as she realized it wasn't William after all.

"Cat? Is that you?"

"It's Joely." She pushed down her disappointment and focused. "What's this all about?"

"This is Trish at the police station. Someone tried to break into your mother's house. You need to get down there as soon as you can."

Zach, a little bleary-eyed after his feast of Merlot and chocolate fudge ripple the night before, staggered into the kitchen in search of orange juice and black coffee. "What idiot calls this early?" he asked as he poured them each a glass of juice. "I want the name and license number."

"Somebody broke into Mimi's house last night. I have to go over there and check it out." Cat was in no shape to go anywhere and wouldn't be for hours.

"I'll go with you."

She almost wept with relief. "You don't have to."

"I figure this way I won't have to grill you later for the details."

"I'll spring for breakfast on the way back."

He groaned and held his head between his hands. "I don't want to hear anything about food for another year or two."

"That bad?"

"You don't want to know." He flung open the doors to Cat's cupboards. "Your sister doesn't believe in pharmaceuticals, but you'd think she'd have some aspirin in the house."

"I have some in my carry-on."

"I'll give you fifty dollars if you can give me two of them in the next thirty seconds."

It took her a little longer than thirty seconds, but he was grateful just the same. She had to push his fifty-dollar bill back into the pocket of his shirt.

"What about the munchkin?" he asked. "We can't take her with us, can we?"

"She's sound asleep. I'll tell Cat to keep an ear out for her."

"I'll make coffee while you get dressed." He pushed her in the direction of the hallway. "Move it. CSI Idle Point is waiting for us."

No wonder Cat adored him. He had the same off-center, wiseass sense of humor her sister had. They really were a perfect couple in every way. If you eliminated sex from the equation, they could go the distance.

Michael Whatever-His-Name-Was had his work cut out for him to come close to measuring up to Zach.

Cat was still busy being miserably sick in the main bathroom, so Joely grabbed her toothbrush and quickly cleaned up in the tiny powder room off the hallway. Annabelle was deeply asleep when she came back into the room, and she dressed as quietly as she could, then slipped back out again.

Cat was in the kitchen with Zach.

"You look awful," she said, before she had the chance to censor herself. "I mean —"

"I know what you mean." Cat poured herself a glass of flat, room temperature ginger ale and leaned against the counter. "Zach told me about the phone call. I'd go myself, but it would have to be later."

"No problem. I figured you're still not at your best in the morning."

"Quite an understatement." She sipped the ginger ale and made a face. "Sorry," she said then raced back toward the bathroom.

Zach stared after her, his face pale. "And they say war is hell." He pushed a cup of black coffee toward Joely. "You did it the right way. Instant family."

No muss. No fuss. No commitment. She knew he didn't mean it that way, but that was the way she internalized his words. A babysitter who was halfway to a Ph.D. in biomechanical engineering and who slept with the lord of the manor on a nightly basis. Was that how William viewed their relationship? Another question added to her list of questions she'd rather not have answered.

Hollywood

The workday started early in Hollywood, too early for Michael's taste, and it all seemed to revolve around breakfast. Lots of breakfasts. So far his schedule for the next two days looked like a series of breakfasts with one dinner thrown into the mix for variety.

For a guy whose brain didn't kick into gear until lunchtime, this was going to be one hell of a business trip.

His first meeting was set up for an ungodly seven a.m., which meant room service caffeine by five so he was awake enough to drive.

You had to drive in California. It was written into the state charter. He'd gone out for a walk last time he was in town and ended up in an LAPD squad car while they ran a make on him.

He poured himself a cup of coffee and stepped out onto the balcony. He was over the limit on sunshine and stepped back into the air-conditioned suite. Too bad he hadn't brought his digital camera with him. Cat would have loved the fusion of old Hollywood and English hunt country. Glitter and chintz. A marriage made in designer hell.

It was the bank of televisions that told a guy he wasn't in Queens anymore. This was a company town, after all, and entertainment was what paid the bills. Even he had to admit there was something pretty cool about watching Katie, Diane, and whoever it was on the other channel all at the same time and still have enough screens for the Food Network, home shopping, and *Entertainment Tonight.*

He put a head on his coffee, then raised the sound on *ET.* Some reporter he'd never seen before was waxing eloquent about some singer he'd never heard before who was about to be featured on an awards show he never knew existed.

Nothing was too small to escape notice. It was a celebrity blitzkrieg of information. If you had had even a flirtation with fame, you were fair game for the reporters and paparazzi. If Julia Roberts slipped out to the drugstore for an extra box of Pampers for the twins, somebody with a camera crew and microphone was waiting to document the event. Innocent dinners, not so innocent lap dances, engagements and weddings and divorces and deaths were all worthy of some airtime. He was grateful nobody gave a damn about the writers.

Katie and Diane went to commercial.

Emeril threw a handful of something into a pot of something else, and Mary Hart crossed her legs.

He raised the sound.

". . . Get well wishes go out to Mimi Doyle, one-half of the classic sixties folk-rock duo The Doyles. Sources in Idle Point, Maine, say Mimi Doyle suffered a stroke yesterday morning and is in intensive care at a local hospital. The Doyles stopped performing in 1978 when Mark Doyle disappeared. Coming up next on *Entertainment Tonight,* we roll out the red carpet for the premiere of —"

Where the hell was TiVo when you needed it?

He crossed the room to the desk where he'd hooked up his laptop to the hotel's high-speed connection. Every show on television had its own Web site. He Googled *Entertainment Tonight,* found what he needed, and waited while the page loaded.

There it was. He hadn't imagined it. Mimi Doyle. Wife of Mark Doyle. One-half of the legendary Doyles. An accident. A fire. Idle Point, Maine.

What the hell were the odds a man would hear the words "Idle Point, Maine" twice in one week? Probably not half as high as the odds he would have spent a few hours there at the hospital and not have a clue.

He glanced at his watch. It was after eight o'clock back home. He grabbed his cell and pressed 1 and waited. She answered on the second ring.

"Michael," Cat said, "it's morning, and I'm seven weeks pregnant. This better be important."

"When were you planning to tell me? When the kid starts college?"

There was a long, guilty silence.

"You saw it?"

"Five minutes ago."

"Wow, *ET* 24/7. What a town."

"Cut the sarcasm, Doyle. Your mother is Mimi Doyle."

"You've known her name for a long time, Michael."

"But I didn't know she was *the* Mimi Doyle. When were you planning to tell me?"

"I didn't think it was that big a deal."

"The Doyles are icons, Cat. They helped define a generation."

"You've been busy this morning, haven't you? Web surfing your way back through pop culture history."

"I didn't have to Web surf. I'm a fan."

"I didn't know that. When were you planning to tell me?"

"That's why you kicked my ass back to New York the other day, isn't it?"

"Yes," she said. "That's not something you can drop into a casual conversation. 'By the way, did I ever tell you my parents used to be famous? And, oh yeah, before I forget, my father went out to buy a new guitar string in 1978, and she's still waiting for him to come home with change.'"

"I get your point."

"I thought you might."

He felt like he had been stumbling through a dark room, and somebody had suddenly turned on the light. "You know what's going to happen, don't you?"

"You're going to start asking even more questions."

He pushed past the defensive sarcasm. "Mary Hart was the opening salvo, Cat. You're going to be swarmed with reporters before the day's over. I don't think you have any idea what's about to hit."

"Nobody's called yet."

"It's early," he said, "and you live in the boonies. Trust me, they're on their way."

"Five bucks says you're way off base."

"Five bucks says I hope you're right."

"What are you doing, Aunt Cat?" Annabelle asked as they crossed the yard that separated her house from her studio.

Cat liked to think of herself as a decent, fair individual, but she couldn't resist having the last word. "I'm texting a message to a friend of mine," she said.

"That's silly," Annabelle said. "You're supposed to talk into a phone."

"You can type into it, too, Annabelle." She showed her the message.

ALL QUIET ON WESTERN FRONT — TOLD YA SO.

Not that she was rubbing it in or anything, because she wasn't.

"You spelled a word wrong," Annabelle said. "Right there."

"That was for comic emphasis."

"What does that mean?"

"Sometimes spelling a word wrong is funny the same way a cartoon is funny."

Annabelle opened her mouth — no doubt to ask another question — when Cat's phone beeped, and Michael's response appeared on screen.

DAY'S STILL YOUNG, DOYLE.

"That's like on the computer," Annabelle said as Cat showed her the message. "Sometimes I talk to my daddy that way."

Cat was sure it was a sign of some faulty character trait on her part, but she took almost wicked pleasure in the fact that Michael was wrong. The phones were silent. There were no photographers hanging from the trees. No reporters hammering on the door for exclusives.

In other words, business as usual.

The short feature on *Entertainment Tonight* had been the result of a slow celebrity news day, not revived interest in The Doyles. Except for a few aging folkies and old friends, nobody would notice or remember.

"Where is everyone?" Annabelle asked as Cat unlocked the door and switched on the lights.

"We all work different hours here, honey. Some of the women have little children they have to take to school or to doctor's appointments."

"Oh."

Her stomach started its familiar descent into rebellion, and she made it into the john without a moment to spare.

"Are you sick?" Annabelle called through the closed door.

"N-no," she managed, rummaging around for the mouthwash. "I'm fine."

"But I heard you."

She rinsed her mouth, then rejoined the little girl. "I'm going to have a baby, Annabelle, and sometimes you don't feel too well in the beginning."

"How can you have a baby if there's no daddy?"

Out of the mouths of babes. "There's a daddy," she said. "His name is Michael. That's who I was sending the message to."

"You don't look like you're having a baby."

"It's still early days, honey. In a few more months I'll be big as a house."

Annabelle giggled. "I asked my daddy and Joely for a baby brother, but they said I'd have to wait."

There was no way on earth she was going to tackle that subject.

"Annabelle, were you serious about wanting to learn to knit?"

"Oh, yes!"

"Come sit down in the chair by the window, and I'll start you on the knitting knobby."

Annabelle was happily knitting away when Jeannie, Taylor, and the others started drifting in.

"Look at her go," Bev said, gesturing toward an industrious Annabelle.

"Great dexterity," Denise said. "I didn't begin to get it together until I was ten."

Cat did a quick head count. Everyone was there. "Listen," she said, "this won't take long, but I need to tell you guys something."

"Really?" Denise said, with a wink for Bev and Nicki.

"It's about time," Jeannie said, looking up from her Louet wheel.

Taylor laughed, dropped a stitch, and quickly recovered it. "We were afraid you were going to try to blame the boobs on water retention."

"You knew?" Cat asked, astonished. "All of you?"

"We figured it out two weeks ago," Nicki said while Bev nodded in agreement.

"Two weeks?" Denise sniffed. "It was longer than that. We probably knew before you did, Cat. There's something in the eyes that's a dead giveaway."

Cat knew exactly what Denise was talking about. She'd seen that look in her mirror almost from the moment of conception. A look of such pure wonder and vulnerability that it rocked her to her very core.

"I'm seven weeks along," she said as they all leaped up to smother her in hugs and well wishes, "which is why you haven't been seeing much of me in the mornings."

"Honey, nobody saw me anywhere for the first nine weeks with my kids," Bev said as she cranked the ball winder attached to the worktable. "The good news is they say it means a healthy pregnancy."

Cat pretended to knock wood against her left temple. "Then this is one very healthy pregnancy."

"Your mouth to God's ear," Nicki murmured, crossing herself.

"It's the guy who drove you up from New York, isn't it?" Jeannie asked.

"Who else could it be?" Denise agreed. "If you were seeing anybody around here, believe me, we'd know about it."

"His name is Michael," she told them, beginning to feel like she should print up the information on business cards and hand them out to interested parties. "He's a screenwriter. He's lives in Manhattan."

The five women stared at her as if she'd suddenly started speaking in tongues.

"You're not going to move down there, are you?" Denise asked, eyes wide. "I mean, not that it's my business or anything but still —"

"Why would I move down there?" Cat asked. "This is home."

"But you two — I mean, once you're married you'll probably live together, right?"

"Who said anything about getting married?"

Taylor started to laugh, then caught herself as the other women shot "knock it off" looks her way. "You mean, you're not getting married?"

"We're not getting married," Cat said. "I'm not moving down to New York. Michael isn't moving up to Maine. We didn't slip up. I didn't forget to take my pill; he didn't forget to use a condom. We didn't have too much to drink, and we knew exactly what time of the month it was. We're two adults who like and respect each other enormously, and we decided to have a child together." She waited for the looks of embarrassment to fade from those familiar faces. "And that pretty much is the whole story."

"We didn't mean to —"

"I'm sorry if I —"

"I hope you don't think —"

"Nothing will change around here," Cat said as she endured another group hug. "If anything, I hope our workload increases,

286

but other than that, I promise everything will stay exactly the same after the baby arrives."

The five women exchanged glances.

"You'll see," Cat said. "There won't be so much as a ripple around here."

The five women, mothers all, laughed until they cried.

Everything was quiet at Mimi's house when Joely and Zach got there. They did a quick walk-through, then Joely and the young police officer walked the perimeter to check for damage.

"What exactly happened here?" she asked him as they joined Zach in the driveway.

"Your next-door neighbor saw two men trying to push in the back door," the officer said. "She turned on her porch lights and called out, and they took off."

"I don't understand," Joely said. "Why didn't they go in through one of the broken windows?"

"Those boards make noise when you crack them open. Some back doors give with no resistance at all."

"Okay, but there's more I don't understand. Why Mimi's house? Look at this place. I think it's pretty clear you're not going to find anything of value in there."

"Depends on what you consider valuable," the cop said. "TVs, VCRs, computers are all fast cash out there."

"I don't think so," Zach said.

Joely and the cop both turned to him.

"Why not?" she asked.

"I think it was paparazzi."

The expression on the young policeman's face was priceless. "Why would paparazzi want to get into Mrs. Doyle's house?" *House* being a synonym for dilapidated handyman's special.

"My mother used to be famous," Joely said. "A long, *long* time ago."

Zach quickly explained about the mention on *Entertainment Tonight*.

"I suppose that could have something to do with it," the cop said, but it was clear he had as much trouble imagining paparazzi running wild through Idle Point as Joely did.

"You don't really think photographers were trying to get into Mimi's house, do you?" Joely asked after the cop left to take another call.

"You still don't get it, do you?" He draped a companionable arm around her shoulders. "Your parents were something very special. Mimi just got national press on *ET*. They practically delivered a road map to her house."

"But it's been years since they made a record together. Mimi quit performing a lifetime ago. What's the point of taking a photo of her burned-out kitchen?"

"Schadenfreude, for starters." That weird little ripple of relief and fascination people felt when they drove by the scene of an accident. "Quick cash from the tabloids, for another."

She shivered at the rightness of his observation. "You and Cat were on the money last night. We really do need to go through Mimi's stuff and push this forward."

"I don't have anything going until this evening," Zach said. "We could do a first pass and make it easier on Cat."

"This place is a train wreck," Joely said. "We'd be better off getting the world's largest trash bag and tossing everything."

But she wouldn't do that. Cat wouldn't let her, and to be honest, neither would her own conscience. It wasn't just Mimi's life hidden away in the damaged house, it was hers and Cat's as well.

If nosy reporters and photographers really were on the prowl, this wouldn't be the last time they tried to get into the house or, even worse, try to find Mimi at the hospital.

"Oh God," she said, grabbing Zach's forearm. "They not only mentioned the town, they said Mimi was in a local hospital."

"Shit," Zach said. "And that's not going to be too tough to find."

They jumped into Zach's car and made it to Idle Point General in under three minutes flat. Joely leaped out at the front door and left Zach to find parking. She dashed through the lobby, bypassed the elevator for the stairs, then raced into the ICU, only to be reminded that Mimi was now in a semiprivate room on the fourth floor.

She took the stairs two at a time and was glad she did when she saw the knot of people surrounding the nurses' station at the end of the corridor. The media onslaught had begun. A beehive of angry voices drifted toward her as she approached. Laquita's controlled alto rose above them. "Absolutely not," she said. "If you persist, I'm calling the police."

"What's going on?" she demanded as she elbowed her way to the desk.

"Good timing," Laquita said. "We were just about to phone Cat."

"Who're you?" A short, dark-haired man edged closer. "Doctor? Lawyer? Daughter?"

"Daughter," Joely said. "Who are you?" *New York Post. Boston Globe. National Enquirer. Star. People. Entertainment Weekly. E!* "Page Six." The list was endless and more than a little daunting.

"No," she said to requests for interviews. "No," she said to requests for photos. "Over my dead body," she said to pleas for ten seconds in Mimi's hospital room with a tape recorder and digital camera.

She leaned close to Laquita. "I want to see her."

"Wait until Security gets here. Otherwise they'll be all over you."

She saw Zach standing, arms crossed over his broad chest, near the other end of the hallway, looking like someone a wise man wouldn't want to tangle with.

"Okay," said a commanding male voice behind her. "What's going on?"

Idle Point General's security team rarely had a chance to flex its collective muscles and show what it could do, and the eight-person team put on a good show. Laquita motioned to Joely, and Zach covered for them as they slipped into the nurses' lounge.

"This door leads to the family kitchen," Laquita said as she held it open for Joely. "Mimi's room is three doors down."

"Thank you for what you did back there," Joely said as they moved swiftly along the hall. "They actually tried to break into her house last night."

"They'd have to go through me to get to her," Laquita said. "Idle Point isn't exactly on everyone's list of hot spots to visit. Any idea how they knew about Mimi?"

"Blame Mary Hart," Joely said. "It was on *Entertainment Tonight*."

"I wonder where they got the information."

"Zach told me that there's good money to be made phoning in tips to the magazines."

"You don't think Zach — ?"

"Not in a million years."

"Just checking." Laquita stopped in front of room 415. "She's sharing with Diane Wills. Mimi's the first bed."

"How is she today?" Joely asked, as her system flooded with adrenaline. Fight or flight at its most basic level.

"Scattered," Laquita said. "Her chronology is shot, and she's not tracking too well. She might not recognize you."

How would I know the difference? Joely wondered as she stepped into the room.

The curtain between the two beds was drawn. Mimi's bruises had blossomed

292

overnight. Her face was a rainbow of purples and deep blues. The railroad track stitches looked starkly black against her pale Irish skin dotted by spots of dried blood. She hated the sight of the dried blood, iron brown and ugly. Why hadn't anyone taken a washcloth and wiped it away?

A pitcher of water and a plastic glass rested on the nightstand next to Mimi's bed. Somebody had placed a small packet of tissues and a washbasin on the folding chair near the bathroom. Joely ripped the cellophane covering off the packet and pulled out a handful of tissues. She dipped one end into the water, checked that it wasn't too cold, then moved closer to the bed.

Mimi's sleep was labored despite the oxygen tubes in her nose. Or maybe because of them. This was why she had opted for the research side of medicine. Hospitals unnerved her. They stripped you of your defenses and reduced you to symptoms and diagnoses. Mimi no longer seemed larger than life. She wasn't the charismatic goddess of chaos who existed in Joely's memory.

She was a vulnerable old woman who was somehow the center of the storm, and the thought of photos of her appearing anywhere made Joely physically ill.

"It's Joely, Mimi," she said softly. "Don't be frightened. I'm going to wipe your forehead."

As if Mimi had ever been frightened of anything but being a parent to her children.

She touched the tissue to her mother's forehead, then drew back, heart thundering inside her chest, when Mimi's eyes snapped open like window shades on a roller.

"I'm s-sorry, Mimi. I didn't mean to startle you."

No response. Those vacant watery blue eyes looked straight at her. Through her.

"See this tissue?" She held it in her mother's line of sight. "I want to wipe your forehead, okay? It'll feel good. I promise you."

Three quick strokes. Mimi didn't even blink. It was like caring for a life-sized doll.

She heard footsteps behind her and turned as Zach entered the room.

"Laquita told me where you were," he said. "Do you mind?"

She was pathetically grateful to see him. "Why do they always leave little drops of blood behind? They can perform brain surgery and lung transplants, but basic hygiene is beyond them."

He stood at the foot of the bed and smiled at a nonresponsive Mimi. "Priorities," he said. "Life and death before aesthetics. They leave the cleanup to the family."

"And what if there is no family?" she persisted. "Would they just leave her lying here with specks of blood all over her forehead?"

He pointed toward the bed. "Keep your tone light," he cautioned. "She's picking up on your distress."

She glanced back at Mimi. He was right. The blank expression had been replaced by confusion that seemed to be sliding swiftly toward panic. "It's okay, Mimi," she said softly, unprepared for the flood of tenderness that rose up inside her chest. "There's nothing to worry about."

"Do you want me to wait outside?" Zach whispered.

"No," she said. "Please stay."

"Hey, Mimi," he said gently. "You knew I'd be back, didn't you? I told you yesterday I couldn't stay away."

Mimi tried to shift position in the hospital bed, but the array of pulleys and tubes limited her options.

"Were you telling the truth last night?"

Joely asked Zach as she touched a damp tissue to her mother's bloodstained cheek. "Did she really try to protect me after the accident?"

"She really did."

"It seems so —" She struggled to find the right words and couldn't.

"Out of character?" he asked, and she nodded.

"Out of character," she said.

"One thing I've noticed," he said as their eyes met across Mimi's bed. "Love doesn't seem to come easy for you Doyle girls. Not even when it's staring you right in the face."

She bent down closer to her mother's ear. "Zach told me last night how you tried to protect me after the car crash. I —" She cleared her throat. "Thank you."

Mimi's eyes opened, and her gaze settled on Joely.

"Mimi?" she asked, leaning even closer. "I know you tried to help me, and I —"

Mimi lifted her head. Her brow knotted as she continued gazing into Joely's eyes.

"Do you know what I'm saying, Mimi?"

Mimi nodded and reached for Joely's hand. Joely's heart started to pound as her mother increased the pressure.

"Wow, Mimi!" she said with a nervous

laugh. "You have a great grip." She glanced over at Zach. "You wouldn't believe how strong she is."

"That's a good sign," Zach said. "Maybe you're getting through to her."

Mimi's eyes were still focused in on Joely, who tried very hard not to dwell on the fact that she couldn't remember ever being the focus on her mother's attention for this long in her entire life.

And on the fact that she liked it.

Mimi's gaze made her feel warm and protected, even though the feelings were probably an illusion. It felt good to be seen. Such a simple thing to ask from a relationship, but it meant so much.

"Tell her about Annabelle," Zach prodded.

Mimi's head turned suddenly in his direction, and Joely felt like the sun had slipped behind a cloud.

"Mark?" Mimi's voice was raw with disuse. The single syllable cracked into two, but the name was unmistakable. "Mark?" Inflection rising, agitation growing more intense.

"Please lie back, Mimi," Joely said. "Everything's okay. I promise."

"Mark!"

"Oh God," Joely said as she realized

what was happening. "She thinks you're my father."

Mimi's face glowed with joy, and she reached out her hands to her husband.

Zach's eyes met Joely's, and she nodded. Was it so wrong to offer comfort? She motioned for Zach to step closer, and he clasped Mimi's hands.

"Hey, Mimi," he said softly. "Lie back. Everything's okay."

"Not Mark," Mimi said. "No." Her eyes closed, and she fell back into the sanctuary of sleep.

Joely's throat tightened as she looked down at the sleeping woman, the stranger who was her mother. Through the haze of drugs, through the neural chaos caused by the stroke, Mimi clung to one singular image, one memory, that nothing could take from her.

"Who are you?" she whispered so low even Zach couldn't hear her. "Why couldn't you love us the way you loved him?"

She didn't expect an answer. It helped just to say the words.

For the first time in her life, Joely looked at her mother and saw past the years and the mistakes and the disappointments. For the first time she didn't see the sorrow or the loneliness or the wasted years. Not hers. Not Mimi's.

She saw a young girl on the brink of womanhood and a guitar player with great hands and a wicked smile.

She saw the future that they believed would stretch straight into forever.

She saw love.

Maybe it wasn't the kind of love she understood. Maybe it wasn't the kind of love she had needed as a child or longed for as an adult. It was messy, incomplete, and it hurt sometimes more than it healed, but it was love just the same.

And she envied her.

Chapter Fifteen

"Are you sure you've never knitted before?" Cat asked Annabelle as she watched the child's small fingers maneuver the yarn along the bamboo needles.

"Louis's mother taught me to crochet a chain," Annabelle said proudly.

"But you never knitted?"

She shook her head, eyes firmly trained on the rectangle taking shape. "Hunh-uh."

Annabelle had rejected the knitting knobby within an hour for the real thing, and now her fingers were flying along.

"She's a natural," Denise said as she checked the gauge on her swatch of handspun Corriedale. "My sister was like that. She couldn't tie her own shoelaces, but she could knit like a dream."

"What's that going to be, Annabelle?" Bev asked. "A scarf?"

"I already have a scarf," Annabelle said. "I want a jumper."

"You're too young for a sweater," Jeannie said. "You should start small."

Why? Cat wondered as she watched Annabelle's needles dance. *Why shouldn't she dream big?*

"You know what," Cat said. "I think a pink tank top with faerie fringe along the hem would be darling on you, Annabelle."

"Faerie fringe?" Annabelle asked, not looking up from her needles.

"Something sparkly and light, like the way the shoreline looks when the sun's going down."

Annabelle frowned and put down her work. "I don't know."

"Why don't we go for a walk tonight, and I'll show you what I mean. That way you can make up your mind about the fringe."

Annabelle considered the offer, then nodded. "Yes, please," she said. "I'd like that very much."

It wasn't at all hard to see why Joely loved the child the way she did. Annabelle charmed without meaning to. She was a serious little girl with a vivid imagination who contemplated the world around her with an adult's intensity and a child's perspective.

Watching Annabelle wield the small wooden needles, her heart felt full to bursting with love. No wonder Joely had stayed away so long. Her life really was in Scotland. She had made a home for herself there and a family. She had no idea what the future held for Joely and William, but she knew that Annabelle was Joely's child in every way a child could belong to a woman who hadn't carried her beneath her heart.

Her hand hovered over her own belly as she thought about the woman who had given birth to Annabelle. Natasha's hopes and dreams for her child were probably the same as Cat's. How had she felt when she learned she was dying, that she would be ripped from the fabric of her baby's life, that her child would be left without a mother to love and guide her?

You don't have to worry, she thought, wishing Natasha could somehow hear her. *Annabelle is loved.*

She had never been more proud of her sister in her life.

"Aunt Cat, I dropped a stitch."

She bent down to take a look. "This isn't bad at all," she said and plucked a crochet hook from the pewter mug at the end of the worktable. "Now watch what I do . . . you're working garter stitch, so we put the hook here . . . grab that thread . . . oops, let me try again . . . okay, got it . . . and now we loop it and loop it again, then seat it on the right-hand needle good as new."

Annabelle reached for the needles, but Cat shook her head. Instead she removed the salvaged stitch from the needle and dropped it two rows.

Annabelle's mouth dropped open in surprise. "Oh!"

"I bet you can do it," Cat encouraged. "Hold the crochet hook like this . . . very good . . . now look carefully at the stitches, and you'll see which way the threads run . . . we're going to grab a loop . . . no, the other way . . . Annabelle, you did it!"

"I did it!" Annabelle echoed. "Now I can make a faerie blanket to keep the rain off the baby's garden back home."

"I thought you wanted to make a jumper."

"I do," Annabelle said. "And a faerie blanket and a pair of bright red socks for Daddy and a scarf for Joely and —"

"Uh-oh," Jeannie called out. "Sounds like you captured another one for our side, Cat."

"Once we get 'em, they stay got," Cat said with a laugh.

Annabelle thrived in the friendly commotion of Cat's studio. She settled in among the chatter, the whirr of the spinning wheels, the rhythmic click of metal needles, and seemed to feel right at home. She was interested in everything and everyone, a little sponge soaking up every drop of information for future reference.

Maybe one day Annabelle would teach Cat's child to use the knitting knobby and then —

She caught herself. Annabelle wasn't her niece, either by blood or by law. She was a lovely and agreeable little girl, but she was only visiting. Cat needed to remember that before she found herself projecting the lot of them into a future that was uncertain at best.

"Cat!" Jeannie called out from across the room. "Your tote bag's ringing!"

Cat dashed across the room to grab her cell phone.

"I was about to hang up and try the studio phone," Joely said.

"Is everything okay with Mimi?"

"She's fine," Joely said, "but you'd better lock the doors and pull the blinds. The paparazzi are in town."

"Paparazzi in Idle Point?" The thought made her laugh out loud. "Very funny."

She wasn't laughing after Joely told her what was going on at the hospital.

"They're at Town Hall looking for marriage and divorce records. They're knocking on doors. Hospital security has them barred from going past the ground-floor lobby, but they already found a photographer hiding in the bathroom in Mimi's room."

"Those sons of bitches!"

"My thoughts exactly. I wanted to give you a heads-up before they show up on your doorstep."

She walked over to the front window. "Too late," she said. "There's a van parked in front of the house with a satellite dish the size of a Toyota on the roof."

"I can't believe it," Joely said. "Nobody's given a damn about The Doyles in over twenty-five years, and now they're acting like Mimi's a rock star."

"Two more cars just pulled up," Cat said, "and I think there's a guy sitting in the oak tree across the street."

"Hold on," Joely said.

Cat could hear Zach's voice in the background.

"What's he saying?" she asked.

"He called Karen, and she said Annabelle's welcome to spend the afternoon with her and the kids."

"That might not be a bad idea. Do you want me to drive her over?"

"Zach will swing by and get her when he drops me off."

She pressed the disconnect button and tossed the phone back into her tote bag.

"Ladies," she said, "you might want to think about working from home for the next few days. It looks like we're going to be under siege around here for awhile."

Bev let out a shriek. "Some guy's looking through the front window at us."

"There's one at the back window, too," Taylor said, "and he has a camera."

"Close the shades," Cat said. "They'll move on."

"If I'd known we were going to have our pictures taken, I would've used a little mascara," Nicki said.

"I'm sorry about this," Cat said. "There's no reason the rest of you should have to deal with it."

"You don't think we'd leave you alone, do you?" Bev sounded highly affronted.

"I'm fine. Joely and Zach are on their way. They'll be here in a few minutes."

"Then we'll stay until they get here," Jeannie said, and this time Cat didn't argue.

"I'm going to let you off with a warning this time," the policeman said, "but don't do it again. We drive on the right over here."

"I'll remember that," William said as he put his passport and driver's license back into his jacket pocket. "Thank you, Officer."

He waited for the officer to step back from the car and allow him to drive away, but he continued to regard William with more interest than the infraction would seem to warrant.

"What brings you to Idle Point anyway?"

"Pardon me?"

"You here on vacation?"

"I have family here."

"Who?"

"Catherine Doyle."

What in bloody hell had he said wrong? He had barely uttered Cat's name when the policeman swung open the car door and ordered William out. He had watched enough American TV shows about cops to know this wasn't a good sign.

"What's your business with Cat?"

"May I ask why you want to know?" he countered.

"I'll let that one slide because you're not from here," the police officer said. "Are you one of those reporters?"

"I'm a financial analyst with Global Banking."

"You sure you're not looking to make some extra change off poor Mimi?"

"My daughter is here with Mimi Doyle's younger daughter Joely. They're staying with Cat."

"How am I supposed to know you didn't get that information off the Web?"

"I'm sorry," he said, "but I don't follow." He had heard Joely's stories about the horrors of life in a small town, but this surpassed even her most grisly tales.

"We take care of our own here," the officer said. "Bad enough we've got those paparazzi disrupting everything at the hospital. But when you start harassing private individuals, we're not going to take too kindly toward you."

"Call Catherine," he said. "She'll tell you who I am."

The policeman studied his face for a full moment. "I'll do that."

Joely peered at the swarm of reporters through a crack in the kitchen blinds. "I say we hook up a garden hose and mow 'em all down."

"Not a bad idea," Cat said as she hung up the phone. "And then let's rip out the phone wires."

"Another reporter?" Joely asked.

"Three in a row. I don't even want to know how many messages are on the business phone."

"Unplug the phone," Joely said. "Karen has your cell number, right?"

"The hospital doesn't."

"So call Laquita and give it to her. She'll put it on Mimi's record."

"I'm so glad I have a brilliant sister. Why didn't I think of that?"

"Hey, my fancy degrees have to be good for something, don't they?" She aimed for light and self-deprecating but fell short of the mark. "Sorry. I was trying to be funny."

"What's going on with your work anyway?" Cat asked, the telephone forgotten for the moment. "When is Clendenning going to secure funding for your department?"

"Soon," she said. "I'm in line for a head slot with a new research group they're forming."

"How terrific!" Cat beamed with pride. "The same area as before?"

She nodded. "Spinal regeneration supplemented by fourth-generation prosthetic devices. It's an exciting field."

"So why don't you look happy about it?"

"For one thing I don't have the position yet."

"But you'll probably get it, won't you?"

"It's in Surrey."

"Surrey as in Surrey, England?"

She nodded.

"What does William say about it?"

"He doesn't know."

"You haven't told him?"

"There's nothing to tell."

"Come on, Joely! If you take the job, you'll have to move. That's a pretty big deal."

"I'll worry about it if and when it happens."

"Great philosophy if you're talking about the weather, but not when your future's at stake."

"Tell me something I don't know."

The phone rang again, and they both stared at it like it had a will of its own.

"Let it ring," Joely said.

Two rings. Three.

"I can't," Cat said. "It might be important."

It wasn't. And the next two calls weren't important either. When it rang a fourth time, Joely feigned a yawn.

"If Diane Sawyer calls, let me know, and I'll pick up the extension."

Cat managed a laugh as she picked up the receiver. "Slow down. I'm having

310

trouble following you. Okay, okay . . . a man is trying to find my house . . . yes, there are a score of reporters outside . . . did you say he's English . . . yes, okay . . . that's fine . . . give him the directions." She turned to Joely. "You'd better sit down," she said. "William's here."

"I think my brain just stopped functioning." She focused in on her sister. "Would you say that again?"

"He's on his way."

"From Japan you mean. He's still in Japan."

"No, he was in Japan, but he's in Idle Point now. In fact, he'll be pulling into the driveway any minute."

Joely hadn't been joking when she said her brain had stopped functioning. Oh, it still managed to keep her vital organs running, but thought, logical or otherwise, had stopped dead.

"I wish you looked a little happier about this," Cat said as she ran down the hallway to change her sweater and run a brush through her hair. "The man flew halfway around the world to see you."

"He's not supposed to be here," Joely said as she yanked off her green sweater and grabbed a red one from the dresser drawer. "I didn't ask him to come here."

She pulled the sweater on over her head and struggled to get her arms through the sleeves.

"Damn damn damn!" She was close to tears as she pulled and tugged.

"What's this?" Cat sounded amused. "You're coming apart at the seams faster than this sweater."

"Annabelle's not even here. This is a disaster."

"She didn't run off to join the circus, honey. She's on a play date at Karen's house."

She tugged the sweater into place, then reached for the brush on top of her closed suitcase.

"Do you see what it looks like out there? Reporters, photographers, those stupid vans with the dishes on them. What's he going to think?"

"I guess he'll figure it has something to do with Mimi."

"He doesn't know the first thing about Mimi, Cat. I haven't told him anything."

"Join the club. Michael found out from Mary Hart."

"I was on the other side of the ocean," Joely said, hating the defensive tone of her voice. "I'd been gone so long that it no longer seemed relevant."

The fact that she was speaking about her own family was lost on neither of them.

Cat was quiet for a moment. "Well, that's not hard to understand in your case. By the time you came along, she wasn't performing very much. That life was never really part of yours."

"You're not listening," Joely said, throwing the brush down onto the bed. "I mean I didn't tell him anything. He knows I have a mother. He knows you keep an eye on her. But he thinks it's because she's frail and old and cultured, not because she's —" She stopped, totally at a loss for words, politically correct or otherwise.

"Troubled?" Cat offered. "Difficult? Mercurial? Crazy?"

"You're getting warmer."

The doorbell chimed, and they locked eyes.

"Do you want to get it?" Cat asked.

Joely shook her head. "It's your house."

"He's your . . . whatever."

"Point taken," she said. "I'll get the door."

She could hear the commotion as she hurried down the hallway. Shouted questions. Car engines. William's cultured tones rising above the throng in protest.

Welcome to my world.

She opened the door a crack and yanked him inside.

"What in bloody hell is going on?" he demanded as she locked the door behind him.

As an opening statement, it didn't bode well.

"Glad to see you, too, William."

He colored slightly. "Where's Annabelle?"

"She's at a friend's house. We thought it was a good idea."

"What in bloody hell is going on?" he repeated. "The street's crowded with news vans. Everyone's asking about your mother."

"It's a small town," she said, trying to break the tension. "They have nothing better to do."

He looked exhausted, strung out, exactly the way anyone would look after spending almost twenty-four hours in transit, and all of the tender feelings she had ever had for him came flooding back at once.

Not that it mattered. The look in his eyes told her everything she didn't want to know. She was relieved when Cat joined them.

"Annabelle has your eyes," Cat said. "It's great to finally meet you, William."

She extended her hand in greeting. William's innate good breeding took over, and he put his anger with Joely aside.

"And you," he said, kissing Cat on both cheeks.

"Joely, why don't you put William's things in the guest room while I make him something to eat. We can figure out the sleeping arrangements later."

Trixie opened one eye when they entered the room, studied William for a moment, then resumed the position.

"Annabelle's in love with her," Joely said as William put his bags on the floor near the window. "She might try to smuggle her home with her."

He nodded but said nothing, as if words were more than he could manage.

"At least now I know why you weren't registered at the hotel." She feigned drawing her hand across her brow in relief. "I was getting worried."

He was clearly immune to her attempts at humor.

"When were you going to tell me?"

"That seems to be the question of the week around here. It didn't seem terribly important up until now."

"What were you planning to do, Joely, leave us a note and the extra house key?"

"I'm not following you. We spoke on the

phone before I left, and you know I took Annabelle with me."

"I'm talking about the position in Surrey."

She had never been very good at pretending, and this was not the right time to start. "They haven't made an offer yet. I figured I would deal with it when and if it happened."

"Congratulations," he said, his voice unnaturally steely. "You got the job."

The floor started to go out from beneath her, and she abruptly sat down on the foot of the bed. "How do you know?"

"I checked for messages at our home number. You should be chuffed."

She felt anything but.

"It's an offer," she said carefully. "I haven't said yes to it."

"You'd be working in Surrey?"

"William, it's only an offer," she repeated. "Don't read anything into it."

But he wasn't a fool. The look of betrayal in William's eyes cut right through to the bone.

"Your sister's waiting for us," he said, then turned and left her sitting on the edge of the bed watching her world fall apart around her.

Chapter Sixteen

"I've got to go," Cat said to Karen as she heard footsteps approaching down the hallway. "Somebody's coming."

"Should I bring Annabelle back there?"

"Hold tight," she said. "I'll call you back as soon as I can."

She put the phone down and was sliding a turkey club onto a platter when William Bishop entered the kitchen.

"Did Joely show you the guest room?" she asked brightly.

"She did, thank you."

His manners were even more impeccable than his clothes. She was a half step away from being awestruck. Good tailoring always did that to her.

"Annabelle's a wonderful child," she said. "I've become very fond of her in just a few days."

The cautious, slightly aloof look in his eyes vanished at the mention of his daughter, a fact that endeared him to Cat instantly.

"Joely said she's spending the afternoon with friends."

"Karen's my friend and my business partner," Cat said, picking up on his unease. "She has three kids, all homeschooled, and a lot of pets. Annabelle has taken over the care and feeding of a baby cria."

"She raises alpacas?"

Cat's eyes widened. "I'm impressed," she said. "Most people have no idea what a cria is."

"Crosswords," he said with a self-deprecating smile.

It wasn't hard to see what had drawn Joely to him almost five years ago. Not only was he easy on the eyes, he seemed genuinely nice once you penetrated that wall of English reserve.

"Anyway, we figured Annabelle would be better off at Karen's than ducking photographers."

"It was intense out there," he said. "I had to threaten one journalist with bodily harm if he didn't get off the bonnet of my car."

Bless her love of BBC television shows. "Bonnet" didn't throw her in the least.

"They tried to break into Mimi's house early this morning. We had to ask for police protection."

"Why are they doing this?" He sounded skeptical which, considering the situation, he probably had every right to be.

Sorry, Joely, but he asked.

"A television show did a piece on Mimi's accident last night. They included the name of the state, the town, and even described the hospital. It's been insane out there all day."

He stared at her as if she was speaking in tongues. "Why would a television show run a piece on your mother?"

"Our parents were famous a long time ago, William. They were folksingers and activists in the sixties and seventies. They left a fairly impressive musical legacy behind."

"I didn't know any of this," he said, and she wondered if Michael had looked half as shell-shocked when he first found out.

"I can remember some of it, but the whole thing, including their marriage, was just about over by the time Joely was born. I don't think any of it has ever seemed real to her."

"Why the interest now?"

"I'm not really sure," she said. "I suppose someone passed along a tip that Mimi was in the hospital, and it grew from there." She told him about the crowd of hungry photographers Joely had fended off near the nurse's station. "A friend of mine says it's going to get worse before it gets better, but I think he's wrong. This is one of those small stories you run on a slow news day. I think it will die a natural death in a day or two."

"Have you issued a statement of any kind?" William asked as she gestured for him to sit down at the kitchen table.

She slid a turkey club toward him. "We closed the blinds. That's about as far as we've gone."

"Issuing a statement makes you seem accessible to the media but allows you to remain in control. We use the technique frequently, especially when a negative financial report surfaces on one of our holdings."

"You spin it," Cat said. "That's what you mean, isn't it?"

"I prefer to call it a preemptive maneuver."

"Maybe I'll type something up and post it on the door."

"You need a spokesperson," he said. "A family member or close friend who'll go out there and read the statement for the camera. Give them their film and a good sound bite, and you might get some sleep tonight."

"I like the note on the door idea better."

"That's not going to be enough. You'll still have the same problem."

"It's an annoyance, but I can live with it," she said. "It's Mimi I'm worrying about. She's alone in that hospital room, and she can't defend herself."

"That's understandable. Anyone would feel that way."

"Is it?" She had to laugh. "It won't be once you learn more about this family."

"Write up a statement," he said as he picked up half of his sandwich. "I'll read it to the press when you're ready."

"You would do that for us?"

"I do it all the time for less important people."

She leaned down and kissed him on the cheek. "Thank you, William. I mean it. Thank you so much."

"Consider it inadequate payment for a brilliant sandwich."

She glanced down at the table. "Let me pour you something to drink."

"Water would be fine."

"Still or sparkling?"

"Tap is fine."

She quickly filled one of her best glasses with tap water and dropped in an ice cube from the freezer tray. "Salud."

He lifted his glass. "To happier days."

She couldn't help but wonder exactly what he meant by that.

Joely stayed in the guest room for as long as she could without risking the appearance of a search party in the doorway. She felt utterly drained of emotion, and the thought of waltzing into the kitchen and making pleasant conversation with Cat and William was almost unimaginable.

So the job in Surrey was hers. She waited for the sense of accomplishment to catch up with her, the sense of pride in her own achievements, but she still felt hollow inside. If she had had any hope at all that she and William would be able to work things out, she never would have encouraged the higher-ups at Clendenning to consider her for the new research group. Surrey had been her fallback position, the neutral corner where she could retreat when her time at Loch Craig came to an end.

Which it was. She had seen that clearly in William's eyes. The thought of what their split would do to Annabelle almost brought her to her knees. They had to find the right way to do this, a way that would protect the child's tender heart and, please

God, keep her in Joely's life.

The sound of laughter from the kitchen caught her by surprise as she ran a brush through her tangled hair. From the look on his face a few minutes ago, she wouldn't have thought William would be laughing again for a long, long time, but apparently he found the older Doyle sister agreeable company.

That laughter would have delighted her a year ago. Knowing that her sister and the man who shared her life enjoyed each other's company would have been proof positive that they were all meant to be a family. Now it only served to remind her of everything she was about to lose.

William was finishing off a sandwich when Joely walked into the kitchen. Cat was hunched over a lined notebook, scribbling furiously with an emerald-green felt-tip pen.

"What are you up to?" she asked the room in general.

William raised what remained of his sandwich in answer, while Cat mumbled something about a press release.

"Press release? What are you talking about?"

Cat waved her off and continued scribbling. She turned to William for clarification.

"A statement for the media," he said. "It might give you all some breathing space."

"So would driving over them with a backhoe."

He stared at her like he had never seen her before.

"That's one way to solve the problem," he said evenly, "but it would create new ones."

"Yes, it would," Cat said. "I'd have to get the driveway resurfaced."

The two sisters looked at each other and burst into raucous laughter and a quick high five.

"Black humor," Cat said to a watching William. "It's a family trait."

"We're not dangerous," Joely assured him. "We just sound that way."

"So I'm not in peril?" he asked.

"The day's young," Cat said with a wink. "We'll see how things play out."

William laughed with her, but Joely could see the hint of unease lurking just beneath his English surface. They were on her turf now, playing by her family's rules. It would be interesting to see how well he managed to adapt.

She caught herself. Interesting but essentially unimportant. Things like blending families, sharing jokes, building traditions, none of it mattered anymore. Instead of planning a future together, they were reduced to planning an exit strategy that did as little damage as possible.

"I promised I'd meet Zach at the house," Joely said, plucking her car keys from the Peg-Board near the door. "We were going to start sorting through Mimi's things." They wanted to do at least one quick sweep in case her mother had any valuables they needed to secure. The real heavy lifting would begin tomorrow.

Cat looked up from her notebook. "I'm going over to the hospital as soon as we get this taken care of. How about I meet you at Mimi's afterward?"

Joely jingled her car keys in her sister's direction. "Sounds like a plan."

William was far too polite to say, "What about me?"

"I can't imagine any of this is going to be much fun for you," Joely said. "Maybe Cat could drop you off at Karen's. Annabelle will be so excited to see you."

Cat gave herself a V8 slap to the forehead. "I should've thought of that. Of course I'd be happy to take you over to Karen's, William. I'd be delighted."

"Don't change your plans for me," he said, favoring Cat with a warm smile. "I have a rental in the drive. All I need are directions."

"I'm off then." Joely hesitated. She placed a hand on William's shoulder for an instant, then quickly stepped back. "See you at Mimi's," she tossed over her shoulder, then made her escape.

Cat did her level best to pretend she hadn't seen or understood the tension between Joely and William, assuming a stance of willful ignorance that fooled nobody but served a very useful purpose.

It hurt to see the tension seep from William's shoulders when the door closed behind Joely. That wasn't the way it was supposed to be. Not after years of being together, building a life together, raising a child together. When the man you shared that life with started to feel more comfortable when you left the room, you were in trouble.

Trouble that not even a big sister could make go away.

She made coffee for William while he read the statement she'd prepared.

"This should satisfy them for awhile," he said. "They live from news cycle to news cycle. This will buy you twenty-four hours, at least."

"I was hoping for a little longer than that." She poured him a cup of coffee and placed it in front of him. "I'm sorry we had to meet under such . . . unusual circumstances. There are occasional moments when we actually resemble a normal family."

He busied himself stirring sugar into his coffee.

"Sorry," she said. "Another example of black humor. It really is a family trait."

"So I'm learning."

Cat backpedaled again. Clearly Joely hadn't felt the need for black humor in Loch Craig. "Maybe it's a Maine thing," she said lightly. "All that sea air and lobster get into your blood."

Leave it to Joely to pick a man even more circumspect than she was.

"Okay," she said, leaning back in her chair. "We have fifteen minutes until I leave for the hospital and a lot of family history to cover. Let's see if I can get you up to speed."

"You mean he flew from Japan to Idle Point to see you?" Zach looked at her with undisguised envy. "Now that's a statement."

"Don't go getting all Hallmark on me,"

Joely snapped. "He's furious with me, and I don't blame him."

They were sitting on the floor of Mimi's living room, sifting through a stack of boxes they had found in her bedroom closet.

"Not good," Zach said after she told him about the job in Surrey. "Why didn't you tell him you were up for the position?"

"I didn't think it would come to anything."

He stared at her. "You didn't think you'd get it?"

Her eyes filled with tears. "Worse," she said. "I hoped I wouldn't need it."

"Did you tell him that?"

"Why prolong the inevitable?" she said. "It's over, and we both know it."

"Don't jump to conclusions."

"I'm not," she said. "It's been a long time coming, Zach. Sooner or later everything ends. I knew that going in."

"Didn't Cat stitch that charming sentiment into a pillow once?"

"Not funny."

"Endings never are."

"Who sounds like a needlepoint pillow now?" she teased gently.

"There's a difference between us," Zach said, "apart from the obvious ones. At least I know I gave it my best shot."

"What's that supposed to mean?"

"You're the smart sister. Why don't you figure it out?"

"You don't know me half well enough to insult me, Zach."

"You're not that tough. I saw you with Mimi this morning. She got to you."

"I'm human," she said. "It's difficult to watch someone deteriorate the way she has."

"And that's the scientist in you talking?"

"That's what I am, isn't it?"

"How about the daughter? What's her take on this?"

She stood up. "I've had enough of this. There's no point."

"Heading back to Scotland?" he shot back. "Or is it Surrey you're running away to this time?"

"Shut up, Zach. You don't have the right to say any of these things."

"Like it or not, kid, there's a bond between us. We both survived that accident and, the way I look at it, there has to be a reason we're still here. I want you to be happy. Hell, *I* want to be happy. There's not much point to anything else, is there?"

"I'm not sure we Doyle women do happy very well."

He rose to his feet next to her. "Cat's on the right track."

She sighed and leaned her head against his shoulder. "God, I hope so." He draped an arm around her, and she closed her eyes. "I always thought she was happy alone. Shows how well I know my own sister, doesn't it?"

"Alone isn't all it's cracked up to be," Zach said, and she laughed. "We're not wired for it."

"You're doing okay." She opened her eyes and looked up at him. "Aren't you?"

"Getting better every day," he said, but he didn't fool her. The pain of loss was in his eyes, and she knew it would be a long time before it went away.

"We'd better get back to work," she said. "Cat will have our hides if we don't make at least a little progress."

"Joe-leee! Joe-leee!" Annabelle burst through the door, shrieking at the top of her lungs. "Daddy's here!"

Joely's stomach tightened into a fist as William appeared in the doorway behind Annabelle. She moved away from Zach's hug but not before William took note of the embrace. She almost laughed at the absurdity of the situation.

Annabelle flung herself into Joely's arms.

"Did you know Daddy was coming," she demanded, "or were you surprised, too?"

"I was very surprised," she said, summoning up her best smile. "Isn't it wonderful, honey?"

"Yes!" Annabelle did a pirouette. "Brilliant!"

Zach stepped forward and extended his right hand. "Zach Porter," he said. "Good to meet you."

"William Bishop." They shook hands. "You're Karen's husband?"

"Brother-in-law," Zach said.

The two men took each other's measure as Annabelle, giddy with excitement, danced through the mess.

"Annabelle!" Joely warned. "Be careful. You might hurt yourself."

"I won't!" Annabelle said. "I'm just twirling!"

"There's broken glass, honey. Come over here where I can keep an eye on you."

She watched Zach watch William watching her and experienced a moment of total disorientation. There she was in Idle Point, the town where she'd grown up, with her gay friend, her English lover, and the little girl she loved like a daughter. For a moment she didn't recognize her own life or her place in it.

"The fire itself didn't do all of this damage," she said, as William's gaze began to take in the wreckage. "The fire department had a hand in some of it."

He nodded, his eyes traveling past the boarded-up windows, the water-soaked wallpaper, the overturned bookshelves. "This is the house where you grew up."

She nodded. "This is it. We moved in with Grandma Fran when I was still a baby, and she left it to Mimi when she died."

She tried to see it through his eyes and almost laughed out loud.

His gaze landed on her. "You lived here with your parents?"

"Mark was long gone by the time we got here," she said as Zach tried to interest Annabelle in a box of old Christmas cards he'd found tucked in Mimi's bedroom closet. "It was just us girls."

"Catherine tried to sketch out your family tree for me over lunch."

"Enough to put you off food permanently, isn't it?"

He didn't exactly recoil, but she could see that her flip comment set him back.

"Sorry," she said. "It's a family thing. When we're nervous, we get sarcastic."

"Catherine told me about that, too." He

met her eyes. "I told her you weren't like that in Loch Craig. She figured it's something in the Maine air."

"I'm glad you two hit it off."

"We did," he said. She could see him relax the slightest bit. "I like her."

She forced her smile wider. "Great!"

Not that it mattered. It wasn't like they were destined to be one big happy family. Cat and William would probably never see each other again once he went back to Scotland.

"What's this?" Annabelle pulled her hand out from underneath a sodden carpet runner and held up a thin metal box.

"Looks like an old cigarette case," Zach said.

"Let me see, honey." Joely turned the damp metal container over in her hand. "You're right," she said to Zach. "Looks like it was some kind of advertising promotion for Chesterfield cigarettes."

"Open it up," William said. "I heard something rattle when you turned it over."

The lid was rusted shut. She fiddled with the latch and then the hinges.

"Let me," William said. "I was master of the keys at boarding school."

Zach's eyebrows shot skyward, and Joely

333

laughed. "English humor," she said. "It's an acquired taste."

William's eyes met hers, and for a second she had a glimpse of the man who had swept her up to his house in Loch Craig and given her a home, but it was gone before she could imprint the image on her heart.

He did something to the hinge with his thumbnail, and the lid popped open like magic. She held out her hand, and he tipped the cigarette case over and a gold ring and three polished stones fell into her palm.

"Pyrite," William said.

"Fool's gold," Zach amended.

Fitting, Joely thought. Her mother's entire life had been built on a foundation of fool's gold. She slid the stones back into the cigarette case, then carried the dented gold ring over to the window.

"Not too close," Zach warned. "They have telephoto lenses trained on the house."

"He's right," William said. "We had to run the gauntlet to get in here."

It was a cheap band, devoid of either artistry or significant gold content, remarkable only for its size. No stones of any kind. No design work etched on the surface.

She slid it onto her right thumb. "This thing is huge," she said. "I could almost fit two fingers in it."

"Is there an inscription inside?" William asked as Annabelle sat down on the floor to play with the three polished stones in the tin cigarette case.

"I didn't even think to look." Rings, with or without sentimental inscriptions, didn't even register on her radar screen.

She held the ring up to the thin stream of sunlight that filtered through a crack in the closed blinds. "I don't think there's anything inside this thing but rust."

"Gold doesn't rust," Zach said. "That's plain old dirt."

"Who said this was gold?" She held the ring closer to the window, turning it slightly so she could get a better viewing angle. "I'm not sure, but I think I see something."

"Let me." William reached for the ring, and she dropped it into his outstretched hand. He held the ring overhead, twisting and turning it until he found the right angle. "I see something . . . it's badly etched . . . there! I think it reads *Mary* . . . no, it's *Mark* . . . with a date." He handed the ring back to Joely. "February 16, 1961."

Zach whistled. "Two days after the Saint Valentine's Day dance."

Two days after Mark and Mimi met, and the whole thing started.

"This is my father's wedding ring," she said to William. "That's Mimi for you. She saves everything."

The attempt at sarcastic humor fell flat, and the two men shifted uncomfortably and tried not to meet her eyes. Annabelle, bless her, was oblivious to everything but the cigarette case and the three polished stones.

"What are you going to do with it?" Zach asked as she turned it over in her palm.

"You mean, after I take it to Tiffany for an appraisal?"

"Annabelle." William crouched down to his daughter's level. "Why don't we go for a walk near the lighthouse?"

"I don't want to."

"I do," he said, "and I'd like your company."

He held out his hand and helped Annabelle to her feet.

"Good going," Zach said as father and daughter disappeared down the front walk. "Why don't you save time and drive them to the airport while you're at it?"

"You're getting on my nerves, Zach," she said. "I think you forget this is my family we're talking about, not yours."

"What are you going to do with that ring?" he asked again. "And don't tell me you're donating it to the Smithsonian. It may not have any sentimental value for you, but it might mean something to Cat."

"I'm not going to toss it in the recycle bin, if that's what you're worried about."

"The thought crossed my mind."

She glanced around the trashed-out room. "I hate this," she said. "You have no idea how much I hate being here."

There were ghosts in every room, memories that only served to remind her of all the ways in which they had failed as a family. A long, sad legacy of getting it wrong.

"Then let's get back to work," Zach said. "We can't leave it all for Cat."

Yes, we could, she thought as they both resumed sorting through the boxes of paper and photos, old shoes and faded T-shirts. If she walked away from Idle Point and this whole ugly mess, Cat would pick up the slack the way she had always done, and Mimi would never know the difference.

But Joely would and, for the first time in her life, that mattered to her.

Chapter Seventeen

Laquita was changing Mimi's IV when Cat arrived later that afternoon.

"I practically needed a security pass to get in here," she said after they exchanged hellos. "Has it been this bad all day?"

"Worse," Laquita said. "Security finally figured out how to keep them corralled in the ground-floor lobby."

"I can't believe this is happening. She's been living here for over twenty-five years, and nobody cared, and now it's like Madonna moved to town."

"Go figure," Laquita said as she stripped off her gloves and dropped them into the proper receptacle. "Maybe the universe finally remembered she's here."

"Maybe that's it," Cat said as she leaned over Mimi and brushed a lock of silvered brown hair off her mother's forehead. "The universe finally woke up." She looked up at Laquita. "How is she today?"

"Restless."

"Is she in pain?"

"I don't think so. She's just unsettled."

"It's not going to get much better than this, is it?" she asked quietly.

"I don't know, honey," Laquita said. "Anything's possible."

"Friend to friend."

Laquita placed a hand on her shoulder and squeezed gently. "Probably not."

Cat nodded as her gaze settled once again on her mother. "That's pretty much what I thought."

"A bit of unsolicited advice: there are some wonderful long-term care facilities within a thirty-minute drive."

"I know. I had a long visit with the friendly people in financial services just before I came up here. They spelled out the options." She let out a long breath. "Why does even thinking about long-term care make me feel like I'm failing her?"

"Because you're a woman, and we think we have to do it all. Don't underestimate yourself, Cat. You'll do what's best for Mimi and what's right for yourself and your baby." She patted her shoulder. "I'd better go touch up my eyeliner. You never know when you're going to bump into a rogue photographer around here."

The visit with the financial office had set Cat back on her heels. Long-term care was a pricey proposition. Mimi had been declared partially disabled a few years back and was receiving a small Social Security stipend, but not nearly enough to make a difference. Cat thanked God she had had the foresight to enroll Mimi under a long-term-care insurance plan and the income to keep the payments current. Without that, the future would look even scarier than it was looking right now.

The restlessness Laquita had mentioned wasn't apparent as she sat there talking softly to her mother. Mimi seemed calm, almost tranquil, as she lay there in bed looking up at the ceiling. Every now and again her gaze would travel from ceiling to door to Cat, then back to the ceiling again.

"I wish I knew what you're thinking," Cat whispered. "I never really have."

Her father had been a shooting star racing across her childhood. She blinked once and he was gone, but the memories left behind were still bright. Mimi was more like the moon, beautiful, changeable, but nothing without the sun.

"I'm going to have a baby, Mimi," she said as she held her mother's hand. "I was waiting to tell you until I was further along, but now's as good a time as any." She told Mimi the due date. She told her a

little about Michael, about their very logical, very adult plan to raise the baby in
two households, three hundred miles
apart.

Suddenly it didn't sound either logical
or adult. It sounded fraught with uncertainty, and she wished she had stopped
with the words "I'm pregnant."

Laquita had told her about the doctors'
secret exit that took her down a back staircase to the basement, which let out at the
far end of the parking lot away from the
lurking paparazzi.

Her cell phone rang as she pulled up in
front of Mimi's house.

"You're famous," a familiar voice said.

"Wait a second," she said. "I'm parking
the car. I need both hands."

"Come on, Doyle," Michael said. "You
don't even have sidewalks up there."

She parked behind Zach's car and
turned off the engine. "We take driving se-
riously up here, Yanovsky, unlike you New
Yorkers."

God, she loved his laugh. The sound
took her by surprise every time.

"So tell me how I'm famous," she said.
"Did you see Julia Roberts walking down
Rodeo Drive wearing one of my sweaters?"

"I was at my agent's office this afternoon. He has live feed pumped in from the studios, all the syndicated entertainment shows, they monitor client mentions, all that."

"Oh no." She didn't need a road map to figure out where this was going. "Another story about Mark and Mimi?"

"Four," he said. "*Access Hollywood* has a shot of you entering the hospital to see your mother."

Her eyes flew to the rearview mirror. "I knew I should've put on some eye makeup."

"So who was the mouthpiece?"

She laughed. "Don't tell me. You're channeling Raymond Chandler again."

"He looked like a male model."

The jealous edge to his voice made her laugh again, louder this time. "I hadn't noticed."

"So who is he?"

Another, wiser woman might have played it out a little bit longer, but Cat had never been very good at romantic game playing. "That's Joely's William."

"I thought he was in Japan."

"So did she. He showed up early this afternoon, jet-lagged and not too happy." She filled him in on the awkward reunion. "The thing is, I really like him. I found myself wishing things were better between the two of them. I wouldn't mind having him as part of the family."

"And Annabelle?"

"Oh, Michael, she's a delight. Funny, quirky . . . I'd say she was an original, but that sounds silly when you're talking about a seven-year-old child. Looking at her makes me —" She stopped midsentence.

"Makes you think what?"

"Ignore me. The hormones just kicked in again. Be glad you're on the other side of the continent, Michael. These days I get emotional over trash bag commercials."

"Nobody likes to see a family break up," he said. "You don't have to apologize for being sad."

"I wish you could have seen them together," she said. "Very stiff. Very polite. Like strangers except there was this current running between them that I'm not even sure they were aware of. A bond you could almost see."

"I thought you weren't a romantic, Cat."

"I'm not. I'm just trying to explain what I saw."

"You were describing how it made you feel."

"You're wrong."

"I know what I heard."

"And I know what I said. I was talking about William and Joely. Nothing else."

"It's not a crime to hope for a happy ending."

"That's the writer in you talking. Happy endings don't translate well to real life."

"It doesn't hurt to try to get close, does it?"

Two vans with satellite dishes attached to the roof pulled up in front of the house.

"Uh-oh," she said. "We've got company."

"Press?"

"Two TV crews," she said.

"Where are you parked?"

"In Mimi's driveway, right behind Zach's car."

"Zach? Who's Zach?"

"I'll e-mail you the cast of characters when I get home. Right now I'd better make a run for the front door."

"I could be there this time tomorrow if you say the word."

"It's enough to know that you would."

"You're a tough one, Doyle," he said.

"Not half as tough as you think, Yanovsky," she answered and then she hung up just in time. Another moment longer and she might have done something crazy and told him she missed him.

★ ★ ★

Karen, bless her heart, had left a picnic basket filled with barbecue chicken, potato salad, and fresh tomatoes in the studio and a pretty amazing note.

Diane Sawyer (!!) phoned about an interview. Says please call her back (!!) on her private cell phone number. I'm holding out for Brad Pitt.

Love,
KP

"Diane Sawyer?" Joely said as they trooped across the lawn to the house. "That has to be a joke."

"I don't think so," Cat said as she unlocked the back door. "Michael phoned. He said the story's being picked up by four or five other entertainment shows tonight."

"We'd better call hospital security and let them know," Joely said. "They may need to hire on some more guards."

They looked at each other and said, "Diane Sawyer!" then burst into tired laughter. The thought of paparazzi roaming wild through Idle Point was surreal at the very least, but the idea of Diane Sawyer leaving phone messages put the whole thing right over the top.

"Just when you thought life couldn't get any stranger," Cat said, and they started laughing all over again.

"Do you think we should have sent William and Annabelle off to the supermarket alone?" Joely asked as they put the picnic baskets down on the countertop in the kitchen.

"The man does business around the world," Cat said as she pulled out a huge container of spicy, juicy chicken. "I think he can handle a grocery store."

Joely opened the refrigerator and searched around for the iced tea. "So what exactly did you two talk about after I left this afternoon?"

"You," Cat said. "Oh, don't look so stricken. You were just one tiny branch on our whole twisted family tree. I figured somebody had better get him up to speed if he was going to go out there and handle the press."

"I thought all he did was read a prepared statement."

"You've been living with him for over four years, Joely. I think he had a right to know a little something about the family he was representing."

Maybe she was tired. Maybe she was just feeling a little raw and vulnerable. Whatever the reason, Cat's words struck an unexpected nerve. "And how much does this Michael of yours know about the family? Give me a phone number, Cat, so I can bring him up to speed, too."

"You know what?" Cat said. "Maybe that's not such a bad idea. Maybe it's time I practiced what I've been preaching."

Leave it to her big sister to know exactly how to take the wind from her sails.

"Don't look at me like that," Cat said more gently this time. "I meant what I said. It's all out there now anyway, honey, and it isn't going to go away anytime soon. Mark and Mimi are the ones who set this whole thing in motion. We're just along for their ride."

Joely poured two glasses of cool iced tea and slid one toward Cat. "I don't like that analogy," she said. "You make us sound like cogs in a wheel."

"When it comes to their lives, that's what we are, honey, that's what we've always been."

Her throat tightened against memories of a childhood spent longing for something she could never have. "Maybe it's easy for you," she said. "You had ten years with them. I barely had ten minutes before Mark walked out."

"And here I always envied you," Cat said. "At least you didn't spend ten years wondering if you were the reason your parents were so unhappy together."

"You're right," she said. "I didn't. But how do you think it felt to know your father walked out the door as soon as you were old enough to eat solid food? You didn't have the market cornered on guilt, Cat. There was more than enough of that commodity to go around."

"And yet here we both are, picking up the pieces for her," Cat said. "Maybe we're as crazy as Mimi."

"There's a happy thought for you," Joely said. "Since she was handing out presents from her gene pool, why didn't she throw some musical talent my way?"

"I wouldn't mind her thighs," Cat said with a shake of her head. "The woman is in her sixties, and she doesn't have a drop of cellulite."

"A touch of whimsy wouldn't kill me," Joely went on. "I can be too literal-minded."

"You? I don't know how you can say such a thing."

Joely flicked some cold iced tea in her sister's general direction, but Cat ducked before the droplets reached her.

"What do you think she would think about all the attention she's getting?" Joely asked.

"She'd love it," Cat said as she emptied the picnic baskets and arranged the containers on the countertop. "She'd be standing out there on the front step giving press conferences every hour on the hour."

"And impromptu concerts," Joely said, and they both laughed. "Remember how we used to cringe whenever she burst into spontaneous song at the supermarket?"

"You cringed," Cat reminded her. "By that time, it had become nothing more than background noise to me."

Joely glanced down at her watch. "When do all those entertainment shows come on? It might not be a bad idea to know what's being said about us."

They dashed into the living room. Cat clicked on the television and did some fast channel surfing. *Entertainment Tonight*, *Access Hollywood*, and *The Insider* were all in commercial.

"Call Karen," Joely suggested. "Maybe she'd monitor one of them for us."

"Great idea!"

Cat grabbed for her cell phone while Joely bounced between the three channels.

"Here comes Mary Hart!" she announced. "I'm beginning to feel like she's our long-lost sister."

"Bite your tongue!" Cat looked horrified. "We have enough skeletons in our closet as it is."

"Brad Pitt . . . Charlize Theron . . . ohmigod, that's you, Cat!"

Cat shrieked and dropped the cell phone as a shot of her, frazzled and tired-looking, blossomed on the screen. "Michael warned me. They got me going into the hospital," she said. "I'm too old for direct sunlight."

"Shh!" Joely picked up the remote and raised the volume.

"Get well wishes go out to Mimi Doyle, half of the legendary duo The Doyles, as she recovers from a stroke in Idle Point, Maine. Mimi's daughters, Catherine — a costume designer for the HBO hit *Pink Slip* — and Joely — a research scientist — issued a statement thanking the public for its outpouring of sympathy to reporters earlier this afternoon, which was delivered by William Bishop, a family friend. Greensleeves Records said in a phone interview that the renewed interest in the groundbreaking singers has them considering a long-awaited 'Best Of' CD. For those of you too young to remember them, this brief clip from the Newport Folk Festival in 1964 will show you what you missed . . ."

There was no way to prepare themselves for the sight of their parents, young and filled with dreams, looking back at them from the screen of Cat's Sony. It had been years since Joely had seen them on screen and the powerful images pierced her heart. Mimi was in a madras granny dress that fell to her bare feet. Her rich brown hair tumbled over her shoulders, gleaming with auburn highlights in the afternoon sun. Her hands were clasped in front of her as she leaned into Mark, her face aglow with the kind of happiness most people never know this side of heaven.

"She's beautiful," Joely whispered. "I'd forgotten how beautiful she was."

But it was Mark who captured them both.

Joely felt like she was seeing him for the first time.

"Look at him," Cat said so softly Joely might have imagined it. "That's our father."

He looked like one of those gods of legend. His tall, lean frame was made for the faded jeans and T-shirt that had been his trademark. The phrase "bad boy" had been invented for him, and he wore it well.

He looked down at Mimi and smiled, and for a second the earth stopped spinning on its axis.

The sound was scratchy, and their voices were all but drowned out by the cheering crowd, but the magic — oh, the magic was unmistakable. While The Doyles were singing, you believed you could change the world.

"Look at his hand," Cat said, moving closer to the screen. "He's wearing his wedding band. Do you think it might be the same one?"

Joely's arms were wrapped tightly across her chest. She felt like she was a half step away from breaking apart from the sheer weight of emotion building up inside her heart.

The picture faded, and the show went to commercial.

Joely stood there motionless while Cat scrambled for her cell phone and spoke briefly to Karen. Cat's words didn't register on Joely. Nothing did. She was a few hundred miles and a million years away, watching something close to genius at work.

"I never understood what it was all about," she said after Cat said good-bye to Karen. "I think I get it now."

"They really were something, weren't they," Cat said, running a quick hand across her eyes.

"You could feel the chemistry right through the screen." She looked at her sister. "Was that real? Was that how you remember them?"

"I wish I knew," Cat said. "Remember, all of my memories are filtered through a child's eyes. I know there was a lot of fighting — Mimi's mood swings were already pretty scary — but when they weren't fighting, it was downright magical."

"So where did it go wrong?"

Cat shrugged. "I asked Mimi that a thousand times, but she wasn't talking."

"Where do you think he is?" Joely asked.

Cat's expression softened. "Dead," she said. "It's the only explanation I can come up with. He wouldn't have left us like that. I know he wouldn't. Sure, he and Mimi probably would have ended up divorced at some point, but he wasn't the kind of man who would walk out on his family."

"Or his meal ticket," Joely said with more than a hint of acid in her tone.

"The meal ticket was long gone," Cat reminded her. "We had already moved from down on our luck to poor and were skidding our way to dirt poor when he left."

"So where did he go? If he was the great guy you say he was, then where the hell has he been for the last twenty-seven years? Can you answer that one for me?"

"I think he needed a break, and he decided to go off on one of those trips of his."

"So he lied to you about the guitar string."

"Probably," Cat said. "He used to walk over to the interstate and hitch a ride south with any trucker who slowed down long enough for him to climb in. Sooner or later his luck was bound to run out. He picked the wrong guy and that, as they say, was that."

"And that's what you think happened?"

"It's as good a guess as any other," she said. "Nobody else has ever come up with anything that makes better sense."

"People don't disappear without a trace, Cat. Not in the real world."

"Then what do you think happened?"

"Maybe he was living a double life," she said. "Maybe he had another family someplace, and he liked them better than he liked us."

Cat shook her head. "I don't buy that. Mimi was the only woman in the world for him."

"Then why weren't they happy?" Joely demanded. "If they loved each other so much, if they were so much 'in love,' then why did it all fall apart?"

"Knowing why wouldn't change things," Cat said. "We'd still be standing here wondering what to do next."

You're wrong, Joely thought. *It does matter.* The only thing that surprised her was just how much it still hurt.

Chapter Eighteen

William proved to be a godsend.

By nine p.m. both Cat and Joely were coming unglued from the endless stream of journalists pounding on the front door, begging for five minutes of their time.

William's cool, very British manner proved a very effective antidote to the circuslike atmosphere growing all around them. Cat quickly learned to pay attention to his suggestions and when he recommended that she hire someone to sit with Mimi at the hospital overnight to protect her mother from photographers, she didn't waste a second and hired one of Laquita's younger sisters.

"I'd worry about that woman in the next bed," Joely said. "What's to stop her from whipping out a digital and selling the files to *People*?"

"Basic human decency," Cat said, "but that seems to be in short supply lately."

There was just so much they could do to protect Mimi and to maintain their privacy without a large expenditure of time and money they didn't have. Zach had stopped by on his way back to Karen's after a business dinner, and he volunteered to sleep at Mimi's house to protect it from trespassers, an offer that made both sisters burst into grateful tears.

"You look exhausted," Joely said after Zach left. "Why don't you call it a night?"

"I was thinking maybe you and William would like to share my room. Morning sickness will have me up at the crack of dawn, so I might as well sleep on the sofa."

"We'll figure something out," Joely said, clearly uncomfortable with the suggestion. "Go phone your boyfriend."

Cat yawned behind her hand. "How did you know I was going to call Michael?"

"He's been texting you all night. The least you can do is pick up the phone."

"He's taking the red-eye back to New York tonight. We'll talk tomorrow."

"You should invite him up for the weekend," Joely said. "The more the merrier."

"Did he put you up to that?"

"I haven't spoken word one to the man."

"Good," Cat said with a wink. "I intend to keep it that way a while longer."

She went into the office to say good

night to William. He had walked unwittingly into a crazy situation that was as foreign to him as lobster shacks and double-wides, but somehow he had managed to step right in and take charge when they really needed a helping hand.

"I just wanted to say good night," she said after he hung up the phone. "I don't know what we would have done without you today."

His eyes lit up when he smiled, making him even more handsome than he already was, which was considerable. Joely had never once mentioned the fact that her William was downright gorgeous.

"I did very little, Catherine, but I'm glad I could help."

He looked so tired, so lonely, that she couldn't help herself. She stepped forward and gave him a swift, impulsive hug that took both of them by surprise.

"I wish the circumstances had been different," he said.

"So do I. It would be wonderful to introduce you and Annabelle to the coast of Maine."

He looked at her curiously, and she realized that he hadn't been talking about Mimi's accident at all, but about himself and Joely.

She said good night and beat a hasty retreat to her bedroom.

"The ultimate faux pas," she said to Michael a few minutes later. "I embarrassed both of us."

"You'll live," Michael said, "and so will he."

"That's a little cold, don't you think?"

"Has he said why he showed up uninvited?"

"Michael! What's wrong with you? You don't sound like yourself."

"Maybe I don't like being three thousand miles away while you're being harassed by reporters."

"I'm fine. Joely and I are both capable of taking care of ourselves. Besides, William's here with us."

"I'd still like to know why he showed up."

"So would I," she admitted, "but it's not the type of thing you can walk up and ask your sister's boyfriend without sounding rude."

"*Is* he her boyfriend? I thought that was over."

"I think it is, but I can't keep calling him 'Annabelle's father,' can I?"

"So where is he?"

"He and Joely are in the living room."

"Where are you?"

"In bed."

"How are you feeling?"

"Not too bad. Morning sickness limited itself to morning today. I could get used to that."

A short silence. "Where did you say you were?"

"You know where I am."

"Feel like some company?"

"Michael —"

"One day you'll say yes," he said. "I just hope it's before you go into labor."

Joely tried to busy herself sorting through the paperwork Cat had brought home from the hospital. Endless reams of paper about assisted living, facilitated living, nursing homes, extended care facilities — an endless number of options that all meant one thing: Mimi needed professional help on a permanent basis.

She and Cat were going to have to sit down together in the next day or so and figure out the gap between what Mimi's various insurances would cover and what her care would actually cost. The trick then would be coming up with the money on a monthly basis to bridge that gap.

She hadn't expected to feel this connection to their mother, this unsettling mix of compassion and pity and love. There. She'd allowed herself to think the word. Despite everything, she loved Mimi. Maybe not the way most daughters loved their mothers. Certainly not close to the way she should. Definitely not the way Cat loved her. But to her surprise the connection between them was there, unbreakable despite her best efforts across the years.

She wasn't going to walk away from the situation this time and leave it all on Cat's shoulders. She had some money in a few different investment accounts — William had made sure she was diligent about building her savings — and if that job in Surrey really was a go, her income would take a giant leap forward.

Just in time, she thought as she slid the papers back into the manila envelope marked Mimi. Her life was about to change in every way she could imagine and the extra money would make it possible for her to contribute her share and more to her mother's care. One small compensation for all that she would lose when she left Loch Craig.

She uncurled herself from the corner of Cat's sofa and stretched. Maybe her sister had the right idea. Cutting the night short suddenly sounded very inviting. Of course there was still the problem of sleeping arrangements, but she and William should be able to work that out without too much trouble.

She walked down the short hallway and stopped in front of the closed office door. She knocked twice and waited. No answer. She knocked again. Still no answer.

"William?" she called out softly, then pushed the door open a crack.

He wasn't there.

It was a small house. There weren't many places where he could be. The bathroom door was wide open. No sign of him there. She walked quickly past Cat's bedroom, shutting her ears to the hushed sounds of laughter and conversation floating through the closed door. Shutting her heart to the sense of envy was harder. Michael Yanovsky was three thousand miles away, but the connection between Cat and the father of her child was strong and vibrant.

She found William in the guest room. He was sitting on the edge of the bed, Annabelle's Tigger on his lap, looking down at his daughter. Annabelle slept on her side, curled around Trixie, her right hand curved beneath her chin.

"She looks like an angel," she said softly.

William nodded, but he didn't turn around.

"It goes so fast," she continued, moving closer. "I feel like I blinked, and she went from toddler to little girl."

Another nod, but he still didn't turn around. A terrible sense of finality rose up between them and she knew the moment had come.

"William," she said, "we need to talk."

"You're right." He stood up and placed Tigger on the nightstand. "We do."

He followed her down the hallway to the kitchen.

"Too bad we can't sit on the porch," she said. "Nothing's better than a summer night in Maine."

"You said you wanted to talk." He claimed a chair at the table.

"I did." She amended herself. "I do."

He looked so tired, so deeply sad, that her heart twisted in sympathy. She had intended to limit the conversation to sleeping arrangements, but she couldn't duck the truth any longer. More surprising, she didn't want to.

"I'm going to take the job in Surrey," she said without preamble. "I spent some time going over the costs for my mother's care —"

He motioned for her to be quiet.

"William." She hit the two syllables hard.

He covered her mouth with his hand. "There's someone on the porch." His lips brushed her ear. "Stay here. I'll see what's going on."

His nearness disoriented her. She couldn't remember the last time she had felt the touch of his lips against her skin, caught his familiar scent. Normally she was a big fan of irony, but this time it left her feeling sad and empty.

She didn't stay put the way he'd asked. She shadowed him all the way across the kitchen, ignoring the scowl he threw at her over his shoulder.

"Flip the switch," she whispered. "Throw some light on the porch."

Men hated to be given directions of any kind, but sometimes that couldn't be helped.

"William," she said, more loudly. "Don't go out there. Just turn on the light."

But he had the bit between his teeth, and nothing but direct confrontation with the intruder, whoever the intruder might be, would suffice. He was, however, a cautious Englishman at heart, and he took a quick peek through the back door curtains before committing himself to a *mano a mano* battle.

"You have raccoons." He stepped away from the door, and the curtains shimmied back into place.

"What?"

"Raccoons," he said. "That's what I heard outside."

"Okay then," she said. "Mystery solved."

He started unlocking the door.

"Where are you going? You said it's raccoons."

"They knocked over Catherine's trash cans."

"That'll keep until tomorrow."

"It'll be worse tomorrow. I'll right them now."

"William, this is ridiculous."

She might as well have been talking to a wall. He was going to go out there and battle rampaging raccoons, and no amount of reason would stop him.

"Fine," she said. "Just close the kitchen door. I don't want the raccoons sneaking inside while you're playing in the trash."

She headed for the living room to double-lock the front door against tabloid reporters and squirrels with disposable cameras. They didn't need to talk. They didn't need to do anything but work out sleeping arrangements for tonight and the few nights remaining to them, and they would do that with as much civility as humanly possible for Annabelle's sake even more than for their own.

It shouldn't hurt this much, she thought as she fastened the chain. She had been expecting it for months. They both had. This whole thing was as inevitable as the changing seasons.

She told herself it was better this way as she slid the dead bolt into place. Better they separated now, before Annabelle grew any older. Children were adaptable. They gave their hearts in response to kindness, and she knew William well enough to know he would never open his heart or Annabelle's home to anyone who was unkind.

That should have made her feel better, but it didn't. It made her feel like she could drink an entire bottle of single malt and not even make a dent in the sense of loss. Cat wasn't much of a drinker, but she had to have a bottle of whiskey someplace. She turned to head back to the kitchen to hunt down something lethal and preferably well-aged when she heard a tap on the front door.

Too high for raccoons, she thought. William must have somehow managed to lock the kitchen door behind him and come around front.

"A second," she said as she started un-latching the front door.

She swung open the door and found herself face-to-face with a medium-sized man in a business suit.

"Ms. Doyle?"

"Joely Doyle," she said. "And you are — ?"

"Robert Quigley. I'm looking for Catherine Doyle."

"This isn't a good time," she said, beginning to ease the door shut. "I recommend you phone Catherine in the morning."

"I've been out here for two hours," Robert Quigley said, "but a Mr. Bishop wouldn't let me speak to her."

Where was Mr. Bishop when she needed him?

"Do you have a business card?" she asked, as the bottom of the door met his well-shod foot. "I'll give it to Cat myself and ask her to phone you."

"Five minutes," Robert Quigley said. "It's very important."

She almost wept with relief when she heard footsteps behind her.

"William," she said without taking her eyes off the man in the doorway, "would you please tell Mr. Quigley that Cat will phone him tomorrow morning?"

"I'll tell him myself."

She turned to see Cat, disheveled but awake, standing behind her.

Robert Quigley stepped forward. "Catherine Doyle?"

Cat nodded.

"Robert Quigley." He extended his hand in greeting, but Cat ignored it. "I have some very important news for you."

"We're not interested in giving interviews," Cat said. "We're not going to open up our family albums to you, and we definitely won't be writing a book."

"That's not why I'm here."

William joined them, and Joely finally started breathing again. The whole thing was getting a little too intense for so late at night.

William looked at Cat, and she nodded.

"You have ten seconds," William said, stepping forward. "This is private property, Mr. Quigley. If you don't leave, we're calling the police."

"I can do better than that, Mr. Bishop," Robert Quigley said. "I can call the media."

"Are you threatening us?" Cat asked. "Because if you are —"

"I told you this wasn't the way to do it, Quigley."

They all stared as a tall old man with thinning gray hair appeared at Robert Quigley's side. Joely wasn't one for déjà vu moments. They always smacked of New Age mysticism and past life regressions to her. But this was something else entirely. She could almost feel the fine hairs on her arms lifting in response to the old man's presence, and she didn't know why.

"Get out," Cat said in a tone of voice Joely had never heard her sister use before.

"Cat, I just want to —"

"Get out *now!*" Cat pushed past Joely and William.

"We need to talk, Kit-Cat. Please don't —"

Cat shoved with all her might and sent the two men stumbling back onto the front porch. She slammed the door shut and locked the bolt.

"You might have opened yourself up to a lawsuit, Catherine," William observed. He fastened the chain. Cat's hands were shaking too hard for her to manage. "They might claim injury."

"They can go to hell," Cat said. "Both of them."

Joely's heart was beating so hard she could barely hear their words. The rush of adrenaline inside her head sounded louder than the ocean. "Do you know that man?" she asked as a ripple of awareness moved its way up her spine.

"I used to," Cat said, her tone steely. "He's our father."

Chapter Nineteen

Joely's face went ashen, her eyes rolled back, and William sprang into action. He crossed the room in a flash and caught her just before she hit the ground.

"The couch," Cat said, her tone still flint hard. "I'll get her some water."

She was so light in his arms. Familiar yet strange. He couldn't remember the last time he had held her this way. It seemed wrong somehow to be aware of the slight frame, the delicate bones, but he registered her physical presence in every cell of his body. He couldn't help himself.

She started to rouse as he laid her down on the soft cushions. He held her gently still as her eyes fluttered open and she looked at him.

"Oh God!" Her voice broke on a sob. "Was that really Mark?"

"Shh," he said, pushing her hair gently back from her face. It was the only thing he could think of to do for her. There was nothing in his experience or in their life together to prepare him for this. "Lie still."

"No." She struggled upright. "Cat!" she called out. "Cat! Was that really Mark?"

"She's in the kitchen," he said. "She went to get you some water."

"We can't leave him out there," Joely said. "We have to let him in, see what he wants."

"Over my dead body." Cat appeared in the archway between the living room and the kitchen. She held a tall glass of water in her right hand.

"That's our *father!*" Joely said. "After all these years, Cat! He's back!"

"No, he's not," Cat said. "He can go to hell."

Joely stood up, swayed, then straightened up. "We can't lose him again."

"Lose him?" Cat's laugh went right through William. "We should be so lucky. Why do you think the son of a bitch is here, Joely? After all these years, we finally have something he wants."

"Fame," William said quietly as the pieces began to fit together.

Cat turned to face him, a look of triumph on her pale face. "Give the man a prize."

"I think she's right, Joely," he said, aware that he was treading out onto paper-thin ice above a very deep pond. "Quigley works for one of the tabloids. He called a few times tonight, but I put him off."

The look Joely gave him marked paid to any hope he might still have for a future together.

"You don't know anything about this," she said to him. "You have no idea how I'm feeling."

"You're right," he said. "I don't." He looked at Cat. "If you need me, I'll be checking in on Annabelle."

And booking a flight back home.

Joely was making every mistake in the book, and there was nothing Cat could do to stop her.

William was a good man, the kind of man a woman prayed for, and her sister was pushing him away with both hands.

All because of a man who had walked out of her life before she was old enough to walk.

"Don't do it," Cat said as Joely ran for the front door. "Mark has no business showing up here after all this time."

But Joely was beyond reason. Cat wasn't even sure her sister heard her. She flung open the door and stepped out onto the front porch. "Mark!" her voice rang out. "Mark, please come back!"

Cat could barely contain her derision. He and that sleazy Quigley were probably crouching behind the bushes, ready to pounce on the next opportunity to promote their self-serving agenda.

The pain hurt so much she could barely breathe. She would rather have gone her entire life believing her father was dead than to have him show up on her front porch twenty-seven years later, acting like he was dropping by for a cup of coffee with his darling daughters.

Joely stepped back into the house. "He won't come in unless you say that it's okay, Cat."

"No, it's not okay," she said. "It's not okay at all. In fact, you can tell him to go fuck himself."

Joely's face reddened. "Please, Cat." The yearning in her sister's voice awakened memories of Joely as a little girl on those nights when the world seemed a very big and very dangerous place, and only Cat could keep her safe. "You had ten years with him. Let me have five minutes."

Cat's hands trembled with rage, and she shoved them behind her back. The depth of her anger shocked Cat. Joely had always been the angry one, the daughter who left town first chance she got. Cat was the mellow daughter, the easygoing one, the daughter who knew how to forgive.

"Please, Cat," Joely said again. "Five minutes. That's all I'm asking for."

"If he's not out in five minutes, so help me God I'm going to hurl him through a window."

"I promise."

Who were they kidding? That was their father out there on the front porch, their *father*. The man who had called her Kit-Cat, the man who used to sit next to her bed and hold her hand when she had a bad dream, the man who had looked her right in the eye and said he was stepping out to buy a new guitar string and walked right out of her life like he was exiting stage left.

"I can't do this," she said. "Talk to him if you want to, Joely, but don't ask me to be part of it, because I just can't."

Joely felt like the world as she knew it had been turned on its ear. A few hours ago she had stood there in front of the television mesmerized by the sight and sound of the father she'd never known, that beautiful godlike man with the burnt honey voice, and now he was standing there on the front porch. Older. Grayer. Not even close to being godlike. The man whose absence had colored every single day of her life until she left Idle Point for school and the world beyond.

I'm sorry, Cat, she thought as she ran to the door, *but I can't just let him go without finding out why he left us.*

Mark was standing on the front porch, shoulders hunched, smoking a cigarette, while Robert Quigley talked on a cell phone.

Joely caught her father's eye and smiled nervously. "Come in," she said.

"She said it's okay?"

"She's giving us five minutes."

His faded blue eyes swam with tears. "More than I deserve," he said, tossing his cigarette into the bushes. "Five minutes it is."

Quigley snapped shut his cell phone and fell into line behind Mark.

"Not this time," Mark said, raising his hand between them. "You'll get what I promised but not right now."

"You owe me," Quigley said. "You wouldn't be here if it wasn't for me."

She closed the door on Quigley and flipped the lock.

"What was that all about?" she asked, inclining her head toward the front porch.

"Did you make some kind of deal with him?"

"You can't get without giving," Mark said with a rueful smile. "He came to me with the news about Mimi. I owe him something, right?"

Not half as much as he owed his wife and children, but she doubted he would understand.

"He's not getting any photos of Mimi in the hospital," Joely said bluntly, "and we're not giving interviews. Let's get that straight right up front."

He looked at her for what seemed like a very long time then shrugged his shoulders.

"So this is Kit-Cat's house now," Mark said, his eyes traveling the four corners of the room. "Your mother lived here when we first met."

"No," she corrected him. "You're thinking of Grandma Fran's house."

"It's been a long time," he said. "I don't have the memory I used to have."

She looked at him for signs of irony and to her amazement found none.

"Would you like something to drink?" she asked. "I could make you some coffee."

"Can't drink coffee anymore." He patted

his chest with the flat of his right hand. "The ticker, you know?"

"I think Cat has decaf."

"Don't want to be any trouble. A beer would be good enough."

"I'm sorry. Cat doesn't have any beer in the fridge. I could pour you a glass of wine."

He shook his head. "It's late. Maybe I better stay clear."

She was aware of the ticking clock, of Cat coiled with rage in the bedroom, of William thanking God he was getting out before her family screwed his daughter up, too.

Mark sat down on the sofa. She sat down in the chair across from him.

"So you're my little Joely," he said, nodding up and down as he looked at her. "You look like your mother."

"No, I don't," she said. "Everyone always told me I looked like you."

"Your mother," he said again. "Same nose. Same eyes. You were a pretty baby. You grew up very nice."

"Thank you."

Is this it? she thought. *First time in twenty-seven years, and this is the best we can do?*

Clearly he felt no connection at all with

her. He was polite and friendly, but she could have been Karen Porter sitting there or any other almost-thirty-year-old woman in town for all he knew or cared.

She almost cried with relief when William came back into the room. He didn't say anything, just stood behind her chair. He had her back, and she appreciated it.

"How is your mother?" Mark asked.

"She had a stroke. Much of the damage is likely irreversible."

"I want to see her."

She was framing a cautious response when Cat's "No!" resounded.

"Kit-Cat!" Mark struggled to his feet as his oldest child entered the room. "Look at you! All grown up."

"I'm thirty-eight," she said as she approached. "Correct me if I'm wrong, but weren't you thirty-eight, too, when you went out to buy that guitar string?"

His brow furrowed. "Guitar string?"

Cat's anger was incendiary. Joely could feel its heat across the room. She had never been more grateful for her sister's antigun stance in her life.

"You know, Mark. Think back. That guitar string you went out to buy the day you walked out on us."

"I — I don't remember that."

"I didn't think you would."

"You look good," he said. "I didn't know which way it would go with you, but you turned out fine."

The look she shot him was withering, but he didn't flinch. "Your five minutes are up."

"Come on now! You don't mean that."

She laughed out loud. "I can't tell you how many nights I wasted lying awake wishing my father would come home, and now here you are, and all I can think of is how much I hate you."

"You're entitled."

"Am I?" She laughed again. "Gee, thanks, Dad. I probably should have run it by you first, but then you weren't here, were you?"

Cat's explosion seemed to stiffen Mark's spine. He stood a little taller and faced down his oldest daughter. "I want to see Mimi," he said. "I know you think I don't have the right, but she's still my wife."

"How would you know? She might have divorced your sorry ass a long time ago."

"She didn't."

"How would you know?" This time it was Joely asking the question. "You haven't talked to her since 1978. You can't possibly know what's been going on in her life."

"Well, now," said Mark Doyle, "that's not entirely true."

"What does that mean?" Cat demanded. "And don't go telling me you were psychically connected."

"We were in touch."

Joely and Cat locked eyes.

"Bullshit," Cat said. "I would have known."

He looked so old, so worn, that for a second — just a second — Joely felt sorry for him. How much he had lost over the years. She wondered if he had a clue about all he had missed.

"You don't know anything," Mark said to Cat. "It's a long story."

"Even longer from my perspective," she shot back.

"Let him talk," Joely said. "I want to hear it all."

"Go ahead," Cat said, "then maybe we can tell you our story."

He locked eyes with Cat, and his defiance surprised Joely. A touch of humility after a twenty-seven-year absence wouldn't have been out of place.

"I hitched down to West Virginia," he said, looking somewhere into the middle distance over Joely's shoulder. "I'd heard about a fiddle player named Ben Carstairs who played with Woody. He was getting on in years, and I wanted to get him on tape and —" He grinned and dragged a huge, bony hand through his hair. "Hell, I wanted to play with him, too, before it was too late. I'd tried to get Mimi to come with me, but she wouldn't leave you girls with anybody, and we both knew bringing you along wouldn't work."

"Why not?" Cat asked. "We had that big stupid van. You could've transported a Girl Scout troop in that thing."

"We weren't good at being parents," he said without apology. "Some people are naturals at it but not us. We loved you, Kit-Cat, but once you showed up, it was never the same again between us. No!" He raised his hand to silence them. "I'm not blaming you. We made our own choices, that much is for sure."

"Your warmth overwhelms me," Cat said. "It's so nice to know we were wanted."

"It is what it is," he said. "I can tell you the way it really was, or I can tell you the way I wish it had been. It's up to you."

"The truth," Joely said. That was the only way they would ever be able to get past it once and for all.

He was a talker, Mark Doyle was. He jumped back into his narrative without stopping for breath. "Kids change things. Nobody will argue that. No matter how strong a marriage you think you have, when those babies start coming, you find out how little you know."

"And how much you still want," Cat said.

He met Cat's eyes. "Yes," he said. "I still wanted more from life. I wanted my wife. We had been together twenty-four hours a day from the moment we met, and I still couldn't get enough of her. I resented the time she gave to you, and she hated me for leaving her behind when I hit the road." He seemed to drift for a moment, then pulled himself back. "Your mother wasn't like other people. I knew that when we met. She wasn't tough like you girls are. She felt things too much. After you two arrived, she was a raw nerve. She would see something on the television or hear something on the radio, and next thing I knew, she'd have sunk so low it would take me weeks to pull her back up to the surface." He looked from Cat to Joely. "By the time you came along, Joely, I had run out of energy. I couldn't do it anymore. She swung high and she swung low, and that sweet spot in the middle just wasn't there to balance us out."

"Why didn't you take her to see a doctor?" Joely asked.

"We saw lots of them," Mark said, "but nothing helped." His gaze hardened. "You took her to doctors, Cat. She still set fire to her house."

"She had a stroke," Cat retorted. "There was nothing anyone could do."

He nodded as if it all made sense on some cosmic level only he understood. "You want to know why I left? Hell, I've been asking myself that all the way up here. Joely still wasn't sleeping through the night, and our tempers were frayed. I figured I'd go down to West Virginia to see Ben Carstairs, give us both a little breathing room. Maybe when I came back, things would be better."

"You fought a lot," Cat said. "I used to lie awake in bed with my hands over Joely's ears so she didn't have to hear it."

"I'm not going to lie to you. We were in bad shape but, may God strike me dead, swear on Woody's grave, I was coming back home again. A few weeks is all. Just a few weeks."

"Fifty-two weeks a year for twenty-seven years," Cat said. "You're the scientist, Joely. You do the math for him."

"Why didn't you come back?" Joely

asked. "Did you fall in love with somebody else? Did you start another family?"

"Nope, nothing like that." He narrowed his eyes at them. "You sure your mother never told you any of this?"

They both shook their heads.

He exhaled loudly but went on. "I went to jail. Now I'm not proud of it, but somebody'd picked my pocket outside of Baltimore, and I didn't have two cents to rub together. When we got to West Virginia, I had to find some way to get money. Hell, I was so broke I couldn't even call Mimi and ask her to wire me some. So I did the only thing I could think of: I robbed a convenience store. Got fifty-six dollars and ended up with fifty-six weeks in the county jail with time off for reasonably good behavior."

"And Mimi knew about this?" Cat asked in a dazed voice. "She knew you were in jail?"

"She knew," he said. "She wrote to me every week while I was in, and I wrote back as often as I was able. I'll bet she still has those letters, too."

"If she did, they're probably gone," Cat said with more than a touch of malice. "There was a fire at Grandma Fran's the other day."

Of course he already knew that. He knew the whole story, or he wouldn't be there, looking to feed off the bones of Mimi's love for him.

"Okay," Cat said, "so you did time in a county jail. Why didn't you come home after you got out?"

"She'd moved back up here by then. Living with Fran in that old sand trap. I told her it was the perfect chance for us to start over. Fran loved you girls. She did a damn better job mothering you two than Mimi and I ever could. Mimi could come down and live with me in the mountains while I collected the old songs, and Franny would bring you two up. Hell, she couldn't do any worse than we were doing. You deserved a hell of a lot better than anything we could do."

"You don't have a clue," Cat said softly. "Not even a small one."

"I asked her more than once to come to me, but she wouldn't leave you girls."

"Easy for you to say now that Mimi's in a coma and can't tell us that you're lying."

"Your mother saved everything," he said. "She'll have those letters. Mark my words, they're somewhere in that house."

"You really did cover all your bases,"

Joely snapped. "Cat told you about the house fire."

He waved a hand in the air, and she was struck by the same long fingers and large hands, the same elegant grace she had seen earlier that evening on TV. "She had a fire-proof strongbox."

"I never saw one," Cat said, "and I know her house inside out."

"It's there," he said. "I guarantee it."

"That's why you came back now," Joely said. "It has nothing to do with Mimi or with us. You want something from that strongbox."

"I came here to see your mother."

"You wasted your time," Cat said. "I'm not letting you anywhere near Mimi."

"She's my wife, Kit-Cat. It's my right."

Cat stared at him with disdain. "I'd say your rights as a husband ended around 1978."

"Not everyone is as strong as you girls are," he said. "I did the best I could."

"You did nothing," Cat shot back. "You left when things got tough, and you didn't come back."

"I sent money in the beginning."

"From jail?" Joely asked. "Come on, Mark. Can't you keep your story straight?"

"After I got out, Joely. I sent Mimi

387

money for a couple years."

"And then what?" Joely persisted. "You got bored. You decided you'd given us enough. You didn't care. You never tried to see us or talk to us. I don't get that. Didn't you ever wonder?"

"It was easier not to," he said with almost breathtaking honesty. "After awhile I got to like my life. They're good people down there in the mountains. They made a place for me."

"Lucky you," Cat said, her voice rich with sarcasm.

"I didn't plan it," he said as if that made everything all right. "The days passed, and you don't realize it, but you're drifting farther and farther away from the things that used to be important."

"Like your family," Joely said.

"Yes," he said. "Like your family. It's easier to just let go of your old life and start over."

Like I did when I left for school, Joely thought. Like she was about to do again when she left Loch Craig.

"But you never really let Mimi go, did you?" Cat asked.

He shook his head. "No, I didn't." Sometimes three or four or even five years would go by where he thought he could cut the ties, and then he would see her face in his dreams or hear a voice that brought the sweet days back to him, and he would pick up the phone or send a postcard. Just enough to keep her hopes alive.

"Do you have any idea what you did to her?" Cat demanded as tears streamed down her cheeks. "She was fragile — you said so yourself! You never gave her the chance to move forward. You didn't have the guts to come back and make a real life with her, so you helped her build a fantasy life that kept your options open and her life on hold."

The room went completely silent. There was nothing left to say. Joely lowered her head, wishing William had stayed in Japan, that he hadn't heard any of this.

"Daddy!" Annabelle's voice rang out. "Joe-lee! I need water, please!"

"I'll go," William said.

"So will I." Joely regretted ever opening the door to the past. It hurt more than she would have dreamed possible.

She wanted to hide herself away in the guest room with William and Annabelle, lock the door and bar the windows against the terrible things that could happen to families when they weren't looking.

Annabelle was sitting up in bed. Her soft

brown hair spilled across her tiny shoulders. She let out a squeal of delight when her father entered the room.

"You really *are* here, Daddy! I thought I was dreaming."

"You're not dreaming," he said as he sat down on the edge of the bed. "I'll always be here for you, Annabelle."

And he would. Joely knew that the way she knew the sound of her own breathing. All the things a father should be, all the things a little girl needed from the first man in her life, she had right there in the father who loved her.

She slipped from the room unnoticed.

Cat was standing in the middle of the living room when she returned. Mark was nowhere in sight.

"Is he in the bathroom?" She angled her head in the direction of the back hallway.

"He's gone," Cat said, her face a shifting canvas of painful emotions.

"He can't be gone," Joely said. "He didn't say good-bye to me."

"Same old Mark. Some things never change."

"Is he coming back?"

"Probably. He hasn't scored his full fifteen minutes yet."

"Maybe he's changed."

"Right," Cat said, "and he's come back to make it up to all of us."

"You sound bitter."

"And you sound awfully forgiving."

"I always thought you'd give anything to see him again."

"So did I," Cat said. "Guess I was wrong."

"He looked so old," Joely said, her voice breaking.

"Twenty-seven years will do that to a man."

"I don't know what's wrong with me," she said, unable to stem the flow of tears. "He never meant anything to me, and now I'm falling apart."

Cat opened her arms to comfort her the way she had been doing as far back as Joely could remember. "Join the club."

Chapter Twenty

Laquita phoned first thing in the morning. "There's a man here claiming to be your father," she said when Cat answered. "He called a press conference for ten o'clock in the parking lot. I know this sounds crazy, but I think he might be the real thing."

Cat, who had been nursing her first ginger ale of the day, closed her eyes. "He is the real thing, Laquita. He showed up late last night with some weaselly PR guy."

Laquita muttered something earthy and highly appropriate to the circumstances. "What do you want me to do?"

"Don't let him anywhere near Mimi," she said. "He's looking for publicity, and I'll be damned if he gets it in some tearstained reunion in her hospital room."

"Gotcha," Laquita said, "but we might run into some problems. Are they still married?"

"I don't know," Cat said, as her stomach did one of those familiar slides toward misery. "I guess so." Then again, up until last night she thought her mother hadn't heard from Mark since October 1978.

"Legally he might have the right to see her."

"I'll be there as fast as I can," she said, then made the ten-yard dash to the bathroom.

"Who was on the phone?" Joely asked when Cat returned to the kitchen. Her sister was scrambling eggs at the stove while the coffeepot did its thing.

"Laquita." She gave Joely a quick rundown.

"What are we going to do?" Joely asked.

"He doesn't deserve to see her." She turned the eggs onto a big serving platter. "Especially not if he's going to use it for publicity."

"We're not waiting for William and Annabelle?" Cat asked as she sat down at the table.

"They went out," Joely said, her face a mask of controlled emotion. "They'll probably grab breakfast in town."

"Good thing William's here," Cat said carefully. "Karen had to take the kids up to Bar Harbor today to see the grandparents."

"Speaking of grandparents, Annabelle's grandparents are coming to Loch Craig next week to fetch her for their annual holiday motor trip. William's taking her back home tonight."

"Tonight? He just got here."

"That's why he came, Cat. Neither one of us would have been comfortable letting Annabelle fly back alone."

"Honey, I understand if you need to go back with them."

Joely shook her head. "I don't think I'll be going back except to pack my things."

"You and William have talked about this."

"We don't need to. It's painfully clear to both of us."

"Talk is good, you know."

"Why start now?" Joely said with a false laugh. "We've done fine without it."

Cat leaned forward and reached for her sister's hand. "You know I never pry —" She stopped as Joely's face registered amazement. "Okay, so I almost never pry, but I think you're making a mistake. I saw the way he looked at you, honey. I see the way you look at him. There's something there worth saving. I know it. Don't let him go without a fight."

"Too late," Joely said as she helped herself to some eggs.

They were so much alike, the two of them. Despite the ten-year difference in their ages, they shared much of the same baggage when it came to men and family. It had taken her thirty-eight years to feel she had not just the right but the wisdom to open her heart to the future. Joely had everything she needed right there in front of her, but the timing was wrong, and she couldn't see it.

There were no shortcuts to happiness. She couldn't draw a road map for her sister and point her in the right direction. It didn't work that way, no matter how much she wished it did. All she could do was be there for her, support her choices —

Or blaze the trail.

She pushed back her chair and stood up. "I'll be right back," she said.

"The eggs were too much, weren't they?" Joely said. "I should have made dry toast for you."

She hurried past the bathroom and ducked into her bedroom. Her cell phone rested on the nightstand. She turned it on, then typed the message that just might change her life:

HOW WOULD YOU LIKE TO MEET MY PARENTS?

She hit Send.

Now all she could do was wait to find out how her story ended.

Annabelle loved the beach. She turned somersaults in the sand and danced along the edge of the surf, singing with the sheer joy of life.

Her happiness was in sharp contrast to the deep, yawning sadness William had been feeling ever since he arrived in Idle Point a lifetime ago. He had been angry when he got there, determined to confront Joely about the job in Surrey, force her to sit down and talk, really talk, about their future and where it was leading, but the sheer drama of what was happening to her family overshadowed all else.

Maybe it was a good thing. Maybe he and Annabelle had been a stopping-off point, a place to rest while she waited for her life to unfold. He hadn't a clue. God knew he hadn't been looking for the powerful connection he had found with Joely, but it had come calling just the same, and he had been helpless to turn away.

Maybe it was the same with her. Maybe given another time, another place, they would have been able to make it work, make the kind of connection that could weather the storms and the years, but he would never know. There was something ironic and terribly sad about meeting the right person at the wrong time in your life and knowing you'd never be given another chance.

He had still been raw from losing Natasha when Joely came into his life. The attraction had been undeniable but his heart was still mending. Joely had never demanded more than he could give. She had been enormously understanding and compassionate and he had thanked God every night for bringing her into his life and Annabelle's.

It took a while before he realized that her undemanding ways weren't born of understanding but of a deep need to keep her own heart locked away.

Only Annabelle had known how to turn the key. He had been too caught up in his own drama to even try.

And now it was too late.

"Hungry?" he asked Annabelle as she took his hand for the walk back to Catherine's cottage. "I hear they make brilliant pancakes in America."

"Could we really?" Annabelle's entire face shone with delight. How little it took to make his daughter happy. It killed him to know what was about to happen and how much it would hurt her.

He waited until they were seated in the tiny restaurant near the newspaper office. He delayed until the pancakes, studded with blueberries the size of marbles, were brought to the table. He postponed saying anything at all until Annabelle had her fill of rich amber maple syrup with a touch of pancake underneath it.

"We're going home tonight," he said as casually as he could manage. "Grandmother and Grandfather Sinclair are on their way to Loch Craig to take you on holiday with them."

"I don't want to go," Annabelle said. "I want to stay here."

"We can't stay here, Annabelle. This isn't our home."

"I wish it was. I like it here."

"So do I, but sooner or later we have to go back to Loch Craig."

"I don't care."

"Your grandparents love you. They look forward to this trip all year. You don't want to disappoint them, do you?"

Her little face brightened. "Why don't they come here instead?" she asked. "They can drive in America!"

"That might be a bigger trip than they were planning, Annabelle. They're expecting to find you in Loch Craig, and that's where we'll be."

Annabelle was distraught. Her entire body registered such black despair that he almost laughed. Sometimes he felt that this wildly emotional, melodramatic daughter of his was a changeling, and the serious, stolid daughter he was meant to have had been spirited away.

How many nights had he and Joely spent discussing Annabelle in excruciatingly minute detail, lovingly examining every facet of her personality, dreaming about the shining future she would one day claim.

Why had that been enough for them? They should have been dreaming about their own future together, the brothers and sisters who would be there for Annabelle when they were long gone, brothers and sisters who would look up to her for love and counsel.

He'd had those dreams, but he had never found the right time, the right way, to put them on the table.

Too late now, he thought as he drained his cup of coffee and gestured for a refill. *Too bloody late.*

"I got your message," Zach said when Cat and Joely joined him at Mimi's house. "It's a joke, right?"

"Mark's here," Cat said as she unlocked the front door. "He showed up last night."

Zach looked like somebody had told him there really was a Santa Claus. He was filled with questions — who could blame him? — but neither Cat nor Joely had the time or patience to answer them.

"I think he's looking to get back in the spotlight," Cat said.

"Maybe he just wants to see Mimi," Zach countered, then looked toward Joely for support.

"Maybe both," she said. "Who knows?"

"I don't care why he's here," Cat said, "but I do want to know if anything he's told us is true." She brought Zach up to date on the chronology of Mark's little vacation from family life.

"Holy shit," Zach said. "What the hell was he thinking?"

"He was thinking about himself," Cat said. "That's the one thing I'm sure of."

She explained about the strongbox and Mark's absolute certainty that it was hidden somewhere in the house.

"It's not going to change anything," she said, "but I have to know if he's lying to us."

"Does it really matter?" Joely asked.

"It matters to me," Cat said. She needed

to know that just once in the twenty-seven years since he walked out that door, her father had wondered if she was happy.

Zach, bless his heart, volunteered to do a target-specific search of the place.

"I'm flying up to Portland tomorrow morning," he said. "I'm yours until then."

"My cell's on," Cat said as she kissed his cheek. "Call me if you find anything."

"He won't find anything," Joely said as they climbed into Cat's Jeep. "Mark made all of that up to salve his guilty conscience."

"It looks that way," Cat admitted, "but it doesn't hurt to check it out."

They struggled to keep up a light smattering of conversation on the short drive to the hospital.

"I didn't know Zach had his own plane," Joely said. "I'm impressed."

"He learned to fly in college," Cat said as she turned into the parking lot. "Who knew he'd be able to afford his own plane one day?"

Life was nothing if not surprising.

Michael had barely cleared the jetway when he flipped on his cell phone to check for messages. The voice mail symbol appeared immediately, followed by the text mail envelope. He clicked on the symbol.

FROM: cat
TIME: 8:07 a.m.

MESSAGE: HOW WOULD YOU LIKE TO MEET MY PARENTS?

A joke, he told himself. Exactly the kind of "gotcha" they liked to perpetrate on each other.

He clicked on the next text mail envelope.

FROM: cat
TIME: 8:35 a.m.

MESSAGE: HOW WOULD YOU LIKE TO MEET MY PARENTS?

He laughed, imagining the scowl on her face as she waited for him to respond with a crack about The Fockers.

He clicked on the third text mail envelope. This one had to contain the punch line.

FROM: cat
TIME: 8:54 a.m.

MESSAGE: THIS IS NOT A TEST. HOW WOULD YOU LIKE TO MEET MY PARENTS?

It wasn't a joke. There was no punch line. This was a love letter.

Twenty minutes later, he and his rented Ford Escort were on their way to Maine.

William and Annabelle stopped by Mimi's house in search of Joely.

"Come and gone," Zach said, up to his elbows in dust. "They're at the hospital."

"They told you their father's in town?" he asked.

"I'm still trying to wrap my brain around it," Zach said. "The guy was my idol."

William took note of the past tense. "Did you know him?"

"He was gone by the time Mimi and the girls moved here. I was a fan."

"From what I've been seeing, he had a lot of them."

"The Doyles were huge," Zach said, wiping his hands on the legs of his trousers. "Everyone out there today owes them a debt of gratitude."

Regret lodged in William's throat like a stone. He knew so little about Joely, about her family. Why had they both been so reluctant to share anything beyond the here and now?

"Annabelle and I are leaving tonight," he said, extending his right hand. "I'm sorry we won't have more time. I'd like to hear about The Doyles."

Zach looked at him for a moment. "I'm sorry, too." He drew his right hand along the side of his trousers once more. "Nothing I like more than a captive audience for my Doyles stories."

They shook hands briefly, then Zach crouched down to make a proper good-bye to Annabelle, who flung her arms around the man's neck and sobbed like her world was coming to an end.

"A thespian?" Zach asked with an amused grin.

"Diva," William said. "I fear the onset of puberty more than I can say."

"Can we say good-bye to Bess and Mamie?" Annabelle pleaded after they left Zach to his work.

"The sheep?"

"Al-pak-ah," she enunciated. "Please! Can we?"

"Karen's not home today," he said.

"Bess and Mamie are."

"You don't wander around private property without permission, Annabelle. You know better than that."

"Where's Joely?" she demanded. "She would take me to see Bess and Mamie. I know she would."

"Joely and Cat are visiting their mother."

"Mimi," Annabelle provided. "Her house went on fire."

He checked his watch. They needed to be on the road to Portland before long. Joely hadn't said much that morning when he told her they would be leaving tonight for Scotland. Still, he couldn't leave without a proper good-bye.

He headed for the hospital.

"The daughters!" a voice cried out as Joely and Cat approached the entrance to the hospital.

Cameras seemed to materialize from nowhere. Reporters literally leaped from the bushes. The only bright spot was the sight of William and Annabelle standing in the lobby.

"We'll get through it," Cat said to Joely.

"We don't have a choice," Joely said. "We're surrounded."

Neither one of them was surprised to find their father at the center of the storm. Mark, still clad in the same jeans and shirt he had been wearing last night, appeared in the hospital entrance like an aging avenging angel.

"They won't let me see her," he announced to his daughters and every microphone within range. "She's my wife. They can't deny me the chance to see my wife."

A reporter stepped into their path. "You're Mark and Mimi's daughters," she said, brandishing a microphone like a weapon. "Are you here to help reunite your parents?"

"We're here to see our mother," Cat said, "if you'll let us through."

"That's why I'm here, too," Mark said as he joined them. "Those fascist bureaucrats won't let me past the lobby."

"Good for them," Cat muttered, then wished she hadn't when the reporter flashed a triumphant what-a-sound-bite grin.

"You're keeping Mark Doyle from his wife and partner?" another reporter asked at the top of his voice. "What are your reasons?"

"Ignore them," Joely whispered. "Don't let them drag you into a fight."

But Cat was already engaged. She dug in her heels and faced down the throng. "My mother had a serious stroke," she said. "She sustained numerous broken bones and is in considerable pain. My first and only concern is her safety and comfort."

Mark? Her mother's voice sounded over her shoulder. She spun around, but Mimi wasn't there. *Mark! Is that you?*

"That's my concern, too," their father said. "I think my daughters know that."

"Your daughters don't know anything about you," Cat snapped, "and maybe —"

"We're going inside, Cat," a familiar voice said. "Don't say another word."

William put an arm around her shoulder and led her into the lobby with Joely, Annabelle, and Mark close behind.

"You don't want to do that, Cat," William said when they were safely inside. "Don't feed the tabloids any more than you have to."

"Tell him that." She gestured angrily in her father's direction. "He's the reason those vultures are out there."

"No, he isn't." Joely touched her arm with a gentle hand. "He didn't set this whole thing in motion, Cat. Jack Willis did."

Cat wanted to argue, but she couldn't. Of course Joely was right. Karen had told her that Willis, one of the volunteer firefighters and a music lover, had passed the news on to his brother in Florida, who immediately phoned in the tip. Jack and his brother cashed the check. Mark was only looking to benefit from the fallout.

"I'm not asking for anything from you girls," Mark said. "I just want to see my wife."

William took Annabelle's hand and stepped away from the family circle.

"No," Cat said. "Absolutely not."

He's coming home any day, girls. Just wait and see. Mimi's clear, sweet voice filled her head.

"I know how you feel, Cat," Joely said. "I feel the same way. But this isn't about us. It never has been."

"Mimi's in no position to make any decisions."

"Then let's make the decision you know she'd make for herself. She's spent twenty-seven years waiting for this moment. I don't want to be the one who takes it away from her."

"He doesn't deserve a second chance."

"No, he doesn't," Joely said. "But maybe our mother does."

Chapter Twenty-one

Mark was quiet as they rode the elevator to the fourth floor. The brash and aging rebel had been replaced by an old man who kept nervously touching his thinning hair.

"She had a stroke," Joely reminded him. "She won't know who you are."

"I understand."

"I'm not sure you do," Cat said. "She's not a young woman anymore."

"I know that."

"She was badly hurt, Mark." Joely wanted to make sure he knew exactly what to expect so there would be no scenes that might upset Mimi. "There are a lot of tubes and machines. We don't want you to be surprised."

"Let me put it this way," Cat broke in. "You do anything to upset Mimi, and so help me God, I'll make sure you're the one in a hospital bed."

His shoulders slumped, and he looked down at the floor.

"Cat," Joely said softly. "Was that necessary?"

"Yes," Cat said. "It was necessary."

The ten-year-old girl who had loved her daddy more than life itself was in that elevator with them, and she needed to be heard. But it was a seven-year-old English girl who was on Joely's mind.

She wished Annabelle hadn't seen that exchange in the lobby. She wished she could spin the hands on her watch the way she had on the night of the solstice and claim those few minutes all over again. She wanted Annabelle to know only the sunny side of life.

Thank God William felt that way, too. He had quickly spirited the child away from the throng and Joely had experienced a pang of sorrow as she watched the two of them disappear down the corridor.

The elevator stopped on four, and the doors slid open. Mark stepped aside so Cat and Joely could exit first, then followed them to Room 415.

The air was thick with tension. You could almost see the sparks of nervous energy coming from Cat, while Joely was sure her heart was going to split open. Mark seemed to be aging right before their eyes. The closer they got to the door, the older and smaller he grew as if the weight of the lost years were grinding him into dust. She didn't mean to, she wasn't even sure exactly why she did it, but she reached out and touched his hand.

"It'll be okay," she said, and he managed a smile.

He still didn't seem to connect with her, but that was okay. She would survive.

She reached into the pocket of her trousers. "I found this yesterday," she said. "I think it's yours."

She dropped his old wedding band into his palm and all of the sweet emotion she had hoped to see washed over his face.

"Thanks," he managed as his long fingers closed around the circle of gold. "She kept it all these years."

Maybe she was a fool but she didn't have the heart to tell him about the long-forgotten cigarette box under the carpet.

"Mimi's in the first bed," Cat said as she opened the door. "Let me prepare her before you say anything."

Mark nodded. Joely had the feeling he was too nervous to speak.

Mimi looked tiny and frail. Her graying brown hair was swept up and away from her heart-shaped face, which only served to highlight the starkness of the black stitches against her pale skin. The array of tubes and apparatus were daunting even now that Joely had grown accustomed to them. Next to her, she heard a low moan from deep inside her father's gut.

"Morning, Mimi." Cat bent on the right side of the bed. "You look pretty today."

Mimi's eyes opened and roamed Cat's face as if the secret of her own identity might be hidden there.

"Hi, Mom." Joely crouched down on Mimi's left side and gently stroked her hand. "It's Joely."

Mimi's gaze shifted in her direction, but there was no recognition in her eyes.

"Mimi, we have a big surprise for you," Cat said. Neither one of them knew how much their mother understood. "Daddy's come home."

No response.

Cat gestured for Mark to step forward and slip into her place. He was shaking so hard Joely was afraid he would break apart.

"Talk to her," Joely urged. "Let her hear your voice."

He opened his mouth, but no sound came out. He cleared his throat and tried again.

"Mimi, I'm here. It took me a long time, but I'm here."

Joely's chest hurt too much to breathe. She grabbed Cat's hand and moved away from the bed.

"Mimi," he said again. "You haven't changed . . . you're still my beautiful girl."

Mimi turned in the direction of his voice. Her eyes, so wild and unfocused before, seemed to gain clarity as her gaze settled on his still-handsome face.

The sisters held on to each other as their father leaned closer to the bed.

"What did you say, Mimi? Did you say something?"

She lifted her head from her pillow, eyes roaming his face for something only she could possibly understand.

"She's upset," Cat said, taking a step toward Mimi.

"No." Joely held on to her arm. "Wait a minute."

He reached for Mimi's hand and Joely saw he was wearing the wedding band at the same time Cat noticed it.

"You gave him the ring?" Cat glared at Joely.

"It belongs to him," she said and to her surprise Cat backed down.

Mimi murmured something unintelligible.

"What does she want?" he asked, not taking his gaze from Mimi. "Am I hurting her?"

"Just talk to her," Cat said, her voice husky.

He did better than that. He began to sing a song Joely had never heard before, a sad lament for a brown-haired girl and the boy who broke her heart. The sound of his voice seemed to soothe Mimi. Her restless movements slowed down. Her gaze met his and stayed there. And then suddenly the room was filled with the sweet sound of her voice rising to meet his the way it had all those years ago.

All her life Joely had searched for a fragment of memory, a whisper of something that would prove to her that once upon a time there had been a family named Doyle, but she always came up blank. How could she remember what she had never known or experienced? Now here they were, the four of them, gathered together in Mimi's hospital room, bound by a common past, by sorrow, and by love.

She reached again for Cat's hand and held tight, wanting to anchor this moment in time and space and memory forever. Flawed and imperfect, this was her family. She didn't have to understand them. She didn't have to like them. None of that mattered. Their blood coursed through her veins. Their hopes and fears and dreams were all part of her, always had been, always would be.

"It's okay," Cat whispered, giving her hand a squeeze. "Everything's okay."

And for a little while, as she watched her parents, it really was.

William took Annabelle to the cafeteria for a snack, but there was a limit to how much time they could spend over a wax carton of chocolate milk and a handful of chips.

Annabelle was bursting with questions. She wanted to know why Joely and Cat yelled at their father. She wanted to know why Mark had been away for so long. She wanted to know why families weren't like the ones she saw on telly, why Joely had looked like she was about to cry.

He tried to explain the nature of sadness to his daughter. He searched for reasons that would make clear something that even he was at a loss to understand. He was reminded of the nature of fog, impossible to grasp and equally impossible to penetrate. He realized he had known only the bare bones of Joely's life before she came to Loch Craig, and those things he didn't know were shaping his future and Annabelle's.

The only thing he knew with certainty was that Joely's heart was breaking same as his.

They finished their snack and he waited while Annabelle carefully carried the tray over to the waste bin. Every now and again he caught a glimpse of Natasha in the way his daughter walked, the tilt of her head, and the pain felt as sharp and new as it had those first terrible weeks. But then it receded and he was left grateful for having loved Natasha, grateful for this child who made each day special.

Grateful that he had met a woman who loved his child as much as he did, a woman who had brought so much happiness into Annabelle's life at a time when he thought happiness was beyond their reach.

When had that stopped being enough for him? Somewhere along the way a sea change had occurred and he began to want more. He wanted Joely to give her heart to him the way she had given it to his daughter, to see her face light up with happiness when he walked into the room.

And what about you? Have you ever told her how you feel?

All those nights they had spent together in their big wide bed and he had never once said the words. Never once let her know the depth and breadth of the feelings harbored inside his heart.

"Where are we going?" Annabelle asked as he took her hand and strode off toward the lobby. "Can we see Joely's mum?"

"That's what I'm going to find out," he said as they boarded the lift.

The car shimmied to a stop at the fourth floor where he was met by a security guard who asked his name.

"William and Annabelle Bishop," he said.

"I'm sorry, sir," the security guard said, "but you're not on the list."

"Please call Mrs. Doyle's room," William said. "One of her daughters will vouch for me."

"Mrs. Doyle doesn't have a phone in her room," the guard said. "Why don't you and your little girl go get something from the cafeteria? I'll send Cat and Joely over when they come down."

"Perhaps you could ring the nurses' station."

"Listen, this is the best I can do. Take it or leave it."

He thanked the guard and took Annabelle's hand.

"We can't leave before we see Joely," Annabelle said. "She'll be worried."

"She knows you have to go home to see your grandparents," William said carefully. "She'll understand."

"Maybe we can sit by the elevator. That way we won't miss her."

He looked at the huge clock suspended over the bank of elevators.

"Thirty minutes," he said, "then we have to leave." Once again time was his enemy.

By the time the nurse came in to shoo them out so Mimi could rest, Joely felt like she had lived five lifetimes.

"We'll grab some lunch," she said to Mark but he shook his head.

"I'm not going."

"You have to," the no-nonsense nurse said. "She needs her sleep more than she needs you yammering in her ear."

"Come on," Cat said more gently than Joely had expected. "Get some lunch, Mark, then you can come back."

He nodded then leaned forward and pressed a kiss to Mimi's cheek.

"She smiled," Mark said with almost childlike pleasure. "Did you see that? She smiled."

Cat opened her mouth to speak then shook her head. Joely smiled. She knew exactly what her sister was thinking. It didn't matter a whit if Mimi had or hadn't smiled. Mark believed it and he left the room on a high.

"There he is!" a female voice called out and a second later he was surrounded by admirers of a certain age, all of whom remembered The Doyles with affection bordering on fanaticism.

"Should we wait for him?" she asked Cat as they watched him sign hospital nightgowns, plastic bedpans, and outdated magazines for his fans.

"He'll be fine," Cat said. "He's in his element."

Joely took a good look at her sister. "You look knackered. Maybe you should go home and have a nap."

"Knackered." Cat gave her a tired smile. "I love it when you go all Brit on me."

"Come on," she said. "I'll walk you out to your car."

They slipped out the back way and crossed the sun-splashed parking lot toward Cat's Jeep.

"You've done your sisterly duty," Cat said as she opened the driver's side door. "Now go back in and find William and Annabelle."

She nodded, suddenly reluctant to say good-bye. "When Mark —" She paused, trying to put her thoughts into some semblance of order. "Was that real?" She gestured toward the hospital behind them. "The two of them, the way she looked at him —"

Cat reached over and smoothed Joely's hair off her face. "It was real," she said. "God knows I don't understand it either, but it was very real."

"Twenty-seven years," Joely said, "and it's like he never left."

"Don't get all sentimental on me," Cat warned. "This is Mark Doyle we're talking about. Wait until the camera crews leave then let's see what we've got."

"I think he's going to stay awhile," Joely said.

"I think so, too." Cat looked at her for a moment. "I invited Michael up for a visit."

Joely felt her eyes widen. "Full disclosure?"

"Meet the parents and everything," she said.

"Wow," Joely said, shaking her head. "Are you sure you're doing the right thing?"

"No," Cat said, "but I did it anyway."

"The times, they are definitely a-changin'."

"I like him," Cat said.

Joely grinned and patted her sister's belly. "I should hope so."

"I'm talking about William."

"You barely know him."

"I know that your face lights up when he enters the room. I know that when you're around him the rest of the world falls away. The three of you fit the way a family should. That doesn't happen often in this world." She reached for Joely's hand and held it tight. "Don't let them go without a fight, Joely. Life's too short. We don't have to make Mark and Mimi's mistakes. We can get it right."

Cat's words lingered as she paced the hospital lobby. If she thought for an instant that William loved her, that they might have a future, she would crawl from there to Loch Craig to prove her love.

Mark was still upstairs holding court and probably would be for the rest of the day. She searched for William and Annabelle in the cafeteria, the solarium, and even the chapel, but they were nowhere to be found. She supposed she shouldn't be surprised. She had been upstairs over an hour and a half. How could you expect a little girl to sit in a hospital lobby with nothing to do?

She checked the clock over the reception desk and then checked it again thirty minutes later. William and Annabelle would be leaving for the airport before long and nothing had been settled between them.

Don't let them go without a fight, Cat had said. Life was too short. Sometimes a woman had to do more than wish on a star to claim her happy ending.

Finally, after another hour of aimless wandering, she walked the half mile to Mimi's house, where she found Zach sitting on what remained of the front porch, nursing a giant bottle of Pepsi.

"I found it," he said.

"Found what?" She grabbed for the Pepsi and took a swig.

"The strongbox Mark told you about. There was a trapdoor in the floor of her bedroom closet. I found three metal strongboxes."

"Did you open them?"

"Not my job," he said with a grin. "But, damn, did I want to."

"Did you call Cat?"

"Not yet. I figured you guys were at the hospital."

"We were. She went back home to take a nap. I've been hunting down William and Annabelle."

"They're gone, honey."

She felt the ground shift beneath her feet. "You mean they went back to Cat's."

"They left for the airport. Annabelle left

Tigger here when they stopped by this morning, so they swung around to pick it up on their way out."

She must have heard wrong. William and Annabelle would never have left without saying good-bye.

"They can't be gone," she said. "I thought they weren't leaving until tonight."

I thought I still had time.

"Check your watch, Joely. It's later than you think."

But not too late. It couldn't be.

"I have to go." She turned and ran down the street toward Cat's house, heart pounding, lungs screaming for air.

There had to be a note, a message, something. He wouldn't just leave that way, not after all the years they had spent together —

Did you ever give him a reason to stay? Did you ever once tell him you love him?

She found the note on her pillow and her hands shook as she picked it up.

Flight number.

Estimated time of arrival.

A promise to call when he and Annabelle got home.

"This isn't enough," she said out loud. It wasn't close to enough. You couldn't live with a man for almost five years, make a home with him, mother his child, and let it end this way.

There was too much left to say. They had shared too much, cared too much, to just let it all drift away. If she was going to lose him, she wasn't going to let him go before she told him how she felt.

He could tell her it was over. He could tell her that they had run their course. But not before she told him that she loved him, not just his daughter, not the life they had made together, but him. William Bishop. She loved his heart, his soul, the sound of his voice, the touch of his hand, the smell of his skin. She wasn't sure exactly when it happened, the moment when her heart opened wide enough to let hope slip inside, but it had happened and now she had one last chance to tell him.

She grabbed the keys to her rental and raced back to Zach's.

"I need a favor," she said, "and it's a big one."

He listened and, bless him, he didn't bat an eye. Romantics never did.

"I'll do it," he said, and before she drew her next breath they had a plan.

They would drop the strongboxes off at Cat's house and then head for the local airstrip where his single-engine jet was hangared.

If she was very lucky, if God was watching over her, she would make it to the Portland airport before William and Annabelle boarded their plane.

And if not, she'd find another way. She wasn't going to give up on their future. Not without a fight.

Cat wasn't a religious woman but she offered up a quick prayer as she waved goodbye to Zach and Joely. It was never easy to put your heart out there on the firing line, to open yourself up to the dangers of love, but oh God how wonderful it was to see that look of embarrassed hope in her sister's eyes as she said, "Wish me luck!"

There had to be one more happy ending out there for the Doyles because it didn't look like happily ever after was in her forecast. No phone calls, no e-mails, no text messages, nothing at all from Michael. The later it got, the more certain she was that she had made a terrible mistake. Michael never played the silence card. He was a talker, a communicator. This silence meant something but God help her she didn't have a clue exactly what.

She glanced about for something to distract her and her gaze settled on the three strongboxes Joely and Zach had dropped off. The plan was to wait until Joely got back from her adventure and open them together but Cat's resolve was disappearing fast.

She tried to pretend they weren't there but they were the equivalent of a thousand-pound pink gorilla in tights. She tried to walk around them, look over them, ignore them, but the lure was too great, and she finally gave in to temptation.

"Oh God . . ." she breathed as she opened the first one and the past tumbled into her lap.

Mark hadn't lied. There were letters. Lots of them. Postcards. Old photos. Mimi's diaries. Handwritten music. Cassette tapes. The whole complicated, painful, messy record of a couple's life together and apart, captured in three dented metal strongboxes.

She scanned a few of the letters, then put them down. They were too intimate, too personal. They cut across the years and threw her headlong into the heart of a complicated, messy marriage between two romantics who hadn't a clue what real life was all about. Maybe one day she would be able to read them all, but her heart was too raw today, her emotions too close to the surface.

In a day or two, if he was still around, she would invite her father over, and they would go through things together. Sooner or later she needed to hear the stories, the real ones behind the legend she had grown up with. She owed it not just to herself but to the baby she carried.

Mark was definitely a wild card. He might decide to publish the letters or write a memoir. He might burn them in a bonfire on the beach. She couldn't predict or control what he would ultimately do. All she wanted was the story of how their family came to be. She wanted to hear about the love that had brought them together, the strange strong love that had survived across the years of separation.

And then she would let it go. The years of resentment. The pain. All of it. Only the story mattered, but she and Joely were the ones who would write the ending.

How quiet the house seemed without Annabelle. She wandered into the guest room and stripped the sheets from the bed. She was halfway to the laundry room when she realized the phone had been quiet for hours.

Had she forgotten to plug it back in? She lifted the receiver and heard the familiar dial tone. Maybe the ringer was off. She dialed herself from the cell. Nope. The ringer worked just fine.

There was no reason for frantic calls from reporters now that Mark was out there granting interviews and photo ops. It was just that she thought maybe Michael would call or text her or something. This silence wasn't his style at all.

She started the laundry then walked into the kitchen and poured herself a glass of orange juice. She had sent him three text messages earlier this morning. At least she thought she had. Electronic communications weren't infallible.

Nothing wrong with resending again, was there?

She sifted through her sent text messages, clicked on the last one, then pressed Send again. She watched as the message turned into an envelope icon, then spiraled off into the ether.

Less than ten seconds later her cell rang.

"Michael!" She felt like a sixteen-year-old high school girl. "You got my message?"

"You sent a message?"

"I texted you three times." Four, but who was counting.

"So what's up?"

She hesitated. Why was it so hard to say the words to him? What was so difficult

428

about saying I love you, I need you, I want you in my life?

"Howwouldyoufeelaboutdrivinguphereto meetmyparents?" she managed in one long rush of words.

"Sorry, Doyle. I'm busy tonight." It didn't take him a nanosecond to beg off.

"Oh," she said. "Well." *Pull it together,* she told herself. *Don't embarrass yourself.* "I didn't mean tonight. You know . . . whenever." Clearly it was a very good thing she made her living with wool, not words.

"I'm going out for dinner tonight."

"You don't owe me an explanation." The hell he didn't.

"Thought I'd get some lobster."

"In New York? There goes your next royalty check." Why was he telling her this? She didn't want to hear any of it.

"Actually I know a place where lobster's pretty reasonable."

"Good for you." She ordered herself not to cry. He was talking shellfish, not the end of civilization.

"Open the front door."

Her heart bounced off her rib cage. "What did you say?"

"Open your front door before these lobsters make a break for it."

She peered out the front window, and

there he was. Jet-lagged. Disheveled. Struggling up the front walk with a bucket of irritable crustaceans and the biggest bouquet of roses she had ever seen in her life.

The man she loved.

Her baby's father.

Her future.

"You could have told me you hated to fly," Zach said as he prepared the small plane for landing at Portland.

"I don't hate to fly," Joely said. But, as it turned out, she did hate flying through the air in a tin can.

"Seat belt fastened?"

"It's been fastened since we took off."

"It might be a little choppy," he warned. "There's some crosswind."

"Just get me there in time, Zach. That's all I'm asking."

It was all she was asking of Zach. God, however, was being bombarded with a steady barrage of prayer, plea bargains, and promises.

Fifteen minutes later, her legs still trembling from the bumpy landing, she ran from counter to counter, desperate for information but nobody knew anything. The electronic signs were no help. And to make it worse, she had the feeling she was too late.

"I spoke to someone at the United counter," Zach said, catching up with her near the first security checkpoint. "They fly to Glasgow via London." He hugged her tight. "I'm sorry, kid. The flight left an hour ago."

She didn't cry, but the sense of loss was so overwhelming she could barely stand. "Okay," she said, stiffening her spine. "Okay."

"Don't cry," Zach warned. "I'll end up giving you the plane and my company if you cry."

"I'm not going to cry," she promised him. She was too numb to do anything but stand there staring up at him.

"So why don't you fly over there yourself?" Zach said after a moment or ten. "They have another flight tonight. You would be just a few hours behind them."

"My passport's back at Cat's."

"We'll go back and get it."

She shook her head. "It's a sign. This was a crazy idea. I don't know what I was thinking."

"You weren't thinking. You were following your heart."

"Too little, too late," she said.

"Maybe not," Zach said. "Look over there."

William, with Annabelle at his side, was standing at the United ticket counter with their backs to her.

She wanted to tear across the terminal and fling herself into William's arms and lay her heart at his feet.

She wanted to hide behind Zach until the feeling went away.

"Go over there," Zach said, placing his hands against her back and pushing her forward. "That's why you came here. Do it!"

"I can't!"

"You can't *not* do it," he said. "This is your destiny, Joely. Go for it."

He was right. She knew he was right. But, oh God, it was hard to face your future head-on when you didn't know the outcome.

She put one foot in front of the other. She tried to remember to breathe. The distance between them seemed to widen, but she kept moving, closing the gap, praying in a way she had never prayed before, until she was inches away.

"William?"

She sounded terrified, which was no surprise. She was terrified. What happened in the next sixty seconds would determine the rest of her life.

He turned slowly, and she saw shock on his face and then —

Oh God, was that disappointment?

"Joely!" Annabelle flung herself around her legs and hugged her tight. "I knew you'd come with us. I told Daddy you would!"

She bent down and pressed a kiss to the top of the girl's head, but her eyes never left William's.

"Don't go," she said, heart on her sleeve, her future in his hands. "Please don't."

"You came all this way to say that?"

Please, God, make him stop looking at me that way.

"You can't — I mean, please don't . . . I —"

"Don't say anything." He placed the palm of his left hand against her lips. She tried to speak, but he shook his head. "I love you, Joely. I wanted to be the first one to say it."

"I love you, too," she said, feeling the truth of it fill her heart. "I love you!" She flung the words out into the world for the first time in her life and they filled her heart tenfold.

Their gazes met and held. She didn't turn away or deflect the moment with a joke. She let him see past her defenses, past the walls she had built up over the years, let him see into her heart.

They drew together, closer and then closer still, until their lips met. The taste and touch of him was familiar yet brand-new.

It was a moment of firsts. Their kiss held all the wonder and promise of the very first time and in that instant their lives changed forever.

"I know you have to take Annabelle home to see the Sinclairs but —"

"I turned in the tickets."

"You turned them in?"

He nodded as Annabelle leaped around them like an excited young filly. "They started boarding the plane. We were next in line. They asked for our passports, and I was about to hand them over when I knew I couldn't go. Not before I told you how I feel."

"What about her grandparents?" Joely asked. "Won't they be disappointed?"

"This was more important," he said. "Our future's more important."

"Our future," she repeated. "We've never talked about the future before."

"You're right," he said. "We've talked around it, over it, through it, but we've never actually talked about it."

"I wasn't sure we had one."

He looked at her. "I wasn't certain you wanted one."

"With you," she said, holding his gaze. "That's the only future I care about. When I got back to Cat's house and found out you'd left, it was like my whole world had crashed down on me. I couldn't imagine my life without you."

"What about Surrey?"

She shook her head. "I'm not taking the position."

"Your work is important," he said. "We could pick up sticks if that's what you want."

"Loch Craig is home," she said. "That's where I want to be."

"Marry me, Joely."

"What did you say?"

"Will you marry me?"

She gasped as he dropped to one knee right there in the middle of Terminal A. William, her reserved and dignified Englishman, was kneeling in a wad of chewing gum, looking up at her with his heart beating crazily on the outside of his chest for the world to see. He was wide open and vulnerable, fearless the way only a man in love could be, and her heart soared.

She thought of her parents on that stage in Newport, beautiful and glowing with love. The look in her mother's eyes when she realized her husband had come back to her. Her father's tears. The new life growing in Cat's belly.

She thought of Annabelle and the weekend visit that had turned into a lifetime.

Nothing about love was easy. It didn't come with guarantees or guidebooks. It didn't promise happiness. It couldn't shield you from pain.

It might even break your heart in two from time to time.

And when it did, she and William would hang onto each other with both hands, and then they would start all over again, better and stronger than they were before.

"Joely?" He looked so painfully unsure of himself. "There's a crowd gathering around us, and I'm here on one knee —"

"Yes," she said, then, "Yes! Yes! Yes!" as the crowd around them burst into applause while Annabelle and Zach did an impromptu jig.

There was no candlelight or champagne, no long-stemmed roses or candlelight. They didn't need the trappings of romance to prove their love. Everything they could ever want was right there within reach.

"Does this mean we'll be a family just like Louis?" Annabelle asked as they followed Zach out to his plane for the trip back to Idle Point. "With the same names and everything?"

"That's exactly what it means." William winked at Joely over Annabelle's head. "We might even be able to produce a baby brother or sister for you."

"I don't want one anymore," Annabelle said. "I want an alpaca."

"The girl knows fiber," Zach said. "I'd listen to her."

"Don't worry," Joely whispered to William. "I prefer a baby to an alpaca any day."

Suddenly Annabelle stopped short and looked up at Joely, her little face aglow with happiness. "Can I call you Mummy now?"

Joely gripped William's hand so hard she almost broke his fingers. "I would be very, very happy if you started calling me Mummy right this very minute."

"Brilliant!" Annabelle declared.

Three months later, on the hill behind their house in Loch Craig, with the people they loved most in the world gathered around them, William Bishop and Joely Doyle (and Annabelle) made it official.

They became a family.

Epilogue

One year later

On the morning of the summer solstice Joely Doyle Bishop woke up to the sound of children laughing outside her window. If there was a better way to wake up, God hadn't created it yet.

She didn't move quickly these days. Her center of gravity seemed to shift on an almost hourly basis. The simple act of climbing from bed in the morning required both cunning and a helping hand.

"William!" she called out. "I feel like a beached whale!"

There was nothing pretty about the sight of a woman in her ninth month struggling to sit up in bed but she had long since said good-bye to things like vanity and dignity.

"I told Annabelle and Louis to play quietly," William said from the doorway. "I'll send them over to Sara's for the morning."

Joely hid a yawn behind her hand then

smiled up at her husband. "Don't," she said. "I love the sound."

"Cat phoned." William placed a glass of orange juice on the nightstand then helped her sit up. "She dreamed today would be the day."

"Her mouth to God's ear," Joely said, rubbing her belly absently. "I'm ready when our son is."

"First babies are usually late," William reminded her. "You may go another week."

"Sadist," she muttered with a laugh. "I'll need my own postal code if I get any bigger."

"You're beautiful."

"You're blind without your glasses," she said, ruffling his hair. "So what else did Cat say?"

"The usual. I promised you'd phone her at the first contraction so she can jump on a plane."

"Michael and Katie might have something to say about that."

William sat on the edge of the bed and she leaned into his warmth. "They're coming, too," he said. "Cat says we started a new Doyle family tradition when we flew back for Katie's birth."

Katie was a five-month-old dictator who had both Cat and Michael wrapped around her tiny finger. Not to mention her aunt, uncle, and cousin in Scotland. It had been a magical, wondrous time and Annabelle was purely delighted to have a baby cousin.

"I wouldn't have missed that for the world," Joely said as a funny little twinge pinched her mid-section. "Cat was —" She stopped as the twinge escalated into something deeper, more intense.

"What's wrong?"

"Nothing." She forced a smile. "Just a little twinge."

"You winced."

"No, I didn't."

"You did it again." He placed the flat of his hand against her belly. "Was that a contraction?"

"I told you it was a twinge," she said. "Nothing to worry about."

"You're two days away from your due date."

"You're the one who said I'd probably be late, William."

"You're in pain."

"I'm not in pain. It just felt strange."

"Strange in what way?"

"I shouldn't have said anything. It's probably nothing more than Braxton-Hicks."

"Again?"

"William, if you're going to drive me crazy, you might as well go to work. I'll phone you if I need you."

"I'm working from home today."

She tried to focus her attention away from the odd twisting sensation in her belly. "On Doyle business?"

"Mark wants me to set up foundations for the grandchildren."

"He doesn't have to do that. We're fine."

"He wants to do it."

"I understand that but it isn't necessary. He's taking care of Mimi. That's enough."

Joely leveraged herself from the bed and walked slowly toward the window that overlooked the garden where Annabelle and Louis were playing. The offers had been pouring in for a year now, ever since Mimi's stroke and Mark's reappearance. The Doyles were suddenly on everyone's radar screen. A CD of their first album shot to the top of the charts and opened up a world of possibilities. Mark had signed a book deal and there was even talk of a movie.

Cat's Michael was helping Mark navigate the dangerous waters of Hollywood, while William kept a sharp eye on Mark's finances. To be fair, money never had meant much to their father. Neither its presence nor its absence seemed to influence the way he lived. For all of his faults — and they were legion — he was the least materialistic person she had ever known.

It was an odd thing getting to know your father for the first time. In his own way, he was as mercurial as Mimi, but he knew how to channel his emotions into the creative process. Songs had been pouring out of him in record number, mournful love songs based on medieval lore, bouncy children's tunes born of Revolutionary War–era folk songs — it was as if he couldn't stem the flow, as if he had to capture it all right now, this minute, while there was still time.

Mark and Zach had become friends but Zach remained in awe of his hero. It was comical to see a millionaire businessman, one who owned a vineyard and a private plane, in thrall to a man who lived in faded jeans and worn work shirts, but that was the case. Zach was helping Mark catalog the astonishing collection of notes and tapes he'd amassed on the history of American music with an eye toward donating the originals to the Smithsonian.

The Doyles were flawed individuals, but together they were still pure magic.

The most surprising fact of all, however,

was that Mark hadn't left Mimi's side once since his return. He had taken over responsibility for her care and seemed grateful for the opportunity. She and Cat had spent many hours on the phone trying to figure out exactly what it all meant, but somehow they always reached the same conclusion.

He loved her. Not in a way either Joely or Cat understood, but it was love just the same, and it was making Mimi's last days happier than most of the years that had come before.

That turned out to be true for both her and Cat as well. They had answers now to questions that had haunted them for years and while the answers weren't Hallmark-perfect, they were finally able to put the past aside and embrace the future.

"Oh!" She clutched her belly as a spasm rippled through her. "Now that was more than a twinge."

William was at her side in an instant. "Shall I ring the doctor?"

"Not yet," she said, focusing on the way the sunlight sparkled in Annabelle's hair as she played in the garden. "It's still early days."

"The doctor said it could be any time."

"William, I promise you I'll —"

"You're not breathing."

"I couldn't breathe," she said when the pain subsided.

"Another twinge?"

She met his eyes. "I think this one was a contraction."

William's English reserve vanished as a big, wide, hundred-watt smile lit up his serious face. He bent down and kissed her soundly. "I'll phone the doctor."

"Brilliant," she said. Calling the doctor would make William feel he had things under control, but Joely knew better.

Doctors were important to a woman in labor but not half as important as her big sister.

"You were right," she said when Cat picked up the phone. "It's time."

"Our bags are packed and we're on our way," Cat said.

"Hurry!" Joely urged. "William thinks we have plenty of time but I have a feeling our boy is ready to meet his parents."

"Don't worry. I'll be there before my nephew makes his appearance."

"Promise?"

"I'll be there in time, honey," Cat said. "I promise."

And wouldn't you know it?

Her big sister was as good as her word.

About the Author

Barbara Bretton is the *USA Today* best-selling, award-winning author of more than forty books. She currently has more than ten million copies in print around the world. Her works have been translated into twelve languages in more than twenty countries.

Barbara lives in New Jersey but loves to spend as much time as possible in Maine with her husband, walking the rocky beaches and dreaming up plots for upcoming books.

The employees of Thorndike Press hope you have enjoyed this Large Print book. All our Thorndike and Wheeler Large Print titles are designed for easy reading, and all our books are made to last. Other Thorndike Press Large Print books are available at your library, through selected bookstores, or directly from us.

For information about titles, please call:

(800) 223-1244

or visit our Web site at:

www.gale.com/thorndike
www.gale.com/wheeler

To share your comments, please write:

Publisher
Thorndike Press
295 Kennedy Memorial Drive
Waterville, ME   04901